Elizabeth Speckman was born and raised in Illinois. She currently resides outside the St. Louis area. She started writing short stories in her youth and has never stopped. Ideas pop into her head and she has to get them down on paper.

To Mom. Without you, this would not be possible.

Elizabeth Speckman

SCARY BEAUTIFUL

AUSTIN MACAULEY PUBLISHERS™

LONDON • CAMBRIDGE • NEW YORK • SHARJAH

Ordering Information:
Quantity sales: special discounts are available on quantity purchases by corporations, associations, and others. For details, contact the publisher at the address below.

Publisher's Cataloging-in-Publication data
Speckman, Elizabeth
Scary Beautiful

ISBN 9781645754497 (Paperback)
ISBN 9781645754503 (Hardback)
ISBN 9781645754510 (ePub e-book)

Library of Congress Control Number: 2020912149

www.austinmacauley.com/us

First Published (2020)
Austin Macauley Publishers LLC
40 Wall Street, 28th Floor
New York, NY 10005
USA

mail-usa@austinmacauley.com
+1 (646) 5125767

Chapter 1

Some would call me a drifter. Others might call me a runaway. I didn't care much what people referred to me as, I just made sure that I didn't stay in one town too long. Staying draws attention. No matter how much you try and keep a low profile, word somehow always spreads and ends up in the ears of those you try to stay away from.

I made sure that I moved about every six months. That way, I was still able to keep up with my schooling. It was tiring though, always moving, always keeping an eye out for familiar faces in crowds, and always being a few steps ahead. It was a wearing thing for me to do, but I did what I had to. I was too young to be so tired.

I had broken promises to people I loved. I had left behind those I said I never would. I left a trail of heartbreak from all the people I had grown close to in other towns and left abruptly without any warning. It was all a part of my life now. I had grown used to it. I did what I had to do to stay alive.

I was walking along the edge of the road where the gravel crunched underneath my boots. Over my left shoulder was slung a bag that carried all that I owned in this life. My dark hair had grown long in the past months and was held back by a simple band to keep it out of my face. A dark scruffy beard covered the lower half of my face.

I had no idea where I was, but it was too warm out for my clothing choices – dark jeans, boots, and a black Henley with the sleeves shoved up.

I took my eyes off the road in front of me to survey my current surroundings. A steep grassy hill rose up on the other side of the road. A sign reading 'Watch For Mudslides' was posted at intervals along the stretch of road. I glanced up the hill before I turned my attention to the other side.

A guardrail separated me and the road from a cliff that dropped off rather abruptly to a beach down below. The air smelled of salt and that dry scent that I associated with sand. It brought me back to a time during my childhood when my dad would take my sister and me to the beach. It was rare that he took us, but it always felt like the best day when he did.

I stepped over the rail and sat down with my legs dangling over the side of the cliff. The fall wouldn't have killed me, but it definitely would have left me broken.

Down below, teenagers around my age were enjoying a day at the beach. There were guys playing volleyball with a swarm of scantily clad girls surrounding them. The guys were so wrapped up in the game that it seemed they didn't even care or know they were being watched. The giggles from the girls drifted up and made me want to vomit. I was never one to go for that kind of girl.

A few girls were lying on the beach with magazines spread out in front of them. And there was a cluster of people in the water. Some were swimming and some were splashing water at one another. There were girls sitting on guys' shoulders and guys dunking each other under water.

Then there was her.

She was a good distance away from the others. She was standing in the water that hit her about mid-thigh. She had her hands raised in the air. I had no idea what she was doing. I guessed it was some form of water yoga. She then tilted her body back until she was floating in the water. Her body just moved with the waves and the current – like she was a part of the ocean itself.

She stayed like that for a while. I didn't understand why those guys down there were giving their attention to those other girls when clearly the most interesting girl was floating further away from them.

After a while, another girl swam down to her floating friend and gently roused her. She twisted her head to look at the girl and a smile lit up her face. She stood up in the chest high water and the two of them just talked for a while until the group of people who were already in the water swam over to join them. Before long, all the volleyball players and their salivating groupies joined in as well. She was quickly swallowed up by the mass of bodies.

As the sun began its descent toward the horizon, looking as though it would crash into the ocean, a handful of the guys exited the water and started to drag armfuls of varying sizes of driftwood to a central location. They made a teepee out of the wood with the larger pieces on the outside and smaller pieces on the inside.

They stood around surveying their work until one guy bent down and lit it on fire. I didn't see him pull a match or a lighter from anywhere, but I sure saw the spark before the wood went up in a blaze.

I rose from my perch on the cliffside and headed down to the beach. I needed to see these people closer up. I was quite fascinated by them.

I sat down on the beach not too far from the bonfire. I made sure to keep far enough away that I wouldn't draw their attention, but close enough that I could hear and see them.

The group that was still in the water began to exit slowly. A few people would walk up to the fire and then a few more until the only person who was left was the floating girl. She was just standing there watching the sun set. She seemed almost fascinated by it – like it was the first time she'd ever seen the sun do that.

Once that fiery ball disappeared, she walked slowly up towards the fire. She was walking at an angle that would bring her nearly right in front of me. As she passed me, she smiled. No one else paid me an ounce of attention, probably because I looked like some sort of beach hobo with my long hair and my scraggly beard.

I glanced at her after she went by me, and I noticed a tattoo running right down the center of her back on her spinal cord. It started just below her neck and stopped right above her black bikini bottoms. I couldn't tell what it was though. Actually, I couldn't see much about her at all other than she had dark hair and a tattoo.

As soon as she arrived at the fire, one of the volleyball players draped his arm over her shoulder and pulled her into his side.

"Hey baby," he said with a lazy smile.

It would figure that she had a boyfriend and one that seemed like a prick too. Why did beautiful girls always fall for the assholes?

She shrugged his arm off. "What do you want?" she asked in a bored tone, like she had been putting up with his shit for a while now.

Clearly, they were not together. Maybe she was one of the smart girls who stayed away from the assholes because she knew that all he'd do was break her heart.

"You know what I want," he said, stepping closer to her. He was a good head-and-a-half taller than she was.

"No," she replied simply.

"Come on, Em. You've had the summer. Let's just get back together. I'll be good. I promise," he begged.

Okay, obviously they had dated. She let out a breath and looked to the side. Her eyes connected with mine briefly before she looked back at the blond volleyball player.

"Mason Monroe never makes promises," she stated.

"Exactly! I am. So please believe me."

She stood there for a moment, processing his words. I thought she was going to actually give in to his bullshit. He had that cocky smile on his face like he knew that her answer would be what he wanted to hear.

"No." She then turned and walked away from him.

He was standing there with his mouth hanging open in disbelief that she had rejected him. One of his friends walked over and clapped him on the back.

"You, my friend, fucked up."

She walked to the other side of the fire and started talking to the girl with white blond hair and a small face. It was the girl who had joined her in the water. I was guessing that they were best friends.

I couldn't hear what they were saying, since the voices of the others drowned them out, but the blond girl kept glancing over at the volleyball player and throwing him a dirty look. He was watching them like a hawk stalking its prey. Then again, I was doing the same thing.

She hugged the blond-haired girl and walked away. I hopped up and followed her. She picked up a bag along the way. She pulled out a pair of shorts and tugged them on and then a set of car keys. She walked down the beach a little way and then up a set of stairs that led to a parking lot. That's where I caught up with her.

"Excuse me," I called.

She stopped dead and slowly spun around. She arched one of her eyebrows up but didn't say anything. Most people would have streaked off to hop in their car and lock the door or ran back to their friends when a stranger approached them in a near-empty parking lot. She was different though. It was like she wasn't afraid of anyone.

"Can you tell me where the high school is?" I asked.

One side of her lips tugged up in a lopsided smile. "It's not exactly open at this hour. And it's still summer, so it's not open at all. Registration for fall is tomorrow though. It's down on Maple Street which is just off Main Street... and you have no idea what I'm talking about, do you?"

I shook my head. "It's actually my first day here. My dad and I just moved. I'm sure I'll find my way though. Thanks," I replied.

"No problem." She turned around and got in a black car with tinted windows. From the four rings on the front, I knew it was an Audi. She fired the car up and pulled out of the parking lot without even stopping to see if anyone was coming down the street.

I had only been in this town, that I didn't even know the name of, for less than four hours and I was already in love with the place. Normally, it took me a few days to decide if I wanted to stay in a particular town or not, but this place hooked me quickly.

I stood in the parking lot for a little while. I usually arrived in a town when it was still light out and was able to navigate around a lot easier. I needed to find a place to crash for the night and go from there.

A few carloads of people pulled into the parking lot. I was guessing they were joining the party on the beach. A couple of guys hopped out the cars with guitars in their hands. Things were going to get all kumbaya-ish and I wanted to hear no part of that.

I walked to the entrance of the parking lot and headed the same way that black Audi had gone. A few houses lined the road that headed deeper into town. Those lucky few had the beach right in front of them. More houses came into view. And none of those houses were in poor condition, nor were they small. And every single one of them had some luxury car parked in the driveway. I never understood why people would leave a fifty-thousand-dollar car sitting in their driveway, yet their garage was full of junk.

I headed deeper into town and found exactly what I was looking for – a liquor store. I might have looked like I was about thirty with all the scruff on my face, but it wasn't alcohol that I was after. I entered the store and a bell dinged above the door. The cashier was on his hands and knees, using rags to soak up a massive spill. From the scent that lingered strongly in the air, I was suspecting it was vodka.

The guy turned his head to briefly look at me. "Stupid punk-ass kids," he grumbled. "Told them they were underage, so one shoves a bottle of Goose on the floor. Oh, he couldn't have picked a cheap bottle of the stuff, could he? Nope, he went straight for the pricy stuff."

He stood up and brushed his hands on his pants. "What I can get for you?" he asked.

"Actually, I just wanted to know if there is a motel or hotel close by?" I asked.

I saw him give me the once-over, taking in my poor appearance. "There's a hotel just up the street, The Perlinian. It ain't cheap though."

"Money isn't an issue," I said, turning and heading for the door.

"Sure you don't want a nightcap?" he asked as I had my hand on the door.

"I don't drink," I muttered before shoving the door open and stepping out into the muggy night air.

I walked further down the street. I was starting to get tired. I had no idea how many miles I had walked today, but it sure felt near a hundred. My legs were aching and my lower back was killing me. I just wanted to drop onto a bed and sleep the aches and pains away.

Up ahead was a brightly illuminated tall building. Windows stretched up the sides, with sliding doors placed here and there at certain intervals and balconies anchored where the sliding doors were. A sign lit up with fat, clear light bulbs in pretty script read:

The Perlinian Hotel
Est. 1856

The front of the hotel was glass. Two revolving doors anchored each side of the building with wooden doors having gold handles in the center. I could see the lobby from the outside of the building. The floors, walls, and reception desk were all shiny black marble. All the light fixtures, tables, chairs, and picture frames were silver. Right in the middle of the lobby was a massive staircase with deep red carpeting and wooden handrails. It went up to the first floor where a landing was such that you could look across the lobby and then continued up to the second floor. It was quite a jaw-dropper.

I pushed through the revolving door closest to me and headed to the reception desk. A middle-aged woman with her blond hair all pinned atop her head glared at me. I was kind of sick of these people assuming I was a vagrant with no money.

"Can I help you?" she asked with plenty of distaste laced in her tone.

I glanced around. "This is a hotel, right? So, assuming the sign outside isn't a lie, I would probably like a room," I stated.

She arched an eyebrow up and leaned forward. "The cheapest rooms in this hotel run at $300 a night. I don't think I need to say more. There is a motel down the street that is probably more your style."

I tugged my bag around to my side and pulled my faded brown leather wallet with the worn corners out and opened it up. I slapped three one-hundred-dollar bills on the counter and stared up at her.

"I'll take one of your cheap rooms."

She stared down at the money and then back up at me. She shoved her chin forward. "We need a credit card on file in case anything in the room comes up missing or is damaged."

I closed my eyes. "I don't carry a credit card. I have enough money in my wallet to buy this fucking hotel, so I don't think I'll be stealing any of your priceless artwork or bathrobes."

12

That little statement had her looking at me in a different light. Why was it that any mention of your worth instantly changed how people looked at you? It was disgusting really.

She cleared her throat and began typing on her computer. "I just need a name Mr....?"

"Marlow."

She stared at me for a moment before typing once again. She then turned and opened a glass-front case with keys hanging on small gold hooks. Each gold key had a tag attached to it with the room number on it. They probably recently updated the hotel, but I was glad to see they retained the old-school lock and key. It was always good to keep some of the grandeur of what the building used to be. Added some history to it.

She slid the key across the desk. "Elevators are just down that way. If you need anything tonight, Mr. Marlow, you can give the front desk a call," she said with a wink.

Yeah, I'd be passing on that. Besides, I was seventeen, a little young for her in my opinion. I nodded my head and grabbed the key. I made my way down the marble hall beside the staircase to where the elevators were. I pushed the '/\' button and glanced at my key. Number 418 was stamped on the key ring.

I stepped inside the elevator that was so polished on the inside that it was like three hundred and sixty degrees of mirror surrounding me. I pushed the '4' button and leaned against the back wall. The doors shut and I felt that unnerving feeling in my stomach. It was the same feeling I had when I was in an airplane, that feeling your stomach gets right as the plane's wheels leave the runway. I hated that feeling. It was like letting some outside force control your body.

The elevator binged as it stopped on the fourth floor and the doors slid open. The same red carpet that covered the grand staircase covered the floors. A sign on the wall across from the elevator read:

< Rooms 400 – 449
Rooms 450 – 499 >

I headed left down the hall and twisted and turned down the proper halls until I finally came to Room 418. I slid the key into the lock and shoved the door open. The red carpet was in the rooms as well. They must have gotten a really good deal on it.

A long hall separated the door from the main bedroom. Along the hall was an open closet with bare hangers dangling and an extra pillow and blanket on the shelf above the hangers. On the floor sat a black safe with the key in it.

On the other side of the hall was an open door leading to the bathroom. It was all bright white and chrome fixtures. It was very… clean.

I walked deeper into the room. A massive desk/TV stand set against the wall. On one half of the wooden piece set a flat screen TV and a channel guide. The other half contained stationery, pens, and binders with menus. Beside the sliding doors set a small square table with two chairs.

And then there was that king-sized bed. It had a charcoal-gray comforter and black sheets. There were four super-puffy pillows in the same black material as the sheets. It was flanked by two black nightstands with chrome light fixtures. On one nightstand set the standard Bible that came in every hotel room.

I dropped my bag on the end of the bed and sat down next to it. I pulled my boots off and stretched my feet out. I reached across the open space and grabbed the remote off the TV stand. I hit the power button and dropped the remote on the bed. I didn't care what was on; I just needed some noise.

I peeled off my clothes, opened my bag, and grabbed out a pair of boxers and headed into the bright bathroom. I was glad I picked this expensive place. It came with all sorts of fancy shampoos, conditioners, soaps, a razor, shaving cream, toothbrush, and toothpaste.

I stepped into the shower and stared at the complex system of faucets and handles until I figured out how to get the water to come out of the showerhead. I gave a few more twists to get the water the right temperature between what felt like the frigid Arctic and the fires of Mordor. I swear all showers have that fine line between ice-cold and scalding hot. This one was no different.

I scrubbed my long hair with shampoo and then washed my body. I let the warm water run down my back for a while. It sort of helped relieve the ache. I shut off the water and then grabbed a white towel from the shelf above the toilet and wrapped it around my waist. I brushed my teeth and then it was time to do something about this beard.

I filled the sink with hot water and shook up the can of shaving cream and squeezed the top. The '*sssshhhhhffffffftttttt*' sound of the shaving cream exiting the can always cracked me up. The white fluff filled the palm of my hand. I rubbed my hands together and then gently coated my dark, ratty beard with it. Then I took hold of the razor.

Twenty minutes of shaving with a semi-shitty razor and my face finally looked like my own. My eyes traveled up to where my dark hair hung. I walked back into the room and pulled a pair of scissors from my bag. I took a handful of the straggly mess and just sheared it off. I cut and cut and cut until it was short and even on both sides and the top was a little longer and stuck up in a sort of Statue of Liberty kind of way.

I felt and looked like myself once again. I was dry by the time I was finished with all the hacking away of my hair. I tossed the towel across the side of the bathtub and pulled on my boxers. I set my bag on the square table and pulled the gray and black covers back and slid into the bed. It was even cozier than it looked. I shut the lights off and fell asleep with the blue glow of the TV playing an infomercial for a juicer.

Chapter 2

I walked in the backdoor of my house that led into the kitchen to my Aunt Kate standing there with her hands on her hips. She glanced up at the clock on the wall and then back at me.

"I said that you could stay out until midnight. It is 12:45, Emily," Kate said in a disapproving tone that would make any parent proud.

"I never wear a watch, and even if I did, I wouldn't have it on at the beach. And I left my cell in the car. I thought I was leaving at a decent time. I am sorry, Kate."

Her hair was the same shade as mine, a dark brown that neared black. She had dark, long lashes that most women would kill for. And they were natural. She had soft brown eyes that even when she was mad still held a kindness.

Kate put up with a lot from her nieces and nephews. One day, when she was single and not tied down without a care in the world, she received a phone call that her sister and brother-in-law had died and she was the guardian of their four kids: the oldest was my sister Camilla, my older brother Drew, my younger brother Toby, and me.

Even though we knew that we were all thrust on her, we did nothing to help. She was constantly getting calls from school about Drew punching someone, Toby breaking an arm, Camilla caught making out with a boy in an unused classroom, and me lipping off to a teacher. We weren't exactly the best kids in the world.

My parents died when I was eight. Camilla was ten, Drew was nine, and Toby was seven. We were still fairly young when it happened, but old enough to know that we would never see either of them again. It was hard on all of us, which was probably why three out of the four of us had attitude issues. Toby was the sweet one, and that was probably because he was the baby.

"It's alright, but just remember that you are still grounded from last week. Your grounding will be lifted once school starts." With that, she walked out of the kitchen, hitting the lights as she went, plunging me into darkness.

Apparently, staying out with friends until four in the morning and getting caught on top of the roof of the school was the cause for a two-week grounding. We hadn't done any damage, but Kate freaked. She yelled at me about respect for private property and something about how this was like a gateway drug into becoming a full-fledged criminal.

She let me out of my grounding for one night. The bonfire at the beach always happened the Friday before school started back up. It was a junior-and-senior-only party. I had left before most of the people had even shown up. I knew that Drew and Camilla would be there, but Toby, being a sophomore, was up in his room.

I walked through the kitchen without the aid of a light. I had lived in the house my entire life, so I could get around in the dark without a problem. In their will, Mom and Dad left Kate the house. It was a tiny consolation for also getting their four children.

I walked through the kitchen, into the living room, and up the steps to where my room was. The second floor opened into a wide square landing. Six white doors were all that was visible. Behind four of the doors were each of our rooms and the other two doors held bathrooms. Kate's room was on the main floor and she had a bathroom of her own.

Four high-schoolers trying to get ready in the morning in two bathrooms was no treat. Camilla and I shared one, and my two brothers shared the other. Camilla was the girl who showered every morning, styled her hair just right, and then applied a ton of makeup. My sister was gorgeous without it, but still insisted that it 'enhanced her beauty.' Needless to say, every morning she hogged the bathroom, giving me about five minutes to get ready.

Camilla had graduated in the spring and was moving out and heading to college. I honestly didn't know who was more excited about her departure, her or the rest of us who lived with her.

I loved my sister, but she was… well, she was a slut. She whored it up with nearly half the guys in the school. She was tall, with long legs, blond hair, and eyes that were seductive. She never went without getting attention from guys.

She had self-respect oozing out of her and never let what anyone said get to her. Only one thing could make her snap and that was what would come out of Drew's mouth on a near-constant basis. He would tease her about being the only one of us with blond hair. He always told her that she was adopted and didn't belong with us. We all knew that wasn't true, even though the only resemblance she shared with us was that her eyes and Drew's eyes were nearly the same color of blue. It was a dark shade, kind of like the color the sky gets as a storm is moving in.

I opened my bedroom door and stepped into my sanctuary. There was only one rule that the four of us held to: Never go into one another's rooms. No one wanted their belongings messed with, so we may have teased and taunted each other unforgivingly, but we never went into one another's rooms without being invited.

As it was, before I even closed my door, Toby was standing on the other side of it. His mouth was tugged up at one corner.

"Did Kate tear you a new one?" he asked.

"Not really. I'm still grounded until school starts," I said.

"Eh, only two more days. I think you can handle that. So, was Mason hovering over you all day?"

"No, he was too busy being ogled by all the other girls on the beach."

Toby shook his head. Toby and I could have passed for twins. We had the same shade of dark brown hair. Our eyes were both gray, even though mine were a darker shade. We had the same oval-shaped faces, straight noses with a little slope at the end, and full lips. He was a little taller than I was, but not much. He had yet to hit a good growth spurt.

"I have a feeling you two are getting back together this year. When Mason wants something, he won't stop until he gets it. Isn't that how you two started dating in the first place?" he asked.

I nodded my head. I was cool with my siblings, but I really didn't want to discuss my relationships with any of them – least of all, my little brother.

"So, ugh, was Thea there?" he asked.

I gave him an annoyed look. "Of course, Thea was there. I really wish you would just ask her out."

"She's your best friend. What if we break up?"

"Well, don't do anything stupid. Just ask her on one date and go from there. Now, would you leave me alone? I'm tired and want to get this swimsuit off," I muttered, glancing down. I was only wearing a pair of black shorts, my black bikini top and flip-flops.

Toby shook his head and headed back to his room as I shut and locked my door. I walked across my room to the window. I was about to shut the curtain so the pervy neighbor across from us couldn't do any peeping when I saw someone in our yard waving their arms over their head to get my attention. I couldn't see who it was, since it was dark out. I unlatched the lock on the top and slid the window up and leaned on the sill.

It was Mason and his best friend Micah. I let out a groan loud enough that they could hear it. Micah chuckled. That earned him a glare from Mason.

"Em, why'd you leave the party?" Mason asked.

"Because you were there," I stated dryly.

"Very funny. Seriously though?"

"I'm grounded. Kate let me stay at the party until midnight."

"Let me talk to her. She loves me. She'll let you come back," he said.

"Kate hates you."

"Why?" He had the audacity to sound affronted by this newsflash.

I tapped my chin with my finger. "I wonder why my aunt would hate my cheating ex-boyfriend. Yeah, no idea!" I muttered sarcastically.

Micah started laughing. Mason glanced over at him and then wrapped an arm around Micah's head and pulled him to the ground. Then they started wrestling and throwing punches at each other. I shook my head. After a few minutes, they stood up like nothing had happened.

"Come on, Em. Just sneak out," Mason suggested.

"Don't think so. My grounding ends in two days and I'm not ruining that for one beach party. There will be more."

"Will you please take me back?" he begged. He dropped to his knees and held his hands together in a prayer position.

I rolled my eyes. "Not going to happen."

"I told you, Mase. You screwed up. That," Micah said, pointing at me, "was your girlfriend."

"Aww, Micah, you are so sweet," I said to him.

"You know it, babe."

Just then, the outside light flicked on that had Mason and Micah throwing their hands up to shield their eyes. Then I heard Kate's voice.

"What are you doing on my property?"

"Just seeing why Emily left the party early. We didn't know she was grounded, Ms. Jensen," Micah said. Kate liked Micah, so it was good that he was talking and Mason was keeping his mouth shut.

Kate walked out into the yard and looked up at me in the window. I could see the glare on her face from here.

"I'm in my room. I can't help it when people are outside my window trying to get my attention," I automatically said on the defense.

"Boys, it's time you left. Emily, close your curtain. Mr. Rayner's lights are still on," Kate said, indicating the pervy, peeping neighbor.

Micah and Mason waved up at me as they left. Kate looked up at me again. "I swear you're the only girl in this town with two guys standing outside her window in nothing but swim trunks and flip-flops," Kate said, shaking her head. She walked back in the house and the outside light went off.

I shut and locked my window and closed my curtain. I yanked on the string that held my bikini top on, and it dropped to the floor. I kicked my shorts off and the matching bottoms. I grabbed a long tee shirt out of my closet and pulled it on.

I loved my bedroom. The walls were a mint green and trimmed in bright white. My bed was shoved against one wall in the corner of the room. Sheer white curtains hung around it with white lights wrapped around the headboard and footboard. Assorted pillows were piled on the bed against the wall.

On my walls were two prints of famous paintings. One was Monet's *Bridge over a Pond of Water Lilies* and Van Gogh's *Starry Night over the Rhone*. One picture was on my wall, and that was an original painting done by Toby. It was of a man standing with trees all around him. It would have been a completely normal painting except for the blue streaks that were coming out of his palms and swirling around him and the trees. It was beautiful.

Against the wall opposite my bed was my white dresser. An assortment of random knickknacks covered the top: necklaces hung on a wooden tree, a small statue of Buddha, a tea light candleholder in the shape of a velociraptor, a piece of a blue broken bottle that had been smoothed by the waves on Lake Superior, and a silvered frame picture of our family as a whole before it had been ripped apart.

Beside my dresser was my closet and next to the main door was my desk that sat my laptop, some pens, and notebooks. The bookshelf above my desk had books stacked horizontally just to make them all fit. I had a bit of a book-buying obsession. It was really my one vice. I couldn't go in a bookstore without adopting one of those lovelies.

I turned on the white lights that were around my bed and shut off the main light in my room. I crawled under the white sheets and comforter and fished my latest read out from between the sheets. I always fell asleep while reading. I was currently in the middle of Kerouac's *On the Road*.

The pounding on my door woke me up. There was no need for Drew to then yell, "EMILY! GET UP!" I groaned, rolled off my bed, and stumbled to the door. I yanked it open and threw my brother a dirty look.

"What?"

"It's ten o'clock. We have to be at school to register in thirty minutes. Get your ass ready," he stated before walking away, shaking his head.

I slammed my door shut and stalked to my closet. I stared into its depths for a while before grabbing out a pair of dark gray jeans and a white tee shirt. A black belt and black heels with sliver stripes completed my ensemble.

I headed to the bathroom and brushed my teeth. I knotted my hair up into a messy bun and threw some mascara on my lashes. A little lip-gloss and I was good to go. I didn't need to spend an hour in front of the mirror like my sister.

I went downstairs and found my brothers in the kitchen talking to Kate. All three of them had a cup of coffee in their hands. I loved coffee as much as everyone else in my family, but I never drank what was made in the house. It wasn't because I was a coffee snob, but because Drew added entirely too many grounds. The shit was like chugging tar.

"Why exactly do we have to leave by ten thirty when registration goes on until three?" I asked. I started rifling through my bag that I had left sitting on a stool from the night before.

"Hotch needs us there early to set up a practice schedule with him," Drew stated.

"Well, we can't disappoint the great and wonderful Hotch," I muttered.

"Emily!" Kate scolded. "He is there to help you hone your skills."

"How much more do I need to hone? I had the hang of it in my freshman year." To prove my point, I snapped my finger while whispering, "*Ignis*," causing a bright flame to roar up from my fingertips.

"NOT IN THE HOUSE!" Kate barked. "I swear one of these days, one of you will burn this place to the ground."

My brothers were chuckling.

I whispered, "*Intereo*," and the flame instantly went out.

"And that, Emily, is why you still need training. You use your gift uselessly. You are still careless with it," Kate stated. "Now, all three of you, go!"

Kate was beyond tired of us. She relished autumn when we were all back in school and she had some peace and quiet, at least until the school called her about one of us. The summers made her stressed.

Drew grabbed his keys off the hook by the door, and Toby and I followed him out to the driveway. Our family had three cars. Kate had her own, which was a gray BMW M6 Coupe. Drew and Camilla shared a car. It was a white Mercedes CLS550 Coupe. Toby and I shared the Black A5.

We dropped into the Mercedes, and Drew drove to Autumn Falls High School. Home of the Maple Leaves! We had the most terrifying mascot. Toby must have been ruminating as I was on our mascots' ferociousness.

"Why can't we be something more aggressive? Seriously, we have the shittiest mascot in the history of school mascots," he stated from the backseat.

Drew looked at him in the rearview mirror. "And what do you suggest a town called Autumn Falls name their high-school mascot?" he asked.

Toby shrugged his shoulders. "Most mascots don't have to do with the name of the town or school. I mean, what the hell can a maple leaf do? Drop an acorn on you?"

"That's an oak, not a maple," I replied.

"See! We're not even the most vicious tree!"

Drew started laughing. "Might as well suck it up, baby brother. You're going to be a maple leaf for three more years."

We pulled into the parking lot that only contained a handful of cars. I knew who each of those cars belonged to as well. We headed inside the building to the cafeteria where tables were arranged by class. We split up and went to set up our class schedule for the next school year.

I had the basics – English, math, history, gym, science, art, and study hall. I shoved my printed schedule into my bag and met my brothers out in the hall.

"Who do you have for homeroom?" Drew asked me.

"Watkins," I muttered.

"Oh, you're in for a treat!" he stated before walking down the hall. He pulled his keys out of his pocket as we neared a normal-looking door. Most people assumed it was a janitor's closet, but they were so wrong.

Drew glanced both ways down the hall and unlocked the door. We headed inside and he quietly shut the door behind us. We headed down the sparely lit narrow hall. An open doorway appeared on each side of the hall. Written over the top of one door was: *Women's Room*. Over the other door was *Men's Room*.

We continued on until we reached the main room. It was a massive room with high rafters. The floor was solid concrete. Along the walls were tables with all sorts of weapons laid out on red velvet. A blue mat was laid out on part of the floor.

This room used to house the pool before the school filled it in and built a new one that had a retractable roof. They left it open during the summer for those who didn't want to go to the beach. It brought in the school a decent amount of money.

Standing in the center of the room were eight people I had known for most of my life, seven of them I had grown up with.

My best friend Thea, my friends Sam and Tyler, Tyler's twin Evan, Micah, Mason, and Mason's sister Bridgette were there and standing just off to the side was our instructor Hotch.

Hotch always wore an expression of having just tasted something bad. He had black hair that was more so gray now. He had wrinkles next to each of his hazel eyes. He was a short man, easily the shortest person in the group of people among him.

"How nice it is for the Porters to join us," he stated. "Are your pyromancer abilities so grand that you do not need training anymore?"

Drew let out a low growl, but did not respond. Toby was silent and even I kept my mouth shut. We knew that Hotch didn't want an answer from us… or a smart-ass remark.

We stood among the group as Hotch began to speak. "My fellow Corlissians, today we will not be doing any formal training. I just want to set up a schedule so that during free periods and after school, you can come here to continue your training. I do expect everyone to be ready on Monday. Enjoy your last two days. If any of you wants to stay and practice, you are more than welcome to. There are a few of you who could use it." He eyeballed a couple of people.

Drew, Thea, Mason, Bridgette, Sam, and Tyler all headed for the door. I looked at Toby. "You coming?" I asked.

"No, I think I better stay. I could use some extra training," he muttered.

"You're a Porter, Toby. Being a pyromancer is in your blood… twofold," I replied.

"I know."

I started to walk away, but paused. "Call me when you're done and I'll pick you up. Okay?"

Toby nodded his head and gave me a smile.

I went outside to where everyone else was standing around their cars. Mason stalked up to me and threw his arm over my shoulder. I quickly shoved it off. He didn't even seem to notice.

"So, wanna grab some lunch with me?" he asked.

"No. I'm still grounded."

"You know, I'm starting to think this grounding is some bullshit excuse you're using to avoid me."

"And I have no reason to avoid you!"

"Emily, I apologized… a lot. I just want things to go back to how they were," he whispered as we neared the group.

I stopped and stared up at him. "I loved you, Mason. I really did. And you broke my heart. I'm not going through that again."

"And I promise I won't do it again!"

"Emily, come on," Drew hollered.

I tore my eyes away from Mason and got into the passenger seat of Drew's car. He just stared at me for a moment.

"Tell me you're not getting back together with that skeeze."

"He's not a skeeze and we're not getting back together," I replied.

"Good. That guy is nothing but trouble, Em."

Chapter 3

I woke up to the sun streaming into the room. I had forgotten to close the curtains and was rewarded for my behavior by being woken up at six a.m. I groaned and pulled the pillow I wasn't using over my head to block out the light.

It was then that my mind started racing. Thoughts entered my brain about all the things I needed to get done today. I needed to find an apartment to crash in until at least December. I needed to go buy some new clothes. And I had to register for school today.

It was always tricky signing up at a new school without a parent or guardian, but I was born with a certain amount of charisma that let me persuade lonely secretaries into doing me favors. I always used the excuse that my dad was out of town on business that just couldn't be avoided. Every school had bought that excuse so far. I was hoping that this school would be no different.

I pulled myself up in bed and stared at the TV for a moment. I had forgotten I'd left it on last night. I was so tired that as soon as my head hit the pillow, I was out. The news was on now. Weather. It was going to be eighty-five degrees today. And apparently, the town I was in was called Autumn Falls.

I leaned over, opened the drawer on the nightstand, and pulled out the phonebook that was in there. I flipped through the pages until I found apartments. I remembered the Audi girl told me that the school was on Maple Street. I looked for apartments that weren't too far from the school. There were only two complexes that were a short walk: Alpha Apartments and Domus Flats.

I crawled off the bed and grabbed a piece of paper off the desk. I scribbled down the two numbers and folded up the paper. Then I got dressed for the day. I pulled on my last pair of clean jeans, a dark gray tee shirt, and my boots. I went to the bathroom to brush my teeth.

I grabbed my wallet out of my bag and shoved the folded piece of paper in there. I grabbed the room key off the desk and headed downstairs. The blonde receptionist from last night was thankfully gone. I stood at the desk and waited for the redhead on the phone to finish her call.

"Something I can help you with?" she asked with a smile. Apparently, clean-shaven guys get better service.

"Can you tell me how to get to a decent clothing store from here?" I asked.

"Oh, all the clothing stores are just down the road. They're just a little further into town. And you're in luck. They're open early since school starts up on Monday."

"Thanks for your help," I said before walking out the door.

I made a right and walked down Main Street. I passed Maple on my way into town and could see the school looming, a massive brick building looking like a typical high school.

A little further down the road had me passing a handful of restaurants, and then there was a clump of clothing stores. The receptionist was right… They were all open.

The first one I came across, I did not enter. There were only white clothes in there – white shirts, white pants, white shorts, and skirts. It was like Frosty the Snowman threw up and this store was his vomit. It made me want to vomit too. I was no fan of white clothes.

The next one I came across had items that were more my style. The store itself was darker with hardly any lights on, and the walls were black. The clothes themselves were a whole lot darker too.

"What can I do for you, man?" a guy with spiky black hair asked from behind the counter.

I walked up front and pulled my wallet out. I slapped five hundred dollars on the counter. "I need jeans, shirts, socks, boxers, everything. Can you hook me up?" I asked.

A wide smile spread onto the guy's face. "Not a problem," he said, walking around the counter.

You know those movies where the main female is choosing a prom gown or a new look and there's that montage of her in the dressing room trying on cheesy outfits until she finally finds that perfect one? Yeah, I didn't have that experience.

I didn't have to try on a damn thing – one of the many joys of being a male. We had standard sizes for jeans and standard sizes for shirts. Two hours of scouring the racks and six hundred and fifty dollars later, I had a new wardrobe.

My new buddy, Colin, who owned the store let me borrow his phone to call on the apartments. He said that Alpha Apartments were where the stuck up people lived. He had a few friends who lived in Domus.

I called on Alpha first, and as luck would have it, they didn't even have any openings. Domus had two flats available and the landlord was willing to show me them both.

Colin gave me directions to Domus. I headed out of the store with two bags of clothes and made yet another right. At the next street, Cedar, I made a right. A few blocks down, I came to Domus Flats. It was an old factory that had been turned into apartments. I was already in love.

The landlord met me out front. "Hey, you must be Mr. Marlow. I'm Davis," he said. He was a man of short stature with a gut. He had a ball cap on, but it looked like he was bald. He wore a smile on his face.

He led me into the old factory while giving me a history lesson on the place. "This used to be an assembly line making buttons. That was before the war though. They had to make parts for guns and tanks during the war. After that, the place fell empty. A man from one of the big cities bought it and he gutted the place. He turned it into a mass book-printing factory. Well, he decided to move his factory closer to the city, and once again, this place was empty. That's when I bought it and turned it into what you see now."

"Well, if you only have two apartments left open, you must be doing a hell of a business. So, it was a good investment," I replied.

"It's stressful at times, but I love helping people. All my tenants are great people too," he said with smile still on his face. I didn't think the guy stopped smiling.

After walking down a long, narrow hall, we came to the first available apartment. It was fully furnished. A kitchen was right beside the front door and the bathroom was across from the kitchen. A wall separated the kitchen from the living room. There was a couch, two chairs, and a TV. Beside the living room was a dining room table. Next to the living room was the bedroom with a queen-sized bed and a nightstand.

"This is the bigger of the two that are available. Let's go check out the other," Davis said.

I nodded my head and followed him out of the apartment and down the hall a little way. We took a flight of stairs up to the second level and stopped outside B12.

As soon as I stepped inside, I knew that I had found my place. The kitchen was to the left of the door. A very small kitchen. A wall rose up on the other side of the kitchen to the only thing that was enclosed, the bathroom. To the right of the door was a couch and TV. At the far end of the open space was a massive window with a sheer white curtain and heavier black curtains that were drawn back. In front of the window was the queen-sized bed with a nightstand on each side.

"How much?" I asked.

Davis started laughing. "Well, you just get right to the point, don't ya?" He paused. "First, I don't make you sign a contract. It's a month-by-month system, so you're not tied down. Everything is included in the rent – trash, recycling, water, and power. There are two laundry rooms on each floor. Rent is $300 a month."

"Done."

Davis shook his head. "Since this month is nearly over, I'll let you pass on the rent. Rent is due on the fifth of every month."

We shook hands, and Davis dropped two keys in my palm. "Good to have you here, Mr. Marlow."

"One question."

"What's that?"

"What does Domus mean?" I asked.

"It's Latin for home."

I dumped my clothes on the bed and left the apartment. I headed to the school to sign up for classes. It was only two blocks away from the Domus. As I was walking up to the school, I saw the Audi girl. Blond volleyball player was talking to her again. I wanted to know what was up with them… badly. Were they a couple? Exes? Friends with benefits?

I headed into the school and followed the signs that read: *Registration*. Those signs led to the cafeteria. All the tables had been pushed against the wall. It was divided up by class rank. I made my way to the junior table. A gray-haired woman helped me.

"You must be new, deary," she said when I sat down. I nodded my head shyly.

"My dad wanted to be here, but he was called out on business at the last minute. Is that going to be a problem?" I asked.

"Not here. Hardly any parents sign their kids up anymore. The students know what they need."

"A very progressive school then," I replied.

She smiled at me and nodded her head. "All right. Do you have a copy of your transcripts?" she asked.

"My previous school said they could fax them on Monday."

"Again, not a problem. We're very trusting here. Let's start with your name then."

"Killian Marlow," I said.

She glanced up from the paper she was about to write on. "Family name?" she asked.

"Yup," I lied.

"Interesting," she said. She started writing my name Cillian, so I had to interrupt her and change it to its proper spelling.

It took an hour to get registered. That lady wore me out with all the questions and filling out forms. I finally stood up with a schedule in hand and a locker number with the combination.

I went back to the Perlinian Hotel. I grabbed my bag out of the room and headed downstairs to check out. On the way back to my apartment, I stopped by a store to pick up essentials – bathroom stuff, kitchen stuff, laundry stuff, and school supplies.

I spent Sunday sleeping in ridiculously late. I remembered to close the curtains the previous night and ended up sleeping away half the day.

I used up the rest of the day by doing several loads of laundry and putting away all my clothes. I put all the bathroom and kitchen things away. I took inventory on what I still needed, pretty much food and a cellphone and I was set.

I headed back into town and stopped by the closest cellphone store. In twenty minutes, I had a new cellphone and was on my way to the store.

The grocery store was small in size, which usually meant that everything was jacked up in price. I was surprised to find that wasn't the case here. I was starting to get the feeling that this town was full of the disgustingly rich. All the cars I had seen were expensive luxury cars. None of the houses were rundown. Most of the houses were two-story solid brick with a concrete driveway and perfectly manicured lawns.

I bought what I needed and headed home. I put away my groceries and made it an early night.

My past haunted my dreams that night. Images of my childhood that I thought I had forgotten came into my mind like a flood.

I saw myself at five years of age, sitting on the piano bench. My feet were dangling down and were nowhere near long enough to reach the pedals. My father was looming over me. I could feel the nervous pinch in my stomach. I hit a wrong key and felt the sting across the back of my hands from the yard stick he was holding.

"Play it again," he'd say in his deep voice.

Even when I would play a set completely right, he would still find something to criticize – my clothes, the way I was sitting, the way my fingers moved across the keys. Because of him, I hated playing the piano, even though I could play any piece in front of me.

"You strive to disappoint me. You play horribly. You are a disgrace to this family and a greater disgrace to the name of Marlow. How you are my son, I will never know."

The image of my father beside the piano blurred away and my little sister replaced him. She was lying on her bed with her teddy bear tucked in next to her. She was ten and I was fourteen.

She looked up at me with her big blue eyes. "Promise, you won't leave me, Killian," she whispered.

"I promise, Zoë," I replied. I didn't know it then, but that turned out to be a lie, a lie I wished I could take back. I loved two people in this world and I had outright lied to one of them.

My sister's image swirled away and was replaced by me at fifteen. My father had dropped me off at school that morning. I was taking some bullshit physics course over the summer. He glared at me as I got out of the car.

"Try and learn something of use today," he said before speeding off. The school stood in front of me, beckoning me to enter it. I turned and walked the other way. I went to the bank instead.

My mom had set up a savings account for me and one for my sister when we were both born. Anytime we would receive money, whether it was from birthdays, Christmas, or just on random occasions, she would take the money and deposit it into our accounts. When her parents died, they left all of their money to their only daughter. Mom took all that money and split it between Zoë's and my accounts. It became an enormous trust fund, a trust fund that our father knew nothing about.

That morning, I took out a small amount. Somehow, over fifteen years, my mom had garnered me a two-hundred and fifty-thousand-dollar savings account. And in minutes, two-hundred and fifty thousand dollars was in my bag and I was on the first bus out of town. I didn't even know where I was headed. I just needed to get away.

The bus rolling down the road faded away and in its place was a girl standing in a parking lot with a grin on her face. She was in black shorts and a black bikini top. Audi girl – the reason I was drawn to this town in the first place, her oddness, her fearlessness, her carelessness… I needed to know more about her. I didn't even know her name.

Chapter 4

"Please, Kate. I won't even stay out that late," I begged. It was Sunday evening and the last night of freedom before school and training began. Everyone was going to be out having a grand old time… except me.

"Emily, you are still grounded. The answer is no."

"This is bullshit!"

"Emily! Language!" Kate snapped. She hated when we cussed and we knew it.

"Thea and Sam aren't grounded. You want to know why they aren't grounded? Because we didn't break into the school. We used the fire escape on the side of the building to get to the roof. You want to know what we did on the roof? We lay there and watched meteorites. Because that's what soon-to-be criminals do!"

"I don't care what you did. You should not have been on the roof of the school. You know how well that building is monitored during the summer. I'm glad you weren't doing anything bad, but you just have to put up with one more night," Kate explained.

I rolled my eyes. "This is fucked up," I muttered under my breath.

"Excuse me?" Kate asked.

"Drew beats people up every other week and he doesn't get grounded. Camilla was a walking whore and she never got grounded. Why exactly do you pick on me? It's not like you're making an example out of me for anyone."

"I'm not making an example out of you. You have so much potential and I feel like you're wasting it."

I crossed my arms over my chest. "Can I ask for one favor, since I'm going to be stuck here tonight?" I asked.

Kate nodded her head. "May I please drive to the store to pick something up and then come right back?"

Kate eyed me for a moment. I thought she was going to say no, until she walked over to her purse and pulled her keys out and handed them to me. As I reached out to grab them, she pulled them back. "You have twenty minutes.

Any later than that and I will call the cops," she said before dropping the keys in my hand.

"The cops!" I uttered, shaking my head. I snatched my purse from the island and headed out the backdoor. I hopped in Kate's BMW and drove to the store. It was full dark out and the roads were packed with my classmates all heading to the beach for the end of summer party.

The store's parking lot was nearly empty. I hopped out of the car and went in the store. I made a beeline for the hair-care products – shampoos, conditioners, sprays, and gels. My eyes were searching for the dyes though. I picked through the selection and found the color I desired.

I went up to the counter to find Micah leaning against it. He straightened up when I neared.

"I see you're not at the party tonight," he said, ringing up my purchase. Micah's parents owned the store and made him work there a lot. The poor guy missed out on a lot of parties because of his obligations to the family business.

"Nope. My last night of grounding. I'm free tomorrow only for school to start and for Hotch to take up my time after school."

"I feel ya. We're in the same boat," he replied. "So, what are you doing tonight?" he asked.

I glanced down at the box of hair dye. "Pissing my aunt off," I said with a smile.

Micah shook his head. "You are one of a kind, Emily Porter."

I always liked Micah. He was one of those guys who could integrate in with any group at school. He was just a likable guy. He had jet-black hair and naturally tanned skin from his Israeli mother. He had big brown eyes that were hidden behind his black-rimmed glasses. He was tall and lean and was rarely seen without a smile on his face. His only downfall was that he was Mason's best friend.

"If you say so." I grabbed the box off the counter and made for the door.

"I'll see the new color tomorrow!" he called out to me.

I waved my hand in the air as I was walking away.

I thanked the moon and stars that Kate was not in the kitchen or living room when I got home. She was in her room and the door was closed. I crept by and when I was at the base of the stairs, I yelled, "I'M HOME!" and took off running up the stairs.

I dropped my purse on my bed and put a ratty shirt on that I didn't mind getting damaged… because it would get damaged.

I went to the bathroom and closed the door. I mixed everything together and stared at the applicator bottle. It was some hellish gray color. I shrugged and went to work. I didn't want all my hair that color, but just lots of streaks. It took some time and patience until I was through. I set the timer for twenty minutes and went back to my room.

I found Kerouac somehow shoved under my fit sheet and plopped down on the floor to read while the time ticked away in the bathroom.

I heard the ding and glanced down at my tee shirt that had new colorful splotches on it. I discarded my clothing and hopped in the shower. I watched as the water went from clear to a light purple to a much darker purple. Once the water ran clear again, I scrubbed myself clean and shaved. I got out of the shower and went to the mirror. My hair was nearly black when it was wet, so I couldn't see anything.

I ran a brush through it and blow-dried it. Then I could see the purple streaks. A smile spread onto my face. I loved it. I loved it even more because Kate was going to hate it. I guess this was what she might have meant by me wasting my potential.

I brushed my teeth, lotioned up, and locked myself in my bedroom for the rest of the night.

My cellphone rang endlessly. I never picked it up though. I couldn't bear to hear the fun that everyone else was having. I glanced at a few texts:

"Miss u, Em…"

"Wish u were here…"

"Stealing Mason from u…"

"Can I ask yur bro out?"

"When did Toby get hot?"

After that, I stopped reading and put my cell on silent.

Toby just stared at me for the longest time without saying anything. "I'm not saying I don't like it, cause I do, but Kate is going to kill you," he finally said after taking in my hair.

"You can hardly even see it." That was a lie. You could definitely see it, but it mixed in good with my natural hair color.

Drew walked out of his room, paused, smiled, gave me a nod of the head, and went downstairs.

His black hair was sticking up on all sides looking like a mess. The thing was that he would leave it like that. His hair was perpetually jacked up and he couldn't care less.

Toby followed in Drew's wake. I took a deep breath and prepared myself for the Monday-morning onslaught of Kate versus Hairgate.

Kate was leaning against the counter talking to Drew and eating a bowl of cereal when I rounded the corner to the kitchen. The spoon she was holding slipped from her hand and clattered to the floor.

"EMILY CHARLOTTE PORTER! WHAT HAVE YOU DONE?"

Drew and Toby wisely held back their laughter.

"Just trying out a new look," I said coolly.

"Is this what you were doing last night? Is this what you did instead of me letting you go out?" she asked, trying to hold her anger in.

"Yes."

"You're dying it back tonight. No niece of mine is walking around with purple hair."

"No, I'm not." That was when my brothers both rose from their perches on the stools at the island and went upstairs. I knew that they stopped halfway up the stairs to listen though.

"No? No? Emily, as your guardian, it is my duty to…"

"It's hair, Kate. I didn't kill anybody, I didn't break in and rob a bank, and I didn't steal anything. I dyed my hair. It will grow out. Leave it alone," I stated.

I turned around and walked out of the kitchen. "We are not done with this conversation, Emily," she said to my retreating figure.

She might not have been done, but I was. I found my brothers scurrying up to the second-floor landing. I went to my room and dressed for the day — black leather leggings, mid-calf black boots, and a white tank top under a dark gray Henley.

In the bathroom, I did my standard routine: brush teeth, brush hair, mascara, lip-gloss, and done. I threw a few notebooks in my bag and a few new pens and pencils. I grabbed my purse off my desk and walked across the hall to Toby's room.

"I'm leaving," I called through his door.

Drew walked passed me fully dressed with his bag slung over his shoulder. "I like the hair, Em," he said quietly before descending the stairs.

Drew drove separately from Toby and me. He and Camilla would always drive together, and Toby and I would drive together. This year, he had the car to himself since Camilla was gone. She was living in the dorms on campus and would not need a car, according to Kate.

Toby opened his door. He was running one of his hands through his hair to spike it up in the front. "I haven't eaten breakfast yet, thanks to you and Kate having your yell-a-thon," he said, focusing on his reflection in the mirror.

"We'll stop somewhere and I'll buy you breakfast," I promised.

He glanced at me. "McyDees?" he asked.

I wrinkled my nose. "Sure." I was no fan of ingesting lard for breakfast, but to accommodate Toby, I would.

"Sweet!" He quite literally shoved the items that were on his desk into his bag and zipped it closed. "Let's roll."

We pulled up into a line at the drive-through. It looked like it was mostly students getting healthy breakfasts at McDonalds rather than ingesting the slop they served in the cafeteria. Can't say I blamed them.

When it was our turn to order, Toby leaned across me and yelled what he wanted at the box. "I WANT THE BIG BREAKFAST AND A SMALL COFFEE!"

"Make that two small coffees," I added in a much more gentle tone.

We inched our way forward and I paid. Then we inched forward some more until we finally got our order. Toby tore into his food, shoving sporkfuls of food in his mouth.

I cringed. "God, it's like watching one of those nature shows right in my passenger seat." I put on my Australian accent. "Today we see the young lion cub eat the scraps of food his mother left for him. Look at how he consumes the food with such vigor. Ah, yes. Now we see him tearing at the sausage patty with those large canines. This is exactly why the lion has those teeth. Oh, now he's using his paws to shovel scrambled eggs into his mouth."

Toby laughed and some food exited his mouth and landed on the floorboard and dashboard of the car.

"Stop doing that when I eat," he said with a mouthful of food while mopping up his mess.

"We have clearly angered the young cub by disturbing his morning meal. Stay tuned for the next episode as we watch the cub interact with his peers," I finished.

"Kate shouldn't have yelled at you this morning," Toby blurted out.

"Wow, you really know how to bring the mood way down," I murmured.

"She shouldn't have though. It's your body and you have to live with the consequences of what you do to it. And like you said, it's just hair."

"You should know that I'm doing this for you. Keep doing whatever it is you do and you'll come off looking like the golden boy after me," I replied.

"That's not funny, Em." He paused and looked out the window. "You're not a bad role model to have. I do look up to you. You're a fantastic pyromancer. I'm no good at it. You have all these awesome friends and I have like two friends. I feel like a slacker coming up behind you and Drew, and even Cami."

"Don't strive to be like us, Toby. Be your own person. And for the love of all that is good in this world, do not listen to what Hotch says to you. I've seen you do pyromancy and you're damn good at it. He's just jealous because everyone in our family is great at it, and even at his best, he had nowhere near our talent."

Toby sighed. "It's just that I feel like I can't compete with you, Drew, and Cami," he said.

I pulled down the street that the school was on. "Well, that's your problem. Don't compete with us. I never even tried to follow in Cami and Drew's footsteps and neither should you. Don't be a slut like Cami, don't beat people up like Drew, and do not have an attitude problem like me. You're the sweet one, kid. Honestly, the three of us should strive to be like you."

That had a blush spreading across Toby's cheeks. He looked up at me. "I'm glad you're my sister, Em."

"Umm? You're welcome?" I replied.

"I mean that if you weren't my sister, you'd be just some student that I go to school with. I wouldn't get these pep talks that make me feel like I can take on the world for the first day of school," he said with a grin.

I pulled into the parking lot that was nearly full. I found a spot near the back of the lot, not that Toby or I minded the walk. Toby split from me when he saw his friends hanging out next to one of their cars.

I walked in the school and headed toward where my group of friends always waited for the first bell to ring. It was at the opposite end of the hall, which meant that I had to walk by everyone else lining the halls.

I still had my sunglasses on, and I shoved them up onto my head as I walked down the hall. I could hear whispers when I passed and could feel the eyes of everyone on me. Maybe leather tights weren't the best choice for the first day.

Who was I kidding? My ass looked fantastic in them. And another thing, I didn't give a fuck what they might have been whispering about me.

Thea's mouth dropped open when I reached her.

"Oh… my… I love it, Emily!" she squealed, reaching up to play with my hair. "Drew said that you'd done something with it, but he wouldn't tell me what."

"Why were you talking to Drew?" I asked.

"No reason. But I did see Toby last night at the beach. When did your brother get hot?" she asked.

"Seriously, I'm not responding to that," I replied disgustedly.

"Ugh, Mason's headed this way and he does not look happy," Thea said, nodding her head down the hallway.

I turned to see Mason stalking down the hall with a pissed-off look on his face. His sunglasses were still covering his eyes. I was guessing he had a hangover from the previous night. I just knew that whatever was about to come out of his mouth was going to have everyone's attention on us.

Chapter 5

The alarm on my cellphone started chiming at 7:15 a.m. I hit my hand repeatedly on it until it shut off. I sat up and stared across my small apartment. A lazy smile crawled onto my face.

I flipped the blankets back and went to take a shower to wake my tired self up. After I was squeaky clean, I stood in front of my closet, staring at the array of clothing choices I had. I plucked a pair of dark jeans and black tee shirt out and pulled them on. My black boots were pretty much a staple to any outfit I wore.

I slipped the notebooks and pens I bought into my bag, shoved my wallet in my back pocket, and left the apartment for my first day of school at Autumn Falls High School.

I walked the two blocks over to the school. The parking lot, which had been nearly empty on Saturday, was now almost full. I headed inside.

All the students were waiting in the main hallway. Towards the front of the hallway, closer to where the classrooms were, was the administrative offices that were visible through the massive windows separating the offices from the hall. It was a good way to keep an eye on students as they congregated in the mornings.

Along one side of the hall were lockers with no locks. Most students leaned up against them or along the other side in front of the offices. A group of students were standing close to the doors that were closed until the first bell rang.

From my vantage point of leaning against two lockers, I was able to view the student body. Nearly all the guys, save for a few, were wearing preppy button-downs with jeans. Some wore vests over the button-downs and others wore ties. A few brave guys wore suits. It was nearing the end of summer, so it was still quite warm out. I didn't know how they were handling this no air-conditioned school in suits. The girls were dressed in their skimpiest summer outfits. They would be able to take on the warm school with ease.

This school clearly did not have a dress code.

I heard a guy beside me whisper to his friend, "There she is."

I turned my head to see who held their attention. And there she was indeed – the Audi girl. She was wearing tight black leather leggings with heeled black boots that stopped halfway up to her knees. On top, she was wearing a dark gray Henley and a white tank underneath. She lifted her sunglasses up and into her hair… her purple-streaked hair. Every single guy in that hallway had his eyes glued to her ass.

"Who is she?" the guy's friend asked.

"Emily Porter." The Audi girl finally had a name. "She used to date Mason Monroe, but she dumped him right after school ended this summer."

"Wait! She dumped Mason? I thought nobody broke up with him?"

"She's the first, so of course he wants her back."

Well, now I knew who she was and who the blond volleyball player was.

"There's Mason now," the guy beside me said. I swear the guys gossiped like girls, but I was sort of thankful for it at the time.

I turned my head to see Mason striding past everyone with his sunglasses still firmly in place. He was in a white button-down with the sleeves rolled up and dark jeans. He had a ticked-off look on his face and he was headed straight towards Emily.

Emily's friend whispered something to her that made her head snap in the direction of Mason. I could see her take a deep breath, preparing herself for what he had to say.

He stopped right in front of her. "Can we talk?" he asked deeply.

"I believe that's what we're doing," Emily replied.

"Somewhere more… private?"

"No," she said with a chuckle.

"Don't trust yourself alone with me?" he asked. I couldn't see his face, but I imagined that he was grinning.

"Oh yes! I've been waiting to get you alone so I can rip your clothes off and have my way with you. How did you know?" she said sarcastically.

Mason's arm extended quickly, and in an instant, his hand was gripping Emily's wrist. "You've had the summer. It's time to end this bullshit." His voice was lower, but loud enough that everyone could hear him in the silent hallway.

He started to tug her with him when another guy intervened. He had a head full of black hair that was a mess. He wore ripped jeans and a button-down that had the sleeves rolled up and was not tucked in.

"Get your hands off my sister. Now," he snapped.

Mason let go of Emily and the two guys were standing nearly nose-to-nose, even though Emily's brother was a good head taller than Mason. They were flexing their hands and I swore I saw a glow appear from their palms. It was obviously just a trick of the light in the hall.

Emily shoved herself in between the two guys. "Not here, you idiots. Calm the fuck down," she said.

"If I catch you even looking at her again, I will break your fucking neck," her brother growled.

Mason backed away a little more, nodding his head before turning on his heels and heading back the way he had come. Clearly, he wasn't finished.

This school wasn't exactly small, so there was no way her brother could keep tabs on her all the time.

School hadn't even officially started and there was already drama.

The bell rang and students started filing through the doors. Some students stayed on the main floor as others headed upstairs. I followed the flow that went up.

I found my locker and dumped my bag in there. I grabbed out a notebook and pen and headed to homeroom.

I sat two seats back from the front row on the side opposite the windows. I was studying my schedule and not paying attention to the other students who were trickling into the room, sitting in front, beside, and behind me.

The bell rang and the teacher walked in. "Good morning! It is lovely to see your bright, young faces on the first day of school! If your schedule does not say Mr. Watkins, then you are in the wrong room." He paused and waited to see if anyone moved. When no one did, he continued on. "Good. Oh, we have a new student joining us this year."

I groaned.

"Killian Marlow," Mr. Watkins said, staring at me. I could feel the eyes of everyone in class on me too. "Would you like to introduce yourself?"

"I believe you just did. No point in me doing the same thing," I replied.

Mr. Watkins nodded his head and glanced down at the clipboard in his hands. He started calling off names.

I felt a tap on my shoulder, so I turned around to see Emily sitting behind me. Her right hand was still in midair from tapping me and her left hand was cradling the side of her face.

"Is your name really Killian?" she asked.

"Yup."

She shook her head slightly. "That's too much of a mouthful..."

"Emily Porter?" Mr. Watkins called.

Emily raised her right hand in the air and then pointed down at herself.

"Ah yes, the third Porter child to grace my classroom, from the famous Porter dynasty."

Emily laughed. "We're not a dynasty, nor are we famous for anything," Emily replied, staring at the teacher.

"Trust me, everyone knows your family mostly due to the reputations of Camilla and Drew."

"Well, I don't know what my sister and brother's reputations have to do with me. Maybe I should go ask Drew, since he does still go here."

"Isn't there another sibling?"

Emily rolled her eyes. "Yeah, my brother Toby. He's the worst of all four of us. You have been forewarned," she said sarcastically.

"So, that makes you the least troublesome of your siblings?"

A smile tugged at the corners of her lips. "I wouldn't say that."

Mr. Watkins cleared his throat and continued on with the roll call.

"Like I was saying, your name is too long." She wrinkled her nose and slanted her eyes in thought. "I'm calling you Lian," she said.

I laughed. "All right. I like it," I replied.

"Oh, I don't care if you like it or not. That's what I'm calling you."

"Ms. Porter!" Mr. Watkins snapped.

"Mr. Watkins!" Emily retorted with the same tone of voice.

"Do you really want to spend your first day in the office?" he asked.

"At least it's air-conditioned," she stated.

"One more word from you and you'll be going to that air-conditioned office." Mr. Watkins stared her down.

I saw her lips twitching, trying to hold back. "Good," she blurted out.

"That's it! Office. Now!" Mr. Watkins barked.

Emily slowly stood up and stretched her back as she did. Then she turned around and bent over at the waist, sticking her leather-clad ass in the air. There were several wolf whistles from the males in the classroom and snickers from the females. She lifted her head up and smiled at me while looking me in the eyes. "I'll see you at lunch." With that, she righted herself and strutted out of the room.

Soon after Emily left did the bell for first period ring. I had math first up, which I was glad for. I hated math and just wanted to get it done and over with.

Mrs. Thomasson was the math teacher. She passed out the books we'd be using for the semester and then briefly discussed what we would be studying. She let students talk for the rest of the period. I sat there and doodled on my notebook.

Second period was English with Mrs. Everett. She was very lively, and you could tell she loved what she did. Her gray hair was all pinned on top of her head. Her eyes were a vibrant blue.

She spoke to the class as she passed out the three books we'd be covering. "I know it will thrill you all to know that we will not be studying Shakespeare this semester." A few hoots went around the room followed by laughter.

The three books she deposited were: *The Prophet* by Kahlil Gibran, *Persuasion* by Jane Austen, and *Looking for Alaska* by John Green.

I silently thumbed through the books as Mrs. Everett told us that we would be covering *Persuasion* first and that we needed to have the first chapter read by tomorrow.

Third period was history with Mr. Van Hough. He was a grizzled-looking man and reminded me a lot of the pictures I'd seen of Mark Twain. He spoke with a rough voice. I had a feeling that he was an ex-military man. He wasn't mean, like I expected him to be, but rather kind. He had soft brown eyes. His hair was starting to turn from dark blond to gray.

He too passed out the history book, but instead of giving us free time, he started lecturing. Students quickly opened their notebooks and started jotting down what he was saying. We were starting off with the start of World War I.

Mr. Van Hough rambled on for forty-five minutes and only stopped when the bell rang. A few students hung back to ask him questions.

I went straight to my locker to deposit the growing stack of books I had incurred in my first three classes.

I walked into the lunch room and pretty much just searched for an empty seat. I didn't think Emily meant anything by seeing me at lunch. I happened to walk by the table she was sitting at and heard a snippet of the conversation.

"I swear you are the only person to get sent to the office from homeroom," a girl said.

"It's not that big of a surprise. Watkins is a jackass," one of the guys replied.

"He probably just has it out for your family. Maybe he had the hots for your mom," one of the other guys suggested.

Just as I thought I was clear of their table, I came to an abrupt halt when someone grabbed the back of my shirt. I instantly prepared myself for a fight, but when I turned around, Emily was smiling up at me. She released my shirt and patted the unoccupied seat next to her.

"I said I'd see you at lunch," she stated.

"That doesn't mean you wanted me to sit with you," I replied.

"Well I do, new guy, so park it."

I slid the chair back and sat down. The table was really quiet.

"So, everyone, this is Killian Marlow, but I call him Lian. Lian, this is Sam Malik," she said, pointing at the guy with dark brown dreadlocks and lightly tanned skin. He had bright green eyes. Half of his mouth was turned up in a smile. His bottom lip was pierced with a hoop wrapping around the center of his lip. He had dark gray plugs in his ears. They were large enough that I could see straight through them to the people sitting behind him. He was one of the few guys wearing a tee shirt. A tattoo dipped below his shirt sleeve, but not enough that I could tell what it was.

"And this is Tyler Mitchell." Tyler had light brown hair, pale blue eyes, and a bored expression on his face. He was wearing a flannel shirt that was open with a tee shirt underneath. Unlike Sam, Tyler didn't have any visible tattoos or piercings.

"And this is my best friend Thea Cole." I remembered seeing Thea at the bonfire. She was the girl with white blonde hair. She had big blue eyes and freckles running across her nose and under her eyes. Her eyes were sort of shaped like a cat, coming to drastic points in both corners. She had full lips and dimples in her cheeks. A tiny diamond in her nose sparkled when she turned her head. I knew from the beach that she was shorter than Emily. Thea was wearing a flowy shirt with a vest over it that was hanging open. She had several necklaces and bracelets on.

"It's nice to meet you, Killian," Thea said in a soft voice. "So, where are you originally from?"

That question used to scare the crap out of me. I just didn't know how to answer it. The truth was never a good answer. You can't simply tell people that you ran away from home.

"I can't really remember," I said. "When I was younger, my dad was in the marines, so we didn't seem to stay in one place for very long. After he didn't enlist anymore, he and my mom divorced and I stayed with him. We still move around the country for his job though," I lied. Every last bit of that was a lie.

Everyone leaned on the table, asking me questions about growing up like that. I was assuming that they had all been born and raised in Autumn Falls. Emily was the only one not asking me questions.

She was leaning back in her chair with her arms crossed, eyeing me skeptically. Once the others were done berating me with questions, Emily asked, "Why don't you live with your mom?"

I turned my head to look at her. "We don't get along very well," I replied. Yet another lie. My mom and my sister were the only two people in this world I did love. "I suppose everyone has that one parent they sort of favor. The one they know they can ask anything of and they'll get it," I added.

Emily didn't reply.

"What? Do you not get along with either of your parents?" I asked.

"Wouldn't know. Both my parents are dead," she stated.

My mouth dropped open. I felt like an ass, but I didn't know. I swallowed down the lump in my throat. "How?" I asked.

Emily glanced across the table at Sam. He shook his head so slightly; I barely noticed it. Emily looked back at me. "Car wreck," she replied simply.

Clearly, I wasn't the only one with secrets in this town.

"Let me see your schedule," Emily blurted out, sitting upright. Everyone else at the table started talking about the schoolwork they had already been assigned.

I pulled my schedule out of my back pocket and handed it to her. She unfolded it and pressed it flat against the table.

"We have science together in next period and study hall in last period with the wonderful Mr. Watkins," she said. She glanced up at me. "What'd you think of Van Hough?"

"I like him. Seems knowledgeable. Though he did start lecturing right off the bat," I said.

"Well, heads up because Mr. Evans will too," she replied, refolding my schedule and handing it back to me.

The bell ending lunch rang out. "I'll see you in science," Emily said as we all stood up from the table.

"Does that mean that you want to sit with me?" I asked with a smile.

"You're catching on, Lian," she remarked. She winked at me before turning around. Thea looped her arm through Emily's as they exited the lunchroom together.

Sam patted me on the back. "Be careful around her," he said. I could see he had a green tongue ring when he spoke. "She's not like the rest of these bimbos. She can make you feel like you're the only person in the room with her in a crowd of people, but piss her off and you'll be wishing you'd never met her," he added. He smiled at me. "See ya later."

As much as I wanted to heed Sam's warning, I didn't see how I could not be around her. Something about her drew me in. She drew in a lot of people's attention actually. I had a good view of all the eyes following her out of the room and it had nothing to do with what she was wearing. It was just her.

Chapter 6

"So, the new guy is fit," Thea remarked as we opened our lockers that were next to one another.

"Oh, I noticed."

"He's a lot more muscly than Mason."

"Don't see what that matters, but you're not wrong," I commented.

Thea laughed. "If you hadn't stepped between him and Drew, they would have started throwing fireballs at each other, wouldn't they?"

I nodded my head. There wasn't a doubt in my mind. They would have started an outright war that no student in this school had ever seen. Drew and Mason hated each other. That hatred even preceded Mason and me dating.

"I'll see you later at training," Thea whispered before walking to her next class.

I nodded my head, even though I had no desire to go to training tonight. I didn't want to hear Hotch criticize every little thing I did wrong. I'd already had an earful from Watkins this morning. I didn't want to end my school day with getting another earful from Hotch.

I grabbed the same notebook and pen from my locker as I had used earlier. I'd probably fill up half of it just with whatever Van Hough was going to be lecturing about.

I headed to the opposite end of the building to where the science wing was located. There was an empty stretch of hall between the science wing and the rest of the school. I suppose that if something blew up, it would only kill those in that wing and spare the rest of the student body.

Lian was sitting at one of the tables in the back. I slid into the seat next to him without a word. I noticed that Mason was in this class too. Terrific!

"So, how's the first day going?" I asked.

"Fine," he said.

Lian was a good-looking guy. He had black hair and green eyes. His shirt bulged wider, going across his biceps and chest, and you could practically see his six packs through his shirt. He was wearing a plain black tee shirt and jeans. Those short sleeves did not hide the tattoo sleeves running down both of his arms. They were both weird geometric patterns in black ink. On his right thumb, there were four black dots in a straight line. He had some leather bands tied around both of his wrists.

"Hey, are there any decent coffee shops around?" he asked. I nodded my head. He smiled. "Can you tell me how to get to one?"

"I can do you better than that."

He made a half choking, half coughing sound which made me giggle and made Mason turn around in his seat.

"I'll show you myself," I finished.

"Umm, thanks," he muttered once he was composed.

"Meet me by the tennis courts after school," I insisted as Mr. Evans walked in the classroom.

Lian nodded his head and faced the front of the classroom. Mason gave me a look before turning around himself.

Mr. Evans started lecturing before even handing out the texts. He was teaching us about meteorology this semester. Mr. Evans absolutely loved teaching students science. I couldn't stand the subject, but he made it at least more bearable.

I glanced over and noticed that Lian was scribbling down notes. I poked him in the arm. "Don't take notes. Evans emails everyone his lectures," I whispered.

"Thanks," he said, laying his pen down and leaning back.

The bell rang, ending fourth period. Lian stood up. "I'll see you in study hall," I said as he walked behind me.

"Unless Watkins kicks you out of that too," he mused.

I wouldn't put it past him. The man would probably tell me to go to the office as soon as I walked in the door. Tyler was right. I think the guy had it out for my family.

Before I could gather all my belongings, Mason was leaning on the table in front of me.

"Can we talk now?" he asked with a smile on his face.

"I have class."

"And? I got you to skip class plenty of times with me last year." He wiggled his eyebrows at me.

I ignored his comment. "I don't see what we need to talk about."

He straightened up and frowned at me. "Us," he muttered.

"There is no us," I said, rising to my feet. "And there will not be an us again. Please, get that through your head." My voice started to rise in frustration.

Mason held his hands up. "Calm down, babe."

"No, I won't! I don't know what I have to do to get it through your thick skull that I'm not getting back together with you… ever." I grabbed my books off the table and walked around him.

I didn't turn around, but from the sound behind me, I was pretty sure he punched the table. I'm sure it hurt him worse than the table.

I sat through history with Van Hough for fifth period and math with Mr. Hilleen for sixth period.

I walked in seventh period, which was study hall. Mr. Watkins glared at me and I smiled at him. Might as well act like this morning didn't happen.

Some girl was sitting in the seat behind Lian. I stood beside her and glared down. "Move," I ordered. She quickly gathered her things and slid out of the chair and sat down across the room.

Lian turned around and laid his arm across my desk. "Are you always going to be behind me?" he asked.

"Would you rather want me to be in front of you?" I retorted.

He cocked his head to the side. "I see no problem with that," he replied.

I picked my stuff up and walked around him and plopped down in the seat in front of him. I turned around as he righted himself in his seat.

"Better?" I asked.

"The view is," he smirked.

I saw his eyes looking over my head and I grimaced. I knew that it was either Watkins or Mason standing there. I turned around, and sure enough there loomed Mr. Watkins.

"This is study hall, Ms. Porter."

"Well spotted."

"That means there is no talking during this hour. Is that understood?"

I smiled at him. "Oh, I understand you perfectly, Mr. Watkins." That fake-ass voice I used to mock people came out.

"I will kick you out of study hall too," he threatened.

"I wish you had told me that sooner. Then I could have tried for the trifecta today!"

I heard Lian sigh behind me. Mr. Watkins shook his head as he headed back to his desk.

I turned my head around. "He just said no talking. You heard that, right?" I asked. Lian nodded his head. I turned my head around and faced the front of the class.

The bell rang for seventh period to begin. I ripped a piece of paper out of my notebook and wrote: *Is it just me or does Watkins have a massive stick up his ass?*

I slid the note behind me and heard Lian snort. His pen clicked and I heard scribbling and he passed the note back.

"I'm pretty sure it's just you. You do seem to get on his nerves rather easily."

"It's all part of my charm, though it doesn't work on everybody." I slid the note behind me and heard him scribble something.

"Point out one person in this room, besides Watkins, who isn't enthralled with you."

I immediately glanced over at the girl who I told to move earlier. And sure enough, she was shooting daggers out of her eyes at me.

"The girl I told to move. She's glaring at me. Wait! Now she's staring at you, you sexy beast!"

Lian started laughing and slapped his hand over his mouth. Watkins lifted his head up. "Something amusing, Mr. Marlow?"

"Yeah, they were just having a grand old time in Sarajevo in 1914," he replied.

I turned around and frowned at him. He glanced at me and shrugged.

"I don't know what you're talking about, Mr. Marlow," Watkins said.

"In June 1914, Archduke Franz Ferdinand and his wife, Sophie, were shot in Sarajevo, thus kicking off World War I," I explained.

"Oh, well… good to know," Watkins said.

"How in the hell did you know that?" Lian whispered.

"History turns me on," I replied quietly.

I heard him groan. "Are you trying to get me in trouble?" he whispered.

I didn't reply.

I heard his pen scribble and he slid the note up to me. *"Seriously?"*

"About history turning me on or trying to get you in trouble? Because the answer to both is yes… seriously!" I wrote back.

"The Battle of Little Big Horn… Thomas Jefferson… Hiroshima… Ulysses S. Grant," Lian whispered.

"Not in class," I said loudly.

"MS. PORTER! Would you like detention today?" Watkins thundered at me.

I almost started laughing. "They actually have detention on the first day?"

"Yes, and I'm the teacher you'd have to put up with."

I crinkled up my nose and mouth in disgust like I'd been sucking on a lemon. "No, thank you," I replied.

"Then please keep your mouth closed for the next ten minutes," he asked in a plea.

I nodded my head. The thought of staying in a room with him for any longer than necessary was good enough to shut me up.

I kept my promise and didn't open my mouth the rest of class. Before the bell rang, Watkins stood up. "I let you all get away with a lot today. Tomorrow, there will be no passing of notes." He looked directly at me. "And no cellphone use," he added, glancing at a few other students. "I do expect it to be quiet in here tomorrow." His gaze returned to me.

The bell rang and cut off anything else he might have had to say. Everyone sprang to their feet and exited the classroom in a hurry.

"Tennis courts," I said to Lian as we parted ways. He nodded his head and went in the opposite direction I was going.

Thea was leaning against our lockers when I arrived. "Ready to go scorch something?" she asked.

"You're not a pyromancer, Thea," I replied.

"No, I get to do other fun things," she smiled while wiggling her fingers at me.

"Actually, I'm not going. Could you cover for me?"

"Ugh, I hate covering for you. Hotch always knows I'm lying. And then he'll call Kate and you'll be grounded for another fortnight."

"No, I won't. Just this one time? Please?" I begged. I was about to bust out the puppy-dog eyes, but she caved before I had to.

"One time, Emily. I'm serious!" She shoved off her locker and walked toward the stairs that went down to the main floor.

I put things in and took things out of my locker and then headed outside to where the tennis courts were behind the building.

Lian was already waiting for me. "Ready?" I asked. He nodded his head.

"So, was that just a normal school day for Emily Porter?" he asked.

"Yeah, for the most part. I may have antagonized Watkins a little more than necessary though."

We walked down the sidewalk that led away from Main Street. Grounders was located away from the center part of town, but it wasn't too far from the school.

"So, what's the story behind these tats?" I asked.

Lian held his arms out so I could have a better look at them. Since they were all black lines, one could easily take colorful markers and fill in the blank spots.

"There's no story behind them. I just started out up here with something simple," he said, tugging his shirt sleeve up and pointing at what looked like a starburst on his bicep. "From there, I just added in different shapes." He held his thumb out. "This though is family-related."

I could tell he didn't want to tell me any more than that about the four dots on his thumb, so I left it alone.

"Do you have any?" he asked.

I tugged up the sleeve on my right arm just enough so that my wrist was visible. Two birds in flight were inked there. "For my parents," I said. I pulled my sleeve back down and stopped to pull the back of my shirt up.

"What is it?" he asked.

"This might sound a little nerdy, but it says, 'Not all those who wander are lost,' in elvish." The writing was running right down my spine. It stretched from the base of my neck to just above my butt.

"You mean elvish as in Tolkien?" he asked as I lowered my shirt back down and continued walking.

"Yes."

"That is pretty cool, Em," he replied.

"Well, unlike you, I do get things inked on me that mean something," I said with a grin.

"No offence taken. It's just addictive is all. That's how I ended up with sleeves."

"They do look awesome though," I said.

We rounded a few corners and there sat Grounders. It was in an old hardware store that had moved closer to Main Street. It was a simple coffee shop. There was a counter at one side of the room and tables occupied the rest of the floor. It was a simple place with good coffee. What more could you want?

Lian held the door open and we went inside. "You want anything?" he asked.

"No thanks." I sat down at one of the tables while Lian ordered. I knew that if I had caffeine late in the day, I would be up all night. I only had coffee in the mornings.

Lian sat down across from me sipping on whatever his fuel of choice was.

"So, where do you and your dad live?" I asked.

"Domus Flats," he replied.

"No way? Those places are awesome," I stated. I had been there a few times for a few parties. They were simple studio apartments, which is what I liked about them.

"It is a nice place. I like it. Hey, we can head back to school. I don't want to keep you all afternoon. I'm sure you have things to do and ex-boyfriends to avoid," he said.

"Hopefully me snapping at him after science will get him to leave me alone for a while."

We stood up and headed out the door. "Let's take the shortcut through the woods back to school," I said.

Chapter 7

"Are you that eager to get rid of me?" I asked.

Emily paused and looked at me. "Was I being that obvious?" she asked with a straight face. I thought she was being serious. Then she broke out laughing at me before turning and heading into the woods.

There was a worn footpath that intersected with the sidewalk. The grass that had once covered the trail was long gone.

I followed Emily, shaking my head. I didn't think I'd ever be able to keep up with Emily Porter.

"So, how are you liking the town?" she asked as we walked through the woods. It was considerably darker and cooler. Fallen twigs and dry leaves crunched under our feet.

"It's a quiet town, so I do like it," I replied.

Emily stopped beside me and threw her arm up to bring me to a halt. She was staring straight ahead with a look of disgust on her face. I thought she was playing a joke on me. I was about to say something when her eyes narrowed. I didn't know what she was looking at though.

She sucked in a breath and turned towards me with enough force that she tackled me to the ground. Just as we both hit the ground, something whizzed over our heads. I glanced up to see a dagger vibrating in the trunk of the tree we'd been standing in front of.

Emily was lying on top of me. She pushed herself up with her hands on my pecs. "Stay down!" she hissed.

She rose to her feet. I twisted my body around but kept to the ground as she ordered. Standing ten feet in front of her was someone in all black. There was a hood pulled up, concealing their face. From the build, I assumed it was a male.

He reached into the folds of his cloak and pulled out another dagger and launched it at Emily.

Instinctually, I was about to tackle her, but before I could even move, she had bent backwards. She was somehow balancing on her feet while her back was arched over. Her hair was grazing the ground.

The dagger the male had thrown was buried in the tree behind her. She yanked both her pant legs up and pulled out two daggers that were attached to each leg by ankle holsters.

As she rose back up, she fired one dagger at the male. It embedded itself in his shoulder. The force of it hitting him made him stumble back. Emily took off running towards him. She jumped and wrapped her legs around him and took him down. She had him pinned to the ground. Without a moment's hesitation, she buried the second dagger in his heart.

The cloaked male began to flicker like he was shorting out and then he was gone. Emily turned around and her eyes were searching the trees. I followed her gaze and realized that both the daggers that were stuck in the trees were gone too.

"That son of a bitch!" Emily growled. She picked up both her daggers and re-sheathed them before standing up.

Then her eyes landed on me. I slowly rose to my feet, using the tree to hold myself upright.

"Is there any chance you'll forget what you just saw?" she asked.

"You mean how you just straight up murdered that… thing?"

She brushed off her pants. "It wasn't real. It was a computer-programmed training module. Sort of like a hologram," she stated.

"It didn't look fake. And what you did sure as hell wasn't fake." It dawned on me that I wasn't freaking out as much as I should have been. What Emily had done was not normal. Teenage girls were not supposed to take down men throwing daggers at them and walk away without even messing up a hair on their pretty little heads.

She walked over until she was standing right in front of me. "It is of your best interest to pretend this didn't happen."

I opened my mouth to protest when she cut me off. "You can tell every person in this town what happened. Look around, Lian. There is no evidence."

She did have a point. I would only come off sounding like a complete lunatic.

"Answer me one question and I'll drop it," I said. I doubt I would ever drop it because it would be burned into my memory forever.

She arched an eyebrow.

"Tell me what you are?"

She let out a breath and shook her head. She glanced around before responding. "Not here." She then turned and continued through the woods just carefree like she didn't just pull some moves that normal humans can't do. I ran to catch up with her.

"Where are you going?" I asked.

"Somewhere more private. I'm going to tell you what I am."

I swallowed down the lump in my throat and followed her. I was already regretting asking her what she was. I probably didn't want to know.

We walked back to school in silence. I was glad that it was a short walk through the woods. On the other side of the woods, we emerged where the football field was. Just beyond that was the school itself.

I didn't know where she was going, but I kept pace with her long strides. She entered the school, went upstairs, and got in her locker. Hers was on the opposite side of the school from mine.

She grabbed her bag out and slung it over her shoulder. She pulled her keys out and handed them to me. Then she ripped a piece of paper out of a notebook and scribbled some message on it before slamming her locker shut. She took her keys back and we went back outside. On our way to her car, she stopped by a white Mercedes and slipped the piece of paper under the driver's side windshield wiper.

I could see it read: *Take Toby home.*

She unlocked the black Audi. Instead of walking to the driver's side, she grabbed my arm and yanked me towards the passenger side. She opened the door and shoved me into the car rather roughly. I was very conscious of the fact that she had two daggers attached to her ankles and who knew what else was strapped to other parts of her body.

She slammed the door shut and walked to the driver's side of the car. She tossed her bag in the backseat and fired the Audi up. She floored it out of the parking lot and just like the first night I saw her, she didn't look or stop as she pulled out of the lot onto the road.

A few minutes after taking twists and turns through town, we were on a straight road with woods on both sides. She hit the accelerator harder. I glanced at the speedometer to see we were doing eighty.

"Are you taking me out in the boonies to kill me and dump my body?" I asked.

She spared me a brief glance. She did not have a happy look on her face. "Killing you is Plan C," she replied.

"What's Plan A and B?"

"Plan A is I tell you what I am and you just accept it and keep your mouth shut. Plan B is I tell you what I am and you freak the hell out and I kill you and dump your body."

You might think she was joking here, but there was no hint of a smile or a smirk on her face. She was stoic and very serious.

"I don't see how I'm not going to freak out. I just saw you murder some dude in the woods and you're acting like it didn't happen."

"First of all, it wasn't real. I already told you it was a module. Nothing more. And second of all, stop talking about it until we get to the place."

I was a little too scared to ask what 'the place' was. I was assuming it would be the place where Emily Porter kills me and leaves some poor sap to stumble upon my decomposing body.

About five minutes of us sitting in silence did Emily slow the car down and turn down a long concrete driveway. Trees lined both sides of the driveway and formed an archway over our heads.

I watched up ahead as the trees parted into a large concrete pad. To the side of the parking area was a single-story house. It was covered in black siding and had a black roof. The roof itself was steep. A porch wrapped clear around the house. Wooden steps descended from the porch and went clear down to the massive lake that spread out in front of it. A few docks jutted out into the lake.

Emily got out of the car and walked up towards the house. I opened the car door and unfolded myself from the passenger side and followed a distance behind her. I thought she was going to go in the house, but instead, she took the steps down to the docks.

As I walked along the porch to reach the steps, I got a good view of the part of the house that faced the lake. Floor to roof windows lined the front of the house. I could see a kitchen to the right of the door and a dining room on the other side of the door. In the center of the great room was a fireplace. Bricks rose up in a tall square on the floor and suspended a distance above that was the flume hanging down. It was an interesting design. Beyond that, all I could see were closed doors and a long hallway.

I headed down the stairs and joined Emily on the dock. She had just sat down on the end of one, with her legs dangling over the edge. I mimicked her pose.

She gazed out across the lake. It was smooth and glasslike without a single ripple disturbing the surface.

"I've never had to tell someone what I am. Everyone who is like me, I've grown up with them. So, please bear with me as I try and get through it," she said softly, not looking at me. I still nodded my head to let her know I heard her.

"I'm what is known as a Corlissian." She looked down at her hands that were in her lap. "We all have powers and are trained to fight. We have enemies too. Our greatest enemy are the Talyrians. They are very similar to us, since they too have powers. Our linages go way back to two brothers who were said to come from Mother Earth herself. One brother was Corliss and the other was Talyr. She gave them both powers to be used in times of need. The brothers got along well and all that, but they started having children who also inherited some of their father's powers. Their children started to hate one another and began fighting because some of the kids didn't get the power they most desired."

She took a breath and looked up at me briefly before focusing on the lake again. "That hatred for one another has trickled down and continues still to this day. The Talyrians live in a stronghold up in the north while us Corlissians have spread out. Small groups of us live all across the nation," she paused. "We have other enemies too. What you saw today, had he been real, was a Midnight Brother. There are also Avids, which is short for Aviditas. It's Latin for cravings and desires. They come into your life seeming like a normal human being, but they constantly offer you everything that you desire. You become blinded by everything they give to you, which is all just an illusion. After they have you, they kill you. The other enemy we have are the Nexes. They are similar to the Midnight Brothers in that they just hunt you down to kill you, unlike the Avids that sort of stalk you for a while. All three of our enemies have one goal in mind and that is to hunt down and kill all Corlissians and Talyrians."

She looked up at me again. I didn't know if she was finished or not, but when she didn't speak again, I figured I could ask her a few questions.

"Okay, if the Corlissians and Talyrians have the same three enemies, then why not put aside your differences and come together to eliminate them?" I asked.

"Our hatred for one another is too strong to join forces. We might say we're going to join up, but once we're standing side by side, that temporary peace wouldn't last. We'd end up killing one another while our enemies stand by and watch us murder one another, thus doing their job for them."

"What powers do the Corlissians and Talyrians have?"

"The Corlissians have psychokenisis, pyromancy, and pulso morsus. Psychokenisis is the ability to move things with your mind, pyromancy is being able to create fire, and pulso morsus is touching someone and causing them pain. The Talyrians have psychokenisis, aquamancers, and pulso metus. Aquamancers can create water, and pulso metus is to touch someone and bring their greatest fear alive inside their minds."

"And what power do you have?" I was kind of afraid to ask. I already saw what she could do with a simple dagger.

She lifted her hands up, forming a cup with them. She muttered something so softly under her breath; I couldn't hear. But the moment the word left her lips, a fire sprang to life in her hands.

I instinctually shrank away from her. I was no fan of fire, yet the girl sitting next to me was holding it without it burning her. She started almost playing with it by letting it dance across her arms. It was like it was a part of her.

She glanced over at me and noticed the look on my face. She whispered, "*Intereo*," and the flame went out instantly. "Any other questions?" she asked.

"No. Don't think so."

"Let this be your only warning. You cannot let anyone, and I mean anyone, know that you know about us. Most of all, don't let the other Corlissians know that you know about us. They have no problem doing things to you to make you forget everything you've heard today."

"I don't even know who the other Corlissians are," I stated.

"You're a smart boy. I'm sure you could figure it out," she replied dryly. She stood up and looked down at me. "Come on. I'll drop you off at your place," she said before turning and walking up the dock toward the stairs.

I stood and dusted off the back of my jeans. I caught up with her as she was walking along the porch. "Whose place is this?" I asked.

"My family's. We don't use it very often." She glanced in the windows as we walked past. In her refection, I could see a sad look in her eyes. Maybe she was remembering happier times up here when her parents were alive.

"It's a nice place," I commented.

She looked up at me as we hit the concrete where the car was parked. "Maybe if you're lucky, I'll bring you back here," she said, sliding into the driver's seat with a wicked grin on her face.

I hadn't even known her a full day and already I was learning a lot about her. I didn't mean about her having powers and being a killing machine or even her ancient lineage. I mean her personality. She went from pissed-off-at-you to flirting-with-you in an instant, from zero to a hundred just like that.

I was standing there outside the car, looking across the lake and taking in its beauty. I felt like I was standing at a crossroads with a huge decision to make. Did I do what my body was screaming at me and just stay far away from this very dangerous girl or did I do what was all wrong and go along with her and enjoy the insane ride she was sure to take me on?

I opened the passenger door and dropped in beside her. She started the car and turned the Audi around and left the lake house behind.

"Sorry if I scare you sometimes," she whispered.

I looked over at her. "Scare isn't the word I would use. Try frighten, terrify, alarm, petrify… Any one of those works better than 'scare.' Scared is being in a haunted house. Being around you is indescribable."

She smiled. "I'll take that as a complement, Lian." I knew she would. She wasn't like most girls I knew… Hell, she wasn't like any girls I knew. Emily Porter was one of a kind.

Emily pulled up in front of the Domus and put the car in park but didn't shut it off. She leaned forward on to the wheel to glance up at the old factory. "What number do you live in?" she asked.

"Already trying to stalk me?" I asked.

"Not yet," she replied distractedly.

"B12," I said.

She leaned back in her seat and furrowed her brows. "The second floor is single apartments, not doubles," she stated.

Well, I was caught in a lie. I figured I might as well tell her the truth, since she did just spill an enormous secret to me.

"I don't live with my dad or my mom. I live here by myself. I've been on my own for a few years now and I just move from town to town."

"How long do you stay in one place?"

"If I like a place, about six months."

"Then I guess we'll have to see how long we can keep you here," she replied with a sly smile.

I was about to say something when her phone started ringing. She reached in the backseat and pulled her cell out of her bag and hit 'answer.'

"What?"

I could hear mumbling on the other end, but no clear words.

"I'll be home in a few minutes. We can talk then." Without a reply back, she ended the call and dropped her cell in one of the cup holders.

"I'll see you tomorrow, Emily," I said, opening the door and slipping out of the car.

"Oh, you most certainly will, Lian." As soon as my door was closed, that black Audi was gone – zero to a hundred just like that.

Chapter 8

I drove straight home after dropping Lian off. I could hear it in Kate's voice that she was pissed at me when she called. I knew that Hotch had called her and told her that I had bailed on training. With my luck, I was in for another grounding.

When I walked in, Toby was sitting at the island in the kitchen doing homework. He kept muttering under his breath so a little flame would pop up in his palm and then he would utter the other world to squelch it. He always did that when he studied. He glanced up as I walked in.

"Kate is really mad at you this time. I'm thinking you'll be under house arrest for a month," he remarked.

"Terrific," I mumbled. "Where is she?"

"Living room," he replied. His attention went back to the book lying open in front of him.

I rounded the corner to see Kate sitting on the couch with a magazine in her hands. She glared at me over the top of it before closing it and sitting it on the table next to her.

"Sit," she said sternly. I did as she asked and sat down in one of the chairs that faced the couch.

"Emily, what am I going to do with you?"

"Military school!" Drew yelled from upstairs.

"Boarding school!" Toby chipped in from the kitchen.

Kate ignored my brothers' suggestions. "We just discussed how important it is for you to go to practice regularly. It isn't a form of punishment. It is for your own good. Hotch is there to teach you things in a safe environment so that you do not get hurt."

"Oh, I didn't realize the woods were a safe environment," I stated.

Kate furrowed her brows. "What are you talking about?"

"I skipped practice because the new guy at school asked if I would show him a local coffee shop. I took him to Grounders, and on the way back, we were cutting through the woods and I was attacked by one of Hotch's Midnight Brother modules."

Kate stood up and stared down at me. "Did the human see?" she asked.

"Well, since we were getting daggers thrown at us, it was kind of hard for him not to see. I made up some bullshit excuse about it being a leftover mod from an old paintball field."

"And he bought it?" Kate asked as Drew and Toby walked in the room.

"He didn't question it," I lied. Lian knew way too much about it at this point.

Kate grabbed the landline phone that sat on the end table and dialed a number. She started pacing back and forth with the three of us watching her. "No more training outside of the school. Do you hear me? A human saw one of the mods. Emily convinced him that it was nothing. You need to be a lot more careful when training."

Kate paused as Hotch replied to her. "What do you mean?" Another pause. "There was apparently a malfunction, so no more from here on out." Pause. "I know that it is an excellent exercise, but it is clearly not stable at this point. No more." She pulled the phone away and ended the call. Toby sat on one arm of the chair I was in and Drew sat on the other arm.

"Hotch said that according to the readouts, there was no human with you. The system only registered you in the area," Kate said, sitting back down on the couch. "That system has been in place since I was in high school. It must finally be wearing out."

The system tracked us during training exercises and Hotch was able to put any of our enemies' modules in front of us for practice. The system monitored who was around you. It picked up humans who were close by and other Corlissians. It had never failed to pick anybody up before.

"Just make sure the boy doesn't start asking questions, Emily. And as for you, you will be at practice tomorrow… and all the days after. Am I clear?"

"Yes," I replied softly.

"Hey, at least you're not grounded this time," Drew said, standing up.

Kate's eyebrows shot up like she had completely forgotten about my real punishment for ditching practice. "And you're grounded this week."

"You are dead, Drew," I said, hopping over the arm of the couch. He tried to make it upstairs, but I caught him around the ankle.

"Andrew, stop tormenting your sister," Kate said in a bored tone.

I glared up at my brother and jokingly whispered the word that those who have the pulso morsus power use to activate their power. "*Dolor*."

Drew's eyes widened and a look of horror crossed his face before a scream ripped out of his throat. I thought he was messing around, but when he didn't stop screaming and start laughing, I knew something was wrong. I took my hand off his ankle and he stopped yelling.

Kate ran past me and tugged Drew up the rest of the stairs to the landing. Toby and I followed. "Toby, go get a cool washcloth," Kate ordered.

Toby ran into the bathroom and came back a moment later with a damp cloth that Kate placed on Drew's forehead.

Toby looked at me. "What the hell did you do?"

I shook my head. "I don't know."

Kate looked at his ankle to see if maybe I had burned him, but with him also being a pyromancer, there was nearly no way I could. His skin was able to hold up against the heat like all pyromancers.

Drew lifted his head. "Pulso morsus," he muttered, staring at me.

"I was only kidding when I said it," I trembled. And I had been. No Corlissians or Talyrians have multiple powers, save for those with psychokenisis who were also healers.

Drew sat up and shoved the cloth off his forehead. He held his arm out to me. "Do it again, Em," he insisted. I stood up and backed away from him, shaking my head no. I kept taking steps backwards away from my family until I was at the bottom of the staircase staring up at them.

I looked down at my hands. What the hell was wrong with me? What I had done was impossible. And it wasn't right either. I felt horrible for hurting Drew.

It was then that the doorbell, which was right behind me, ding-donged and about made me come out of my skin. Instead of answering the door, I took off through the living room.

I could hear feet pounding down the steps. Kate answered the door as I rifled through my bag trying to find my car keys. Drew grabbed my arm to stop me.

"DON'T TOUCH ME!" I shouted.

"Emily, I'm fine. You didn't hurt me. Seriously!" he replied softly while carefully removing his hand from my arm. Toby stood in the area between the kitchen and living room, watching in silence.

Just when I thought the day couldn't get any worse, Kate walked into the kitchen followed by Hotch. I let out an audible groan. Hotch didn't say anything but he walked over to me and shoved Drew out of his way. He grabbed my hands and forced them palm up and stared intently at them, like they were going to magically tell him all the secrets of the world.

He dropped one of my hands but kept a hold of my other hand. He looked me in the eyes. "Say it," he ordered.

I may not have been fond of Hotch and I may have dreamed of making him suffer for some of the training I've had to do, but I did not want to purposely hurt the man.

"No."

"Emily, say it!"

I shook my head no while trying to yank my hand out of his grasp. Hotch then pulled a low blow. While keeping a firm grasp on my hand, he pulled a dagger out from his belt, put Toby in a headlock, and had the dagger pressed up against his throat.

Kate let out a yelp and covered her mouth with her hands. Drew's eyes were about to pop out of his head. Toby's eyes were darting around the room until they landed on me, pleading for me to help him.

With a shaky voice, I muttered, *"Dolor."* Hotch released Toby and the dagger clattered to the ground. I ripped my hand out of his and glared at him as he recovered from the pain I had sent through him.

He leaned against the island to support himself. He stared at me in awe and shook his head slowly back and forth. "Amazing," he whispered.

"There is nothing amazing about it. This isn't right," I spat before walking around him and everyone else.

Kate followed behind me. "Emily, we need to talk about this."

"Leave me alone!" I yelled, running up the stairs. I slammed my bedroom door shut behind me and locked it. I leaned my back against the door and slid down until my butt hit the floor.

I didn't eat that night. I didn't even leave my room. After hours of sitting on the floor and staring at the wall across from me, I finally dragged my ass up and changed into my jammies and crawled in bed.

I was hoping to doze off for a few hours, but I only lay there and stared at the mosquito netting above my bed. After a while, I stared at my hands.

There was no way this was real. I tried to convince myself that this was some huge practical joke being played on me and that tomorrow we'd all have a laugh about how fun it was to scare the shit out of me.

As much as I wanted that to be true, there was no denying my reality: I had two powers that were equally deadly. How had I lived for seventeen years and had not known there was another power lying dormant inside me?

I knew that morning was quickly approaching, and as if to welcome me into the new day, my alarm blared next to me. I slapped my hand on it to shut it up but I didn't move. I hadn't slept at all. A few minutes later, there was a knock on my door and Drew's voice came through, "Em, get up!"

I grunted and rolled over. I turned my lights on and went to my closet. I grabbed a pair of white shorts and a black sweater with three-quarter-length sleeves out and pulled them on. A pair of black flip-flops and I was set.

I went to the bathroom and twisted my brown and purple hair up into a messy bun and did my regular bathroom routine. I headed downstairs and could hear my brothers in the kitchen talking to Kate. I stood at the base of the stairs and listened like the nosy butt I was.

"What did it feel like?" Toby asked.

"It fuckin' hurt. I guess the best way to describe it would be like getting hit by lightning, a bus, and a train at the same time," Drew replied. "It's not a good feeling. I still feel lightheaded from it and she didn't even have a hold on me for that long. I can't imagine what kind of damage she could do if she doesn't let go."

"But you've been shocked by others who have pulso morsus, so have I, but that's all it feels like... a little shock," Toby stated.

"Whatever Em has packs way more of a punch. What could have caused this, Kate?" Drew asked.

"I don't know. Hotch said he was going to scour some books to see if this has happened before. I have a feeling he's not going to find a thing."

I took a deep breath and rounded the corner to the living room and kitchen. Kate smiled brightly at me. "Good morning, sweetheart. What would you like for breakfast?" she asked.

In all the years Kate has been our guardian, she has never made us breakfast... not once. We always fended for ourselves in the morning.

"I'm not hungry," I muttered, sitting in the stool next to Drew, but scooting it a little way away from him. I heard him let out a noise.

"You didn't eat anything last night for dinner. You must be starved."

"I'm fine, Kate. I'll eat when I'm hungry."

"Emily..." she started.

"Can we please just end this awkwardness? Yes, I am some sort of Corlissian abnormality. I'm just going to have to suck it up and learn to control it and use it properly. Now, can we go back to being as normal as we were before?"

I heard three "Yeah, sure" and I was satisfied.

Drew slid off his stool. "And just so you know, you didn't hurt me, Em," he stated.

"Lightning, bus, train," I replied.

"Shit," Drew muttered under his breath, making Toby laugh. Drew walked out of the kitchen and went upstairs to get himself ready. Toby followed him up a moment later.

"They're scared of me, aren't they?" I asked Kate.

"No, it's more so being weary around the unusual. We've all grown up as strictly pyromancers. That's all we've had to learn about since we were young enough to understand what we were. Now all of a sudden, someone with an extra power emerges in the family. It's just throwing them off is all. They'll get used to it."

"I don't know if I'll get used to it," I replied.

"Don't think of this as something bad, Emily. It is a gift. But this is something we're going to have to keep quiet about. The last thing we need is for the Talyrians to hear that one of the Corlissians is sporting double powers."

I nodded my head. It was bad enough having to watch my back for Midnight Brothers, Avids, and Nexes. All I needed was Talyrians making attempts to get me too. Unlike the others, the Talyrians would probably run tests on me to see if they could duplicate whatever was going on inside me.

I got off the stool and went upstairs to gather my things. Toby was standing in my doorway ready to go before I was. That was a rarity.

We walked out to the car and I tossed Toby the keys. "You drive. I'm too tired," I said. A grin spread across his face. I hardly ever let him drive.

There was silence for half of the trip until Toby finally spoke. "I think it's kind of awesome, Em. You having two powers. I know you don't think much of it, but you'll be a force to be reckoned with if we ever go into battle. I can see you shooting fire out of one hand and making people scream in agony with your other," he beamed.

"Well, I'm glad someone is happy about this other power of mine," I replied.

We arrived at school and I stayed in the car until the bell rang. I didn't really want to see anyone at the moment. For some reason, my friends could always tell when something was wrong with me. They would badger me about it until I just got sick of hearing them. I was sure this morning it was written all over my face that there was something seriously wrong with me.

Once the bell rang, I headed up to my locker and thanked the heavens that Thea wasn't there. I might be able to keep things under wraps until at least lunch… if I was lucky.

I went to homeroom and passed by Lian without a word. He turned around in his seat. "You feeling okay?" he asked.

I shook my head no. Technically, I was feeling fine. It was just that my brain was coming up with unsavory scenarios as to what was wrong with me and well… there clearly was something wrong with me.

"You mean that I don't get to experience snarky Emily today?" he asked.

That made me laugh. "The day is still young, Mr. Marlow."

As Mr. Watkins was taking attendance, Sam walked in and handed him a note. Watkins' eyes landed on me. *Oh, fuck.*

"Ms. Porter, you are wanted elsewhere," he said, holding the note out to me. I stood up and grabbed my things off my desk, ruffled up Lian's hair as I walked by, and headed out the door next to Sam.

"What is this all about?" I had a damn good feeling, but I wanted confirmation.

"Is it true?" Sam asked. "That you have another power?"

I nodded my head. "Em, that is so cool."

Sam was one of my best friends, my cohort for troublemaking, but I was so sick of people telling me how great it was that I had two powers. Why was I the only one having issues with it?

We headed down to the main floor where the plain door was that led to the old pool room. Sam checked both ways to make sure we were alone before unlocking the door and quickly shutting us inside.

I could hear the voices of the others as soon as we entered the long hallway. And sure enough, the group of Corlissians were all gathered on the blue mats awaiting our arrival. We sat down among the rest of our peers while Hotch stood in front of us.

"I'm sure the word has spread among you that one of you has been granted a second power. It was only discovered last night that Emily also possesses pulso morsus."

No one seemed shocked by this news, so clearly they all knew. Of course, my big-mouth brother Drew had told everyone already. Butthole.

"I stayed awake all of last night searching through my library and even making phone calls to see if this had ever happened before. I am pleased to tell you that you are all sitting beside the only person of our race to possess two powers."

That's when everyone turned to stare at me. Talk about feeling like the bearded lady at the circus. Step on up to gawk at the freak show!

"Did it occur to you to check the other members of my family to see if maybe they also have hidden powers?" I asked. That got those eyes off me.

Unfortunately, Hotch was already nodding his head. "I made them try it last night before I left your house. I got nothing from them. Emily, your power is more potent than anyone here who was born with pulso morsus. Come up here, please."

I stood up and walked around the others on the mats and stood next to Hotch. "I was thinking last night about what you can do and it got me thinking that maybe there is more locked inside you. So, I want to try something," Hotch said.

More? I think two powers were more than enough.

Hotch held his arm out to me. "Grab me," he stated. I sighed and wrapped one hand around his wrist. "Now I want you to say *timor*."

"What the hell does that mean?" I asked.

"Will you please just do as I ask for once and not bombard me with questions?" he grunted.

"Fine." I took a breath and whispered, "*Timor*."

Hotch dropped to his knees immediately. His eyes were squeezed shut and his lips were pulled back, revealing his teeth. I let go of him and stepped back.

He fell forward but caught himself before his face planting on the floor. He turned to me and the look of horror on his face was replaced with a smile. That man had serious issues.

"What was that?" Tyler asked.

"She has three powers, as I suspected," Hotch stated, standing up.

"What else can she do?" Drew asked.

I already knew what Hotch was going to say before the words came out of his mouth. I felt sick. "Pulso metus."

Everyone stared at me again, but instead of gaping at the freak, they were glaring at me like I was the enemy. And they had every right to. I had an enemy power in my body.

Drew stood up with a look of rage on his face. "How is that possible? She's our sister, for fuck's sake. Yet it's like she has Talyrian blood in her veins. Is she also an aquamancer?"

"I don't think so," Hotch replied. That answer wasn't comforting for me at all.

I hadn't even come to terms with having two powers, and now all of a sudden I had three, one of which was a Talyrian power. That word kept replaying in my head: *Talyrian, Talyrian, Talyrian, Talyrian…*

My hands started to shake and I felt the tears spilling down my cheeks. Thea jumped up and wrapped her arms around me and shoved my head against her shoulder.

"I don't want this," I whispered. "I don't want any of it."

"I know, babe," she said, running a hand up and down my back in a very motherly way.

I looked at Hotch. "Take it out of me. Please, find some way to get it out of me."

"Emily, it's a miracle what you are."

I pushed Thea away from me. "A miracle? I'm a freak even by Corlissian standards. I don't want this in me. How do I have a power that only Talyrians have in them?" Tears were flowing down my face freely.

Hotch just stood there and stared at me like everyone else was. My breath felt like it was caught in my throat. I started gasping for breath. Thea shoved me to the ground.

"She's hyperventilating!" Normally when someone announces that a person is having trouble breathing, people give that person some room, but not my fellow Corlissians. They all gathered around even closer.

Thea began muttering the word that healers used on people. Being someone who had the pyschokenisis power, she was also a healer.

I could slowly feel my body relaxing under her touch and my breath became normal again. I looked at Hotch. "What if Cami is like me? Maybe it's just us females?"

He looked at Drew who shrugged his shoulders. Hotch nodded his head. "Call Camilla. She should come in," Hotch said to Drew.

I looked around at all the other Corlissians I had grown up with. The look in their eyes made me ill. They were looking at me like I was not one of them anymore.

Chapter 9

I was not a morning person, nor was I one of those people who loved school, so I was surprised by myself when I woke up before my alarm went off. I was actually excited to go to school. There was only one reason I felt that way, and I was lucky enough that she even noticed me – Emily.

I sat down in homeroom and tried not to stare at the door like a freaking stalker. Emily walked in a moment before the bell rang. She looked exhausted, like she barely slept the night before. I hoped that she hadn't lost sleep because of the secret she had told me the day before. I knew that she could get in serious trouble if anyone knew that I knew, but I wasn't planning on telling a soul.

She sat down behind me and I turned around. "You feeling okay?" I asked.

She shook her head no instead of actually replying to me. I kind of got freaked out that she was shying away from me because of what I knew.

"You mean that I don't get to experience snarky Emily today?"

She laughed at that. "The day is still young, Mr. Marlow," she replied with a smile.

Just then, Sam walked in the door and handed a note to Mr. Watkins. "Ms. Porter, you are wanted elsewhere."

Without a word, she stood up and grabbed her belongings. As she walked past me, she ran a hand through my hair playfully and then she disappeared out the door with Sam.

I walked in the lunchroom and was disappointed when I didn't see Emily sitting with her friends. In fact, she wasn't in the cafeteria at all.

I passed by the table they were all sitting at. I thought it would be weird to join them, since the only one I really knew was Emily. But Thea must have thought otherwise.

"Killian! Come sit with us," she practically hollered.

I turned around and took the seat next to her with the only vacant one being where Emily would have been sitting.

"Where's Emily at?" I asked.

"Some family issue. She should be here shortly," Tyler replied.

A guy who was in my second-period English class walked up and stood between Sam and Tyler. He was an exact replica of Tyler.

"Any word yet?" he asked.

All three of the people sitting with me shook their heads no.

He took a deep breath and nodded his head before turning away to return to his table.

Tyler looked at me and grinned. "Did that freak you out a little?" he asked.

"A bit. I didn't know you had a twin."

"That's Evan. He's my evil twin. As you can see, he hangs out with the king douchebag," Tyler said, indicating Mason.

Then Emily walked in the cafeteria. She looked even worse than she did this morning. Her hair was coming out of the bun and her eyes with rimmed in red and slightly puffy. Her nose was red too.

She plopped down in the seat next to me and stared ahead with a blank look on her face.

"Em?" Sam said to get her attention. She turned her head to look at him. "What happened?" he asked.

"Cami is like Toby and Drew. It's just me for some reason."

"Did Hotch say anything can be done?"

"To what? Remove it? Nah, I'm stuck with it. He has no idea why I..." she broke off and looked at me. "Hey, Lian!"

"Hey, Emily!" I replied.

"How is your day going?" she asked.

"I'm assuming clearly better than yours."

A small smile appeared on her face. "You don't have to assume that one. I know I look like I've been through a war. I feel like I've been through a war. I think I just need a hot bath and a long sleep. Maybe that will make me feel better," she remarked lazily.

"But it won't actually make you better," Tyler stated.

Emily turned her gaze on him. She looked straight up, pissed. "You really want to say something stupid to me, Ty?" she snapped.

Tyler held his hands up in surrender. "No, thank you," he gulped.

I was really confused. I knew that what they were discussing was clearly Corlissian-related and they were treading lightly around the subject matter since I was sitting there. I wished they would just speak openly about it, since I did know what they all were. I knew that whatever was going on was about something happening to Emily. I wondered if she would tell me or if I was going to remain in the dark about this piece of information.

The bell to end lunch rang out and everyone got up from their seats. Thea grabbed Emily and practically pulled her out of the cafeteria. Then I heard a fragment of what Sam said to Tyler: "Man, Emily was just plain dangerous before. Now she's straight up lethal."

I thought Emily was lethal before. Even though the thing was computer-generated, she had no problem shoving a dagger into its heart. I couldn't imagine what happened to make her even deadlier.

In fact, I thought all Corlissians were on the same skill level. I figured that since Emily knew how to use a dagger pretty damn well, they all did. So what exactly has the other Corlissians fixed with a combination of fear and awe for her?

When I walked into the room that my science class was in, I saw Emily was already sitting at our table. Mason was leaning on the table across from her.

"I'm sort of hoping that this will finally scare you off from trying to get back together with me," Emily stated.

"Well, it's scary as hell, make no mistake. But on the other hand, it is kind of hot how powerful you are. Don't think a little jolt is going to keep me away from getting you, babe."

Mason straightened up when I sat down next to Emily. A smile spread onto her face. "Oh, Mason, I don't think you've had the pleasure of meeting my new friend, Lian."

Yeah, I knew exactly what she was doing and I didn't give a fuck that she was using me to taunt her ex. I was more than happy to play along.

Mason gave me a small head nod and then directed his attention back to Emily. "I'll see you later," he said deeply. He then turned and headed back to his seat.

Emily let out a breath. "Sorry about that."

"You mean using me so your ex would leave you alone? It's no problem. Can't say I've ever been used like that before."

"And I can't promise it will never happen again," she replied, arching her eyebrows.

I leaned towards her and dropped my voice. "What is going on exactly?" I asked.

The smile that had been on Emily's face disappeared. Her eyes darted around the room. "I can't tell you. I'm not even sure what's going on," she whispered.

"But it's something with you, right?"

She leaned back on her stool, balancing it on two legs. "Yeah, it's me."

"Is it something with the..." I trailed off and held my hand up and wiggled my fingers while blowing on them.

Emily started laughing. "Is that supposed to be me doing pyromancy? And, stop doing that!" She punched me in the arm and it smarted. She sure didn't look like she could pack a punch, but there was one thing I was learning about Emily – looks can be very deceiving.

"No. It has nothing to do with that. I'll tell you some other time once I have a chance to figure it all out," she added.

I nodded my head as Mr. Evans walked in the door. The bell rang and he began his rambling lecture about meteorology.

I sat down for my last class of the day in the study hall. I was sure this was a pointless class to have. And it being the seventh period, it was pretty pointless for us all to sit around for an hour just to go home. Hardly anyone studied in study hall, especially since it was the last class. Now, if it was during any of the other periods, sure there would be people studying for tests and finishing papers.

Emily sat down behind me. I turned around in my seat. "I thought you were sitting in front of me now?" I asked.

"I prefer staring at the back of your head," she replied with a smirk.

You know when you just have a feeling someone is staring at you. Then you look up and there actually is someone staring at you. Well, I had that feeling. I glanced across the room and sure enough the girl Emily had told to move yesterday was staring us down.

I leaned forward and whispered to Emily, "We have an audience."

Emily turned her head to see who I was talking about. She smiled brightly at the girl and even gave her a little wave before turning her attention back to me. "I think she's insanely jealous that I'm talking to you and she's not. I could make her stop if she's bothering you."

"And just how would you go about doing that?" I was sort of afraid to ask. Emily's version of stop was probably along the lines of a dagger to the chest or catching hair on fire or who knows what else.

A smile flitted across her lips. "I'd ask her to not stare at you." I knew she was straight up lying.

"Really? Just ask her nicely?"

"I didn't say anything about me being nice." Emily leaned back in her chair. "What do you want me to do, Lian?"

"Leave the poor girl alone," I whispered.

Mr. Watkins walked in and his eyes landed directly on Emily. "Oh, I see you've decided to join one of my classes today."

The smile on Emily's face fell away. She was glaring at the man. "I didn't know it was a crime to leave homeroom with a note?"

"But you didn't stay for attendance, so technically you were not in school today." I was starting to think that Watkins was pushing her buttons for no reason whatsoever. He definitely didn't want to push the ticking time bomb behind me any further.

Emily stood up and I should have grabbed her wrists to force her back down. Not that it would have helped anything. Emily had a really bad attitude.

"What is your problem with me exactly?" she asked. "I have done absolutely nothing to you today for you to be such a massive asshole to me. I'm not sure if it's some fucked up form of jealously or what, but I would appreciate it if you would leave me the hell alone. Pick on someone else."

Watkins' face started to turn bright red. "You think I'm jealous of a seventeen-year-old girl with a bad attitude? Oh, that is hardly where my derision comes from. It is your whole family that makes me sick. And I'm starting to think with the way you flirt with every guy in this school that you're nothing more than a whore like your sister."

That was the worst possible thing he could have said to her. I reacted before Emily could. I think she was momentarily stunned at what he had said to her. I stood up and blocked her from getting to him.

"Emily, don't. He is not worth it," I said, leaning down so I could look her in the eyes. I recoiled slightly from her. Her eyes were gray... a dark gray. I had stared into them enough in the past two days to know that simple fact. But the eyes glaring at me now were glowing violet.

"EMILY!" I said. She sort of jumped and blinked, and in that instant, her eyes were back to normal. She looked up at me.

"I'm going to kill him, Lian," she whispered in a deadly voice that made my skin crawl.

She took half a step back and sat back down. She crossed her arms over her chest and just glared at Watkins.

I turned around. "Was that really necessary? You know she was in homeroom. She was sitting right behind me. What you said to her was completely out of line."

"Mr. Marlow, sit down," he stated.

"You know why no student in this school shows you even an ounce of respect? It's because of shit like that!" I sat back down.

Mr. Watkins sat down at his desk and shook his head. He went entirely too far. And I knew that what he'd said to Emily would cost him dearly. I just didn't know what the hell she would do to him. I had a feeling that she was sitting behind me running scenarios through her head.

When the bell rang, ending the school day, I stood up and Emily was still sitting there with her eyes unblinking and locked on Watkins.

"Em," I said to get her attention. She looked up at me and rose to her feet. As soon as we were out of the classroom, that cloak of hatred disappeared instantly. Her moods shifted so quickly that I didn't even try to keep up with them.

Instead of heading the other way, she walked beside me. "I have a question for you."

"What's that?" I said, stopping at my locker. I spun the lock and opened the door. Emily leaned against the locker next to mine.

"What are you doing for dinner tonight?"

That made me stop and glance at her. "Are you asking me out?"

Emily cracked a grin. "Not yet, dear boy. Now answer my question."

"Umm, probably ordering take-out or something. I don't know. Why?"

"Because you're coming to my house for dinner tonight. My aunt always cooks way too much food. I think she still has it in her mind to cook for five people instead of four. So, I'll pick you up at 5:30." She didn't wait for a response because there was no question. She left no room for argument, to say the least.

I watched for a moment as she walked down the hall. Her hair was a mess, her makeup was long gone, and still nearly every guy turned his head to look at her. How did I get to be the lucky guy who she actually paid attention to? It might have been one of those forever-unanswerable questions that the world may never know.

I'd spent the rest of the afternoon doing some school work that needed to be done and doing a few dishes. I was that kid that did their homework right when they got home because I liked to have the rest of the evening to not worry about it.

At 5:23, there was a knock on my door. I opened the door to find Emily standing there leaning against the door frame with a grin on her face. There was also a cut above her right eye.

"What the hell happened to you?" I asked.

She stood upright and glanced into my apartment. "Tiny accident at practice," she replied absentmindedly. Then she ducked under my arm that was holding the door open and entered my apartment.

"Tiny accidents don't cause cuts," I replied as she walked around my apartment.

"They do when you get in the way of flying objects. It was my fault for not paying attention." She then stopped and looked at me. "You ready?"

"Sure," I said, shaking my head. People got cuts on their foreheads from hitting it on low hanging objects or by getting in a fight. Emily got a cut on her forehead because she walked into the area of another Corlissian practicing psychokenisis.

She headed for the door and I followed her out. I locked my door and then we headed out to her Audi that was sitting along the curbside. She hopped in the driver's seat and started the engine. The familiar smell of leather invaded my nose as I slid into the passenger's seat.

I focused my attention on the direction Emily was driving. Not that I was planning on stalking her or anything, but I just wanted to remember how to get to her house.

She made several turns through the neighborhood until she pulled onto the driveway of a two-story brick home. There was a white porch along the front and a garage out back. Two other cars were in the driveway ahead of hers: a BMW and a Mercedes.

"Does anyone in this town drive a hoopty?" I asked.

Emily started laughing. "Nope. We're all rich and complete snobs about it." She opened the door and got out of the car. I followed her around to the back of the house. The same bricks that lined the house also formed a patio out back that held a table, chairs, and a fire pit. The backyard spread out a good distance to where a wooden fence separated it from another backyard.

Emily opened the backdoor and was immediately yanked forward into the arms of a woman who looked almost just like her, only older. She had dark brown hair and the same oval-shaped face. Her eyes were closed, so I couldn't see if they were gray or not. She was a little shorter than Emily, but not much.

"I was so frightened. All day! Hotch called me this morning and told me about what happened. Emily, how have you been dealing with this all by yourself?" She opened her eyes and her brown eyes locked on to me.

She let go of Emily and stood up straighter. "I hope you don't mind, but I brought a friend home for dinner. His dad is out of town and he doesn't need to be eating fast food. Oh, umm, Kate, this is Killian. Lian, this is my Aunt Kate. He's new at school…" she trailed off.

Kate walked forward and shook my hand. "It is so nice to meet you. You are most welcome for dinner. Emily's always telling me I make too much food, but with two boys in the house, you never know. How about you go show Killian around. Dinner will be ready in about ten minutes."

"Thanks for having me, Ms. Porter," I replied.

"Actually, it's Ms. Jensen. I'm Emily's mom's sister, but please call me Kate."

Emily nodded her head for me to follow her. "So, this is the kitchen," she said. "And this is the living room," she continued. I followed her as she made a big show of giving me the grand tour. "Kate's room is over there," she said, pointing past the small hall that ran under the stairs to a closed door on the other side.

"And now I'm going to show you my room," Emily said loud enough that Kate could hear.

"Keep the door open, Emily!" Kate called back.

"Can't make babies with the door open!" Emily yelled.

"EMILY PORTER!" Kate scolded.

Emily laughed as she headed up the stairs and I dutifully followed. She stopped at the top of the stairs and motioned her arm for me to enter the first room on the left.

I'm not saying I had sat down and considered what Emily's bedroom looked like, but I must say that was not what would have come to mind.

I guessed I was expecting weapons hanging from the walls, black curtains and bed sheets, and blood-red walls. It was very airy and girly with lots of soft colors.

Emily dropped her bag on her bed and walked over to her closet to kick her flip-flops in. I sat down at her desk chair.

"Can I ask you something?"

"You can ask me anything, Lian. I have almost nothing to hide," she replied with a grin.

"Today in study hall, you were about to murder Watkins and I was standing in front of you." She nodded her head that she remembered. "Why were your eyes glowing purple?"

She furrowed her brows and walked over and sat down on the end of her bed. "Purple?" she repeated. I nodded my head. "If anything, they should have been glowing blue, but since we are in eavesdropping distance of my brothers, I would prefer not to talk about it here."

"So, add that to my growing list of things I need to ask you about when we're alone?"

"Oh, most definitely," she said with a smile.

There was a knock on her open door. A guy with black hair stood there. He was wearing dark gray sweatpants and a white tee shirt. His hair was a mess.

"Kate said dinner is ready." He glanced at me and nodded his head. I returned the gesture with a nod too.

Emily sighed as she slid off her bed. "Lian, this is my older brother Drew," she said, introducing us.

"Ah yeah, I think I heard Mason talking about you today. Something about standing in his way. I don't know. That guy is an ass," Drew said, shaking his head and walking downstairs.

Emily and I were on the landing outside of her door when the door across from hers opened. Out stepped a boy who looked almost like Emily's twin brother. They had the same dark brown hair, oval face, and their eyes were both gray, though hers were slightly darker. He was a bit taller than Emily.

"And this is my younger brother Toby. Toby, this is Lian."

"Hey, nice to meet you. Hurry up, I'm starving," Toby said as he darted down the stairs.

"And you've practically met my whole family now," Emily stated.

"Who's missing?" I asked.

"My sister, Camilla," Emily said as we headed downstairs.

We sat in the kitchen where the six-person table was. All the food was set out on the table and there was a place setting in front of each chair. Even when I lived with my parents, we never had a meal served like this. It was pretty much a fend-for-yourself-or-starve household. We didn't have quality family time together.

"So, tell me something wonderful that happened today?" Kate asked as everyone started filling their plates.

"Emily let me drive the car this morning," Toby said.

Kate smiled and nodded her head.

"I saw my sister bring Hotch down," Drew stated with a mouthful of potatoes.

Kate gave him a look of displeasure. I was sure he was discussing Corlissian stuff at the dinner table with a normal human joining them. I was sure that was in their *'Corlissian Handbook of Things not to do around Humans, Volume 2.'*

"Emily, your turn," Kate said.

"I refrained from murdering a teacher and burying his body under the goalpost on the football field."

"Which teacher?" Drew asked.

"Fucking Watkins."

"Emily, language!" Kate hissed.

"Oh, sorry. That motherfucker Watkins," Emily rephrased.

Kate sighed and shook her head. Drew and Toby were cracking up.

Just then, the front door opened and in walked a girl with blonde hair. She was wearing white skinny jeans and a white sheer top with only a white bra on underneath it. She had on bright blue heels that had to be at least six inches high. She walked right over, dropping her purse on a chair in the living room and sitting down at the vacant chair.

"What the hell are you doing here?" Drew asked rudely.

"I do still live here," she said as she started filling her plate.

"No, actually you don't. You moved out last weekend. Therefore, you do not live here."

"Well, I was going to head back, but I decided to have dinner with my family first. I missed you guys. I did come all the way back just to see if I'm a freak like my sister... Well, I am a freak but in a totally different context..."

"Camilla, this is Killian, Emily's friend. He just moved here," Kate interrupted.

"Ohhh, Emily, he's cute. No, he's hot. So much better than Mason. I don't know what you were thinking. Even I wouldn't sleep with him, yet you had no problem..."

"Camilla, shut the fuck up, please," Emily said rather calmly.

"Emily, language," Kate stated again.

"Well, tell her to stop running her mouth!" Emily snapped.

"Camilla, leave your sister alone," Kate said.

"Well, tell her not to sleep with skeezy guys."

"Camilla, no one likes you. You're adopted. Go back to whatever whore hole you crawled out of," Drew said.

"I don't know why I even bothered coming here. Drew, you're an asshole!" Camilla pouted.

"It has been quiet without you here," Toby stated.

"Thank you, Toby."

"Oh, that was not a compliment," Toby clarified.

"Yes! My little brother has finally learned the art of messing with Cami!" Drew stated.

"Fine. I'm leaving. And I won't be back for Thanksgiving or Christmas..."

"Good!" Drew and Toby said at the same time.

Camilla shoved her chair back and marched out of the house, slamming the front door behind her.

I looked over at Kate who was sitting there with her head in her hands. "Your parents would be so disappointed in how you treat one another," she whispered.

"The three of us treat one another fine. It's just her. She acts like she's the queen. She needs to be put in her place!" Drew stated.

It was quiet for a moment. "So, that was my sister, Camilla," Emily said, finally breaking the silence, causing everyone to start laughing.

Chapter 10

After dinner, Lian and I were sitting in the living room, since Kate didn't want us to be in my bedroom unsupervised, because having Drew in the room next to mine and Toby across that hall wasn't enough.

Kate had put Lian through the twenty-questions routine she ran on anyone of our friends. What do your parents do? Where are you from originally? How do you like school? How do you like the town? Am I annoying you?

"I have something kind of embarrassing to ask you," Lian said.

"Hmm?" I muttered. I was flipping through my copy of *Persuasion* trying to remember where I'd left off.

"I'm assuming by the way you blurted out that little fact about the Archduke yesterday that you know history fairly well. Is there any way you could tutor me? I'm horrible with remembering dates that things happened and those kinds of questions are always on the tests," he asked.

I looked over the top of my book. "Are you just asking me because of what I said yesterday about history turning me on?" I asked.

He furrowed his brows. "Actually, I'd forgotten you said that. Seriously."

"Well, it's kind of rude to forget something like that. Girls don't go around telling you what turns them on every day, Lian," I scolded.

"Emily, you are not a normal girl, so normal circumstances do not apply to you," he replied.

"That's true. Fine, I'll tutor you," I said with a shrug. "Are you really that bad at remembering dates in history?"

He nodded his head. "I can't remember when D-day was or when Pearl Harbor was bombed."

"June 6th, 1944 and December 7th, 1941 at 7:48 a.m. How do you not know two of the most important dates in U.S. history?"

"How in the hell do you just whip those dates out?"

I shrugged my shoulders. I didn't know. It was something I found fascinating, so it stuck in my brain better than anything dealing with math.

I leaned my head back against the couch cushion and closed my eyes for a moment. It had been a long day and I really hadn't had a moment to myself to process it all yet. I should have been freaking out a whole lot more about these newfound powers that I had, but actually I was sort of trying to forget I even had them. I wasn't planning on practicing and getting comfortable with them. I wasn't even planning on using them… ever.

"So, when can we start?" Lian asked.

My eyes popped open. "Start what?" I blurted out.

He turned his head. "You tutoring me."

"Whenever you want. We'll probably have to do it here though. Kate watches me like a hawk all the time. I think she's worried that I'll turn into Camilla."

"I think that's the last thing she needs to worry about with you," he replied, turning his attention back to the history book that was balancing on his knees.

It was sad that a guy I had just met yesterday seemed to know me better than my aunt who had known me my whole life and who had raised me for half of it.

Kate walked in the living room drying her hands on a kitchen towel. "Emily, it's getting late. You should probably take Killian home. When you get back, we need to talk. And what happened to your eye?"

I closed the book I'd been reading and tossed it on the coffee table. "I'll tell you later," I muttered as I rose to my feet. I nudged Lian's leg with my knee. "Let's go!"

"Thank you for dinner, Ms. Jensen," Lian said to Kate.

"Oh, you are welcome. Come back anytime," Kate replied.

He stood up and set my history book on the coffee table. He followed me through the living room, the kitchen, and through the backdoor.

"You've been quiet," I said when we were outside.

"Sorry. I was more so just observing your family. It's not how my family ever interacted."

"Trust me that was not a typical night for us. It has been quiet without Camilla around. I love my sister and I will fiercely protect her, but she just has a really hard time getting along with the rest of us," I explained.

"You're all really close. I guess that has something to do with being a Corlissian," he said.

We got in the car and I started it and backed out of the driveway. "It has nothing to do with being Corlissian. It's how families are supposed to be. After my parents died, the four of us tried to shut people out, but Kate wouldn't let that happen. She kept us going and tried to make sure our lives stayed as close to the same as they were before."

I pulled up to a stop sign and just stared straight ahead.

"Em?" Lian whispered.

"I don't know how she did it. She had four kids thrust upon her and…" I paused. "When did she have time to grieve? Her sister died." I looked over at Lian.

"I'm sure you were too young to realize it," he replied.

"I was eight. We made everything so much harder on her than it had to be. I know you could argue that we were acting out because of what happened, but we did push things entirely too far sometimes."

A car honked its horn behind me. I turned my head and hit the accelerator. I drove the rest of the way to his apartment with all the ways I'd made Kate's life a living hell running through my head. And that was just me… not all the things my brothers and sister had done too.

I pulled a U-ey in the road so I could drop Lian on the side of the road that the Domus was on. He sat there for a second with his hand on handle to open the door. I thought he was going to say something, but instead he just whispered, "Good night." He was out the door and walking up to the front doors of the apartment a moment later.

A shadow passed behind him and cut across the front lawn. A moment later, it vanished into the shadow of the old factory. I was out of the car and walking up the sidewalk. Both my hands were behind my back, palming the daggers that were holstered to me.

Lian appeared in the doorway. He opened the door a fraction. "Did I forget something?" he asked.

"No, go back inside," I hissed. My attention went back to where the shadow had been. I glanced at him quickly. "I'm serious, Lian!" He hesitated and then I heard the door click shut.

I took off running across the front of the building into the shadows. I turned and was sprinting around the side when I collided with someone. We hit so hard that the impact threw us both back. I was on my feet as quickly as I could get with both my daggers in my hands, ready to attack.

"Em?"

"Mase?" I squinted in the near darkness that surrounded us. "What the hell are you doing here?"

"Sam, Micah, and I tracked four Brothers here. We've got them trapped on the rooftop. Wanna play with us?"

Even in the dark, I knew he had that grin on his face. I rolled my eyes. "Are they really Brothers or are they just mods?" I asked.

"Oh, they're real. Hotch stopped using the mods since you and lover boy were attacked yesterday. What's going on with you two anyway?"

"Do you really want to discuss my relationship with the new guy or can we go murder some Brothers?" I asked.

"Careful, Em, you know I get frisky when you talk about murdering our enemies," Mason replied.

I shoved past him and headed to the back of the building where Sam and Micah were waiting.

"Hey, Em!" Sam beamed.

"Hi!" A light from the back of the building showed that all three guys were in their fighting leathers. Sam had his dreads tied back. All three of them had their daggers in their hands.

"Let's go!" Mason commanded.

We all holstered our daggers and used the offset bricks of the building to climb the side. The guys paused just at the edge and carefully peered over. I didn't pause. I hauled myself up, and on the other end of the roof stood four Brothers.

They were all wearing the black cloaks that hid their identities. In their hands were their long swords that they preferred to use for up-close combat. They looked exactly like the mods that Hotch used.

A moment later, the guys stood on either side of me. Their daggers were in their hands. It was us four on one end of the roof facing a Brother on the other end of the roof. It was quiet, weirdly quiet actually.

Mason took a step forward and Micah and Sam followed suit. The Brothers they were facing advanced toward them. The only ones who remained motionless were me and the Brother across the way from me.

Once the others were slashing at one another with daggers and swords did I take a step forward. The Brother mimicked my movement. I didn't draw either of my daggers. They were both safely strapped to my back.

I brought my hand up and waved at the Brother as he neared me. He tilted his head to the side, almost trying to figure out what I was doing. After a moment, he waved back. Sam paused a moment from fighting to see what the Brother was waving at. He gave me a funny look before taking a step back and driving his dagger into the Brother's heart. He dropped to the ground and Sam wiped his bloodied blade on his leathers.

Sam could have gone to help Micah or Mason who were still fighting to my right, but instead, he stayed right where he was and watched with curiosity as the Brother and I continued our walk towards each other.

We stopped ridiculously close to each other. I stared up into his dark hood. I couldn't see anything. For all I knew, the Midnight Brothers were faceless. Or maybe they were so hideous that it was better that no one saw them.

The tip of his sword was resting on the roof. He took a couple of deep breaths and tipped his head to the side. A smile spread onto my face.

"You can't get a read on me, can you? Am I Corlissian or am I Talyrian? You don't know because you can smell both races in my blood. I confuse you, don't I?"

A growl was my only response from the Brother. He brought his sword up, but I took a step back and easily ducked out of its way. He swung it back the other way. I easily avoided the blade. It was almost like he was moving in slow motion.

I took a step forward and shoved my left foot down on his right foot and then I kicked my right foot up. I made a direct hit right under his chin. My plan was to just cause him to stumble back and throw him off for a moment so that I could draw a dagger and finish him. But I didn't have to draw a dagger. My foot hit his neck with enough force that his head snapped back.

I heard the crack of his neck breaking. His headed tipped back and hit his back. The only reason it didn't fall to the ground was because of his cloak. His body hit the rooftop a moment later.

"The fuck?" I glanced over at Sam who was staring at the body lying at my feet. His eyes traveled up and met mine. "Please, show me how to do that tomorrow!"

I didn't reply. I turned my head to see Micah dispatch his Brother. And then I saw the Brother Mason was doing battle with tackle him. And they both went right over the edge of the building.

"MASON!" I screamed.

Micah was closest and he dropped down after him. Sam and I hit the ground a moment later. Mason was lying on the ground, biting back the scream that wanted out. His shin was bent forward.

I could handle blood and all sorts of disgusting injuries that could probably make a doctor nauseous, but I could not look at a broken bone without wanting to vomit.

Micah and Sam were both gone searching for the Brother who somehow managed to hobble away from the fall. Mason held his hand out to me. I crouched down next to him and held his hand.

"How bad?" he grunted.

"Your left leg is snapped." I reached around and tapped my back pockets when I realized that my cellphone was in my bedroom. "Do you have your cell on you?" I asked.

Mason shook his head no. "Neither do Mic or Sam," he muttered.

"Shit. Okay." I pulled one of my daggers out and placed it in his hand, since I didn't know where his were. "I'll be right back. Okay?" He nodded his head and tightened his grip on my dagger.

I took off running to the front of the building. I yanked open the front door and hauled ass up to the second floor and pounded on Lian's door. He opened it wearing only a pair of pajama pants.

"I would have dressed a little nicer if I knew I was getting a late night visit from you," he said with a smirk.

"I don't mean to be rude, but this is not a time for joking. I need your cell."

Lian nodded his head and I followed him into his apartment. He handed me his phone that had been resting on his nightstand. I dialed Hotch's number from memory. He picked up on the second ring.

"We have a problem. Mason took a fall and broke his leg," I blurted.

"Where are you?"

"Domus. He's out back. Sam and Micah are searching for the fourth Brother. He managed to escape from the fall."

"I'll be there in five minutes." The call ended.

I handed the phone back to Lian. "Thanks." I turned to leave the apartment, but he caught my arm.

"Are you okay?" he asked. He had his hands on my shoulders and was squatting down slightly so he could look me in the eye.

I nodded my head. Then I shook my head no. "I just decapitated a Brother with my foot." Even saying the words aloud didn't help to make them seem true to me. I couldn't believe what I had done.

"You did what now?" Lian asked.

"I'm sorry. I have to go. I didn't mean to bother you, but none of us had our phones. I didn't know what else to do," I stuttered out.

"You didn't bother me. You never bother me," he whispered. He let go of my arms and I gave him a brief smile before leaving his apartment and making my way back outside.

Sam and Micah were kneeling next to Mason when I arrived. "Hotch is on his way," I stated. They nodded their heads. Sam slipped his arms under Mason's armpits and Micah gripped his right leg and they easily lifted him up. They carried him around to the front of the building just as Hotch pulled up to the curb. They carefully put him in the backseat and Hotch took off to the hospital.

The three of us hopped in my car and followed. It was silent for half the ride there. I loved Sam dearly, but like most Corlissians, he had a big mouth.

"Are you going to tell me how you just kicked that Brother's head clean off his neck?"

"I don't know how I did it. I was just going to make him stumble back. It was not my intention."

"You kicked his head off?" Micah asked. He was leaning forward with his forearms resting on the headrests of the front seats.

I nodded my head. "Please, don't tell Hotch," I begged. I already felt like enough of a freak having three powers, with one of those powers being Talyrian. I didn't want any more unwanted attention on me, no matter how awesome the guys in my car thought it was.

When we arrived at the hospital, Micah leaned across the front desk and used his Micah charm to ask the lady where Mason was.

"You mean the handsome young man with the grumpy old jerk?"

"Yeah, that sounds like Hotch," Sam muttered, making me laugh.

Micah nodded his head. "They took him up to the second floor. You can find the waiting room across from the elevator," she replied.

We followed her instructions and sat down in the near-empty waiting room. The only person there besides us was a middle-aged guy. His knee was bouncing up and down rapidly and he was kneading his hands together – all signs of nervousness.

Micah leaned in close to me. "Are you going to show us how you did it at least?" he whispered.

"You want me to demonstrate on you?"

Micah leaned back. "You know you are a badass, Emily, but you are scary as fuck too. And that was before all the…" he trailed off and waved his hands around me.

"The multiple powers that I want nothing to do with?" I finished for him.

"At first, it freaked me out. I mean having an extra power was unheard of. Two extra powers isn't even the stuff of legends. But for one of them to be Talyrian… well, it just takes a little while to process that information. But I think it's pretty awesome now."

"Yeah, the only ones who had multiple powers were Corliss and Talyr. And how long has it been since they've roamed the Earth?" Sam added.

I was saved from hearing any more of their flattery for my powers by Hotch walking towards us. "I need to call for one of the twins to fix him up later. He wants to see you. He's in Room 219," Hotch said, looking directly at me.

"Why?"

Hotch sighed and shook his head. He turned away and pulled his cell out to call on either Tyler or Evan to heal Mason now that his leg had been set.

Sam patted me on the back as I stood up. "Try not to kill him," Sam whispered.

I gave him a dirty look over my shoulder as I headed down the hallway toward Mason's room.

I peered my head around the door that was open about halfway. Mason was sitting on the bed with his broken leg bound in a hard white cast resting on the top of the sheets. He had a bruise on his forehead and left cheek too. His hair that was always combed and gelled to perfection was a mess. He actually looked vulnerable sitting there fiddling with the edge of the cast. It kind of made me remember why I did fall for him.

I knocked on the door and shoved it open the rest of the way. He brought his head up and smiled at me. He patted the edge of the bed next to him and scooted over so I could have more room. I sat down next to his legs.

"What'd you want?" I asked.

He leaned back on his pillows and pulled his shirt up. My dagger was stuffed into the holster at his waistband. He handed it to me and I quickly shoved it next to its twin on my back. The last thing we needed was to be seen wielding daggers in a hospital.

"Thanks for lending it to me," he said softly.

"I couldn't leave you completely undefended."

I looked around the room. I hated hospitals. I hated the way they smelled and the quietness of them. I hated the sad faces on the people seeing their loved ones and the nervousness on the faces of those waiting to see their loved ones. The only place that was less happy than a hospital was a funeral home.

"Is that all then?" I asked. I didn't want to linger any more than necessary.

"No." He sat up a little straighter. "Can you do me a favor?"

I shrugged my shoulders.

"Can you please just sit there and listen to me for once?" he pleaded.

"Fine," I reluctantly agreed.

He took a deep breath. He looked down at his leg that was covered in white plaster and he smirked. "This was my fault. I kept glancing over at you to make sure you were all right. I know you can handle your own self, but it was our first time fighting real Brothers and I was nervous that something was going to happen to you. The Brother took advantage of that and tackled me. We probably shouldn't ever fight together again, just because I can't concentrate when you're around," he smiled at me.

I looked down at my arms and started playing with the hem of one sleeve of my sweater. I knew in his own way he was complimenting me, but I wasn't one who enjoyed compliments on my ability to fight.

"Emily," he whispered. I looked up at him and there were tears in his eyes. "I am so sorry for what I did to you. I could make up a thousand excuses for cheating on you, but they would mean nothing to you. What I did was completely unforgivable and I would do anything to take it all back."

He looked up at the ceiling. "I miss you. I really do. I just miss getting to hold your hand and the way that you would smile at me. I miss you jumping on my back for a piggyback ride. I miss all of that. I was so fucking happy with you and I ruined it because I got scared."

"Scared of what?" I asked.

He lowered his head and closed his eyes. When he did, a few tears slipped down his face. "You were the first girl I'd been with for longer than a few weeks. We were together for nine months and…" He took another breath and opened his eyes. "You were the first girl I could see myself with permanently."

My mouth was hanging open now. "Mason," I whispered.

"But I fucked it all up. I know I don't deserve a second chance with you, but if you would maybe just consider it. I mean, imagine if we did get married and then our kids would be super powerful."

I flinched and stood up quickly while shaking my head no. "I can't have kids. I won't have kids," I blurted out. I hadn't even thought of all the consequences of these extra powers in me. I would pass them on.

"Em?" Mason said, softly reaching for me, but I stepped away from his hand.

"I will not pass this Talyrian curse on to anyone," I snapped. I turned and left the room, with Mason calling my name behind me. I turned the corner and ran right into someone.

I looked up. "I'm sorry, Ty– Ev– Sorry," I stuttered out. I walked around whoever it was. I was so messed up that I couldn't even tell the twins apart.

Sam, Micah, and Hotch were all gone, so I assumed that Hotch had taken the guys home. It was a good thing because I really wasn't in the best state of mind for dealing with those two.

I got in my car and headed home with everything Mason had said swirling in my head.

I pulled the car in the driveway and leaned my head on the steering wheel. I about screamed when someone pounded on the passenger-side window. Kate was standing there looking madder than I had ever seen her.

In everything that had happened, I never even thought to call her. All I was supposed to do was take Lian home and come right back. I knew exactly what she was thinking happened. She wasn't even close to the truth.

I got out of the car and prepared myself for the coming shit-storm I was going to have to talk myself out of.

"Emily Charlotte Porter, you are never allowed to see that boy again. Am I understood?!" she thundered.

"I wasn't screwing Lian if that's what you think. I was fighting Midnight Brothers on the roof of the Domus with Sam, Micah, and Mason. Mason fell off and we had to take him to the hospital when he broke his leg. You can call Hotch or any of the guys to confirm this." I made to walk inside, but I turned to look at her. "I'm not Camilla, Kate."

Kate was on my heels, and once we were in the kitchen, she grabbed my arm to stop me. "I will call Hotch, but you promised me we would talk when you got home. I don't care that it's 1:43 and you have school today. Sit."

She released my arm and I sat down on one of the stools. "Now, tell me about the cut on your forehead for starters."

"I wasn't paying attention at practice and Thea had one of those old metal lockers in the air and I turned around and caught the corner of it with my head."

Kate sighed. It was like me not to pay attention in practice. "And about the powers you now have? How are you dealing with that?"

"Still processing really." I looked up at her. "How can two pureblooded Corlissian pyromancers pass on a Talyrian power?" I asked.

"Emily, if I had the answer to that, I would gladly give it. I know your mother and father were Corlissians through and through. And why it was only you and not any of the other three, I don't know. This is something we may never get an answer to. The best thing that you can do is learn how to use these powers to better defend yourself."

"I have no issue learning to use pulso morsus, but I will not learn to use pulso metus. I want nothing to do with that power."

"Emily, you were blessed with it for a reason."

"Blessed? This is no blessing, Kate." I buried my face in my hands.

I felt Kate's hand rub up and down my back in a motherly manner. "I'm sorry, sweetheart. How about we talk about it later? I'm sure you're exhausted. Go get some sleep." She kissed my temple softly and I knew that she had left the kitchen and went to her own room.

I crawled into bed and just stared at the canopy until my alarm went off. How long was it that a human can survive with no sleep? Five days? Two weeks? Whatever the actual number of days it was, I might be putting it to the test.

Chapter 11

I had just sat down in homeroom when Emily walked in the door looking like hell. Her hair was in the messiest bun I had ever seen in my life and she had no makeup on. She was at least dressed well. She had on a blue-and-white-striped shirt with a navy skirt. She had a dark brown belt and dark brown heels too.

"You look ravishing this morning," I said sarcastically.

She replied by raising her hand and flipping me off. Goody! She was in a chipper mood. It seemed like it was not the day to tease Emily. I decided not to turn around and ask her if she was okay. I had a feeling she'd probably flip me off again.

Watkins walked in just as the bell rang. He paused and looked around the room. "Emily Porter," he stated.

"Present. Present. Present. I'm here in your classroom, so now you cannot mark me as absent," she blurted out.

"I wasn't taking attendance yet, but thank you for your enthusiasm. I was just going to tell you to clear your schedule after school because you and Mr. Marlow both have detention with me due to your outbursts yesterday in study hall."

"Fuck," Emily muttered. "Oh, I cannot wait to serve my sentence with you later today, Mr. Watkins," Emily said aloud.

That had me turning around. She had a wicked grin on her face. She was planning something and I honestly wanted no part of it, even though I was sure to be there and I was probably going to be threatened to keep my mouth closed. I was not looking forward to detention.

After Watkins took attendance and the bell rang, everyone filed out in the hallway to go to their first period. I needed to talk with Emily before I could even concentrate on classes. I grabbed her and pulled her to the side of the hallway. She didn't even put up a fight; she just let me drag her.

"What are going to do to Watkins?" I asked quietly.

She shrugged her shoulders. "I haven't really decided yet. There are just so many ways I could torture him. I'll think of something before the day ends." She started to walk away, but I yanked her back.

"Are you ever going to tell me what's going on?"

She looked up at me. "I really don't owe you an explanation for anything. You're not Corlissian, Lian."

"Yeah, well, I do know an awful lot about you and might I remind you that you came to my apartment at 12:30 last night to use my phone and oh, yeah, you told me you decapitated a dude with your foot. I think I do deserve an explanation."

She leaned back against the lockers that ran along the walls. I knew that she hated the position I had her in. I knew too much about her and I was really giving her no choice in the matter. Then again, she could very well still kill me and no one would ever find me. Like Sam had said, Emily was lethal.

"Do you have plans Friday evening?" she asked, not looking at me.

I snorted. "Yeah, I'm just such a popular guy with so much on my plate right now."

Emily glared up at me. "I'll pick you up at seven." She shoved off the lockers and continued on down the hall.

Emily didn't show up to lunch, nor was she in science. She did stroll into study hall looking like her usual self. She had makeup on and her hair was far less messy than it had been in homeroom. The only thing that altered her appearance was the tear in her skirt that went up almost to her ass.

She dropped her books on the desk behind me and looked down at me. "I'm sorry that I was a rude bitch to you this morning," she apologized.

"It's all right," I replied.

"It's really not. There is so much shit going on right now in my life, but I had no excuse to take it out on you."

I smiled up at her. "I really didn't take you for the kind of person who apologizes."

"Oh, I normally don't. So, this is a one-time thing. Don't expect another one," she said, sliding into the seat behind me.

"What happened to your skirt?" I asked. She glanced down at the tear in it. It was almost like she didn't even realize it was there.

"Snagged it in the training room," she muttered, playing with the fray.

"Is that where you were during lunch and science?"

She looked up at me and nodded her head. "We had to tell our trainer exactly what happened last night."

"What did happen last night?"

She smiled as the bell rang and leaned in toward me. "You'll have to wait until Friday, Lian."

The final bell of the day rang and all the students rose to their feet to leave. Emily and I remained where we were. I did move over one aisle so I was sitting next to Emily rather than in front of her.

"Your detention begins now. You'll get to leave in an hour so long as you behave," Watkins said.

I heard Emily snort beside me. She was clearly not planning on staying the whole hour. I saw out of the corner of my eye that she kept looking towards the door that was at the rear of the room. Soon enough, the noise in the hall died down until it was complete silence in the school.

Emily raised her hand in the air and cleared her throat to get Watkins' attention, since he was looking down.

"Yes, Ms. Porter?" he said in a bored tone.

"Do you know any Latin words, Mr. Watkins?" she asked.

"Do I look like someone who would know Latin, Ms. Porter?" he replied.

"No, you look like a pedophile or someone who'd have a sex slave locked up in their basement," she whispered.

I started laughing and had to turn it into cough so I wouldn't get in trouble... again.

Emily stood up and slowly walked toward the front of the room where Watkins' desk was.

"Ms. Porter, sit down," Watkins said when he noticed her moving toward him. She shook her head no. "Do you want another detention?" She shook her head no again.

She did a little jump and front-flipped onto his desk with both feet landing at the same time. And might I add that she did this in heels.

She was crouched in front of him. "You will stop picking on me. You will not pick on or even talk to my brothers. And you will most definitely not speak of my family ever again. If you do, you will be in such a world of hurt that no doctor on Earth will be able to help ease your suffering. Am I clear?"

"Ms. Porter, have you lost your damn mind?!"

"AM I CLEAR?!" she yelled.

"Are you threatening me?"

Emily laughed. "I don't threaten. I just make promises that I am very good at keeping."

"I am a teacher for the state of..." Watkins started. Emily wrapped her hand around his wrist and whispered something. Watkins' eyes bugged out, his mouth opened, and a scream tore out.

Emily let go. "If you talk about my family in any way again, I will make it sure that you don't even remember your own name. Don't fuck with me again."

Emily stood up, hopped off the desk, and walked down the aisle. She paused to grab her books. She nodded at me, and after what I just saw her do, I dutifully followed.

"I'm guessing I'll have to wait until Friday to learn what you just did to our teacher."

"Teacher is a pretty loose term. He doesn't actually teach us anything. But yeah, you'll have to wait," she replied.

I barely saw Emily the rest of the week. When we were in the same class, she was extremely quiet. Even on Friday after school, she didn't say anything, so I wasn't sure if we were still on or not.

Seven o'clock came and went with no sign of Emily. I was starting to think that maybe her solution to having to tell me anything was just to ignore me. I wasn't going to let that happen though.

A little after eight, there was a knock on my door. I opened it up to find Emily standing there in leather pants, a leather corset, and a leather jacket. She had on black boots that stopped just below her knees. She had on a belt that had daggers holstered all around her waist. Straps on the belt stretched down to her thighs where two more holsters were holding throwing stars. I could only imagine what other weapons she had strapped to her that were hidden.

"Sorry, I'm late. Practice ran over. I would have called but I don't have your phone number. That is something we'll have to remedy."

"So, do you just walk around town like that?" I asked. It was kind of hard to take my eyes off her in all that leather.

She glanced down at what she was wearing. "Only when I'm hunting assholes who want me dead. Otherwise, we aren't exactly permitted to wear our fighting leathers. My sister tried to wear it one year as a Halloween costume. Our trainer put the kibosh on that real quick."

I didn't say anything. I was just staring at her. Emily snapped her fingers to get my attention. "Let's go before you start drooling," she stated.

I grabbed my wallet and keys and followed Emily. We passed a guy in the hall that immediately turned to stare at her as well. "Where you stripping tonight, baby?" he called.

"Just in your dreams," Emily replied. "I don't know if it's a complement or not to be referred to as a stripper," she said when I was walking beside her.

"It is if you're one of those high-class strippers. The ones that cost like $5000 a night."

"Are we still talking strippers or did we make the jump to prostitutes? I sure am way too covered to be a prostitute, Lian!"

"And I would never refer to you as a prostitute, Emily. I do actually value my life," I replied.

We got in her car and she drove a route I was already familiar with. We were going to the lake house.

"Why do you take me to the lake to tell me Corlissian stuff?" I asked.

"Less chance of us being overheard. You're in enough danger knowing even what you do about us. Any Corlissian finds out a human knows what we are and that human won't live long after. I'm just being careful is all."

Emily pulled her car down the long driveway and brought it to a stop in front of the house. As soon as she killed the lights, we were plunged into darkness.

"Here," she said, pressing something that was hard and plastic in my hands. I fumbled for the switch and ended up blinding myself. Emily started laughing, so I shined the light in her eyes.

I followed behind her and kept the light at the ground so we could see where we were walking. I was expecting her to head down to the dock, but instead, she unlocked the door to the house. She hit the switch that was next to the door and illuminated the whole front part of the house.

She shut and locked the door behind us. She pulled her jacket off and tossed it on the back of one of the dining chairs. Sure enough, there were holes all around the back of the corset that daggers were stashed in.

"You can look around or whatever. I need to change out of this. Bridgette thinks the corset makes it so that us females are stylish while we're fighting. I'm glad she has her priorities straight."

Emily walked down the long hallway hitting another switch that showed just how long the hall was. Emily disappeared into one of the doors along the left side. I could hear the sound of metal being laid on a wooden table. It was probably going to take a while just to unload all those weapons off her.

I was mistaken. Emily was a pro. Not five minutes later did she walk out in a pair of a black jeans and a white tank top.

"All right, time to talk," she muttered, walking out the door and heading down to the docks. She plopped down on the same one as Monday. She bent one leg up and leaned her back against one of the posts that held the dock up. Her other leg was hanging down skimming the water. I sat down beside her.

"So, what are you dying to know?" she asked.

"Okay. What happened last night?"

"Sam, Mason, and Micah tracked four Brothers and had them trapped on top of the Domus. I assisted them. The Brother that Mason was fighting tackled him and they both went over the edge of the building. Mason broke his leg and we took him to the hospital."

"You said something about kicking a dude's head off."

Emily scrunched her nose up. "Yeah. That happened. What happened is exactly what it sounds like. The Brother I was fighting, I kicked him right here," she leaned forward and put her hand right where my throat met the underside of my chin. "And his head just popped off. Actually, it made a crack, not a pop. Next question."

"What other power do you have?"

She leaned her head against the post. "Why are you assuming that I have another power?" she asked.

"I'm not assuming. I've heard bits and pieces of hushed conversations and after seeing whatever it was you did to Watkins yesterday kind of confirmed it."

"It's not just two powers I have now. It's a whopping three! I have been bestowed the 'gifts' of pulso morsus and pulso metus. What I used on Watkins was pulso morsus. It just sent a wave of pain through him."

"I thought you said that only Talyrians have pulso metus?" I asked.

Emily turned her head and gazed out across the lake. The area surrounding the house was lit up from the light pouring out of the wall of glass.

"I did say that. And at the time, that was accurate information. For some reason, I have a Talyrian power in me."

"And none of your brothers or sister has it, do they?"

Emily shook her head no. I could see her eyes were shining. "I hate who I am," she whispered.

"Emily, you can't mean that."

She turned her head toward me. "You didn't see the looks of the people I have known my entire life. It was disgusting. They were staring at me like I was the enemy. Everything I've been taught to hate is something that is a part of me. You can't understand what it's like, Lian." She held her hands out and they were shaking. "How can I not hate myself?"

"There's got to be something you can do," I suggested.

A weak smiled slid onto her face. "Powers are permanent things, Lian. We can't just get rid of them when we don't want them."

"What are you going to do then?"

"Pretend like I don't have it. I'm not going to use it."

"I'm guessing you're the first person to ever have that many powers," I said.

"Aside from Corliss and Talyr, yes I am."

"How is that possible?"

She shrugged her shoulders. "No idea and no one knows why. Both of my parents were Corlissian, so there is no reason this should have happened. It's almost like I'm a fluke."

"Don't say that."

"It's the truth," she whispered.

"What happens if the Talyrians find out about you?" I asked.

She looked up at me. "I don't want to even think about that, but I imagine I'd either be killed or kidnapped. They may keep me alive and see if there is some way to replicate what I am. An army of Talyrians with multiple powers would mean annihilation for the Corlissians."

She flicked her toes around in the lake, making droplets of water scatter across the smooth surface.

"Any other questions?" she asked.

"Not that I can think of at the moment, but will you do something for me?" She arched an eyebrow up. "I want to know what pulso morsus feels like."

"Are you fucking insane? I'm not doing that!"

"Come on, Em. I'm serious."

"I know you're serious and I'm saying no."

"Why?"

"Because I don't know how to properly use it yet. And..." she trailed off.

"And?"

She pulled her foot out of the water and sat cross-legged in front of me. "I found out I had it when Drew and I were goofing off. I grabbed his leg and said the word. He started screaming and I thought he was just playing along like I was really hurting him. Only he didn't stop. That next morning, I heard him talking to Kate and Toby about what it felt like. He said it was far worse than any other shock he's gotten from someone else with pulso morsus. For some reason, mine is more damaging. I'm not doing that to you just so you can know what it feels like."

"I guess I'll just have to pull a Watkins and piss you off so much that you do it to me," I teased.

"Oh, Lian, I am the one person in this town that you do not want to piss off. I can do far more depraved things than sending a little shock through you." A wicked grin curled the corners of her lips up.

"Emily, I mean this in the kindest way possible, but you really terrify the hell out of me sometimes," I said.

She pulled herself up and looked down at me. "And you've only had the pleasure of knowing me a week. The fun has only begun for you."

"I technically haven't known you for a week yet," I acknowledged.

"Actually, you have. I do believe that last Friday night you asked me where the school was," she smirked.

"How did you know that was me?" I inquired.

"You may have been rocking some long-ass hair and a nasty beard, but all that mess didn't hide your eyes, Mr. Marlow. You have very alluring green eyes." She gave me a wink and shoved off the post.

I watched her as she walked back up the dock toward the house. I shook my head and sighed as I stood up and made my way to the house. Of course this whole time, she knew that I was the creepy hobo-looking guy who approached her in a parking lot to ask for directions to the school. She never even hinted that she knew who I was.

Emily was pulling her leather jacket back on when I walked in the open front door. "Don't forget your daggers," I reminded her.

"Please, I have daggers stashed all over the place. There are about thirty in my car alone," she replied.

"Time to take me home?"

She looked at me with furrowed brows. "No, not now that I have you alone and all to myself," she smiled.

"Are you trying to seduce me, Emily Porter?"

She laughed. "Seducing you would be entirely too easy. I do like a bit of a challenge. But, no, tonight I am not going to seduce you. You're coming home with me because I believe I am your history tutor and I believe we have a quiz on Monday."

"Wow! Way to show the new guy how you spend your Friday nights," I replied.

"If you're good and if you learn something, I'll take you to the party at the beach later. Better?"

"That's a lot of 'ifs,' but I'll take the deal."

Emily killed the lights and locked up the house and we headed to her car in the dark, with me holding the flashlight once again.

"What do you need a flashlight for when you have flames that shoot out of your hands?" I asked.

Emily stopped and I didn't realize it. I ran right into the back of her. She turned around and whispered something, causing a flame to ignite in her left palm. I flinched back when she did it.

"That's why," she stated before whispering another word to stifle the flame.

Chapter 12

"I want to do one more test with you to see if we've covered everything," Hotch said.

I was standing in the training room when I should have been in the lunch room with everyone else. Hotch had sent me a note this morning, telling me to meet him at the beginning of lunch. I thought he had found something out about how to deal with my other powers. Now it seemed he wanted to see if I had any more. I was half expecting him to tell me that I was an aquamancer too.

I just stared at him blankly for a moment. "What do you want me to do?" I asked.

He tapped his bearded chin and glanced around the room. He then grabbed one of the daggers off the wall and stood in front of me. Instinctually, my hand went to my back where two of my daggers were. Hotch smiled and shook his head.

"I'm not going to fight you, Emily. I know that you could easily take me down. I want you to remember one word and when I tell you to, I want you to say it. Okay?"

"What's the word?" I asked.

"*Sanare*," he stated. It was another Latin word. I knew it well enough to know that was the main word that the healers used. That word had never passed my lips before.

Hotch nodded his head silently, asking if I was ready. I nodded my head in return. I really wasn't, but I didn't want to be stuck in the training room during the whole lunch hour.

Hotch took the dagger and ran a clean line across his forearm. Blood immediately started pouring out of the cut. I glanced up at him and he was watching the blood ooze from his arm.

"Now," he muttered.

I held my hand over his cut arm and whispered, "*Sanare*." The blood flow slowed, and then stopped completely.

"Say it again," he advised.

I said it one more time and the skin started to pull itself back together. The only evidence that he'd had a cut on his arm was the blood that was starting to dry on his arm.

I took a step back from him. "Anything else?" I asked harshly.

He smiled and shook his head no. He was really enjoying the fact that I had all these powers and abilities. It was how I imagined a proud father would look at their child who had just accomplished something great. The only thing was that he was not my father and he was not the reason that I had these powers.

I turned and walked toward the hallway that would lead me out of the room. Hotch called out to me. "You're a healer, Emily!"

"Yeah, I got that," I mumbled under my breath.

From the short walk from the training room to the cafeteria, I had managed to clear my mind of what had just happened. Sam and Thea could read me like a book. If I had even the slightest hint of aggravation on my face, they would know something was up and they would hound me until I broke down and told them. This was something I didn't want to share at the moment.

I walked into the lunchroom and saw everyone sitting at the table as usual. I took my spot between Thea and Lian. Everyone got really quiet when I sat down. Clearly, they had all been talking about me just before I arrived… I wonder what on Earth they could have been discussing. Hmm?

I ignored the other Corlissians and turned my attention to Lian. "So, how'd you do?" I asked.

A smile spread onto his face. "I got fifteen out of fifteen, right?"

I had helped him study for the history quiz we were having today. I was expecting him to do well, mostly because I was an awesome tutor, but I didn't think he'd get them all right.

I turned to everyone else at the table. "Did you hear that? Lian got an A!" We all stood up on our chairs and started making a whole lot of racket by cheering and whooping.

Lian sat in his chair and stared up at us like we were the biggest weirdoes on this planet. We normally only did it when someone got an A on a test, but Lian was new and he sucked at history. It was a well-deserved cheer session.

"I should have sat by myself on the first day, but no, I just had to sit with this group," he said once we all took our seats again.

"You know you love us. Don't deny it!" Sam smirked.

"Seriously though, thank you so much for tutoring me," Lian remarked.

"It was my pleasure, but just because you did good on one quiz does not mean we're done."

Lian smiled as the bell to end lunch rang.

Thea and I headed up to our lockers. And, of course, my best friend had to say something.

"You and Killian look so cute together."

"We're not together though," I replied.

"No, but you should be. And Mason was staring you down the entire time. What happened with you two at the hospital?"

Seriously, every Corlissian had a big mouth.

"It was nothing," I muttered. It was far from nothing, but I really didn't want to bring it up.

We stopped at our lockers and I glanced both ways down the hall to see that no one was around.

"If I tell you something, will you promise me to keep your mouth closed?" Thea nodded her head. "No, I want you to say, 'I promise not to say what you tell me, Emily.'"

Thea sighed and held her hand up like she was pledging something. "I promise not to say what you tell me, Emily." She arched her eyebrows and waited.

"I'm a healer."

Thea stood as still as a statue, just staring at me blankly. I snapped my fingers in front of her. She blinked and shook her head. "Do you have psychokenisis too?"

"No."

"Aquamancer?"

"God, I hope not."

"Emily, part of me thinks it's cool you being this powerful, but a bigger part of me worries what having all these powers will do to your body. There is a reason we are only given one power to deal with. You have four now, and three of the four are seriously deadly. I just hope this doesn't bring you harm."

"It's not like I asked for this, Thea."

"I know that. It still doesn't keep me from worrying. I just wish that we knew the reason why you have them and why no one else in your family does."

I shrugged my shoulders. "Just don't say anything, okay? I know Hotch will tell Kate, and if she tells Drew, then everyone will find out. But for now, can we keep it quiet?"

"I won't tell a soul. Pinky swear." She held her right pinky out and I wrapped my right pinky around hers. "Pinky swear," we whispered together.

I sat down next to Lian in science right before the bell rang. "Close call," he whispered.

"My life is full of close calls," I muttered.

Mr. Evans pushed a TV into the room and fumbled around with the DVD player for about five minutes before another student got up to help him.

Once it was all set up, he stood in front of the TV to tell us about the wonderful weather movie we were going to be watching. I was so enthralled that I just stopped listening to him.

A few minutes later, he killed the lights and hit play. 'The World's Weather' appeared on the screen. Just below the title was the year 1975. So, we were going to be watching an old-ass movie.

"I guarantee every guy in this film is going to have a pornstache," I whispered to Lian.

He started laughing. Mr. Evan's glared at us as best as he could in a nearly dark room.

"And all the ladies are going to have big, flammable hair," he added.

"No doubt!"

Sure enough, the first guy to appear had a hairy caterpillar on his upper lip. Lian's body was shaking from holding in the laugh. I was almost expecting a commercial for Aquanet halfway through the movie.

A little flicker of light to my right caught my eyes. Mason was using pyromancy in the classroom where several people could very well see it, just to get my attention. He then leaned back and tossed a note on my desk.

I opened it up and narrowed my eyes just to see what it said. Mason had horrible writing as it was, and trying to decipher it in a dark room was not pleasant on my eyes.

"What's up with you and the new guy?"

He could have easily gotten caught using pyromancy just to ask me a stupid question. Mason might have been a damn good fighter, an amazing pyromancer, and he wasn't bad to look at, but sometimes he was really fucking dumb.

I didn't have a pen out, so I grabbed the one that was in front of Lian and wrote back a response, one I knew would really piss him off.

"Nothing really. But you should know that he is so much better than you were. You could take a few pointers."

I tossed the note back to him and waited. He had to lean in close to read it. A moment later, he stood up so fast that the stool he'd been sitting on hit the ground. He turned around and I could see his eyes were glowing blue. Corlissians' eyes only glowed blue when we were really furious.

"Here we go," I said.

"The fuck?" Lian breathed.

Mr. Evans turned the lights on as Mason made his way to where we were sitting. His eyes didn't look quite as bright with the fluorescents on.

Mason stood right in front of Lian. He was flexing his fingers really wide and then tightening them into a fist.

"KEEP YOUR FUCKING HANDS OFF HER! TOUCH HER AGAIN AND I WILL PUT YOU IN THE MOTHERFUCKING HOSPITAL!" Mason thundered.

Lian glanced over at me and I was smiling like a fool. He knew that it was all my fault this was happening. Then Lian did something I did not expect. He stretched his arm over and draped it across my shoulder.

Mason's face was deep red, and from how tight his jaw was, he had to have been biting down on his teeth. Mason hopped up on the table and I saw his hand go to his back. I knew he was stupid, but I didn't think he was stupid enough to pull a dagger out in the middle of a classroom, a classroom full of students with their eyes on him.

I hopped up on the stool that I had been sitting on and swept my leg under his. He hit the table, and as soon as he did, I stepped onto the table and pinned him down.

"Pick on someone your own size. And don't tell people not to touch me. I can do that on my own, baby."

"MR. MONROE! MS. PORTER! PRINCIPAL'S OFFICE NOW!" Mr. Evans shouted.

"Emily didn't do a damn thing wrong," Lian snapped.

"Would you like to join them?" Mr. Evans replied. I shook my head no at Lian, and he clamped his mouth shut.

I stood and glared down at Mason who was still on his back on the table. So many thoughts raced through my brain, of horrible things I could do to him, none of which involved the twins that were strapped to my lower back. I could fuck him up with my bare hands. I could see him screaming like a baby on this table and it would only take one word to do it.

I glanced around the room and saw that every eye in that room was on me. I stepped over Mason and jumped down from the table, grabbed my bag off the floor, and walked out the door.

I heard the door open and close behind me. Feet pounding down the hallway came to a halt right next to me. I didn't even look over at him.

"What the fuck was that in there, Emily?"

I threw my hand up, caught him in the throat, and shoved him until his back slammed into a locker. "I think you deserve to answer that question more than I do," I hissed. "Your eyes were glowing, Mason. You were using pyromancy. And you were reaching for a dagger IN—THE—MIDDLE—OF—A—CLASSROOM!"

He shoved his arm up and snapped my hand free of his throat. "It's disgusting, you and him. Being with a human is almost as bad as being with a Talyrian."

"I'm not with him. I'm not really into trusting too many people after my last boyfriend started fucking every girl in the school while we were still together."

"That is not fair and it was only three girls."

"It doesn't matter how many, Mason." I shook my head and started to walk down the hall when he grabbed my arm to stop me.

"Can we ever have a normal conversation?"

"No. Get your hand off me!" He reluctantly let go of me and followed a short distance behind me down the hall.

I stopped before going into the office and faced him. "I think we should fight tonight."

He arched his eyebrows up and smiled a little. "I don't want to hurt your pretty face though, Em." He reached up and ran his thumb along my jaw.

"And I really want to hurt your pretty face, Mason," I replied, smacking his hand away.

"You're on."

I opened the door and we both went in to tell the principal what happened and to hear what our punishments were to be. Mason got a week of detention for starting a fight and I got two days' detention for instigating the fight.

That night, after detentions were served and practice was over, Mason and I met at Culver's Field. It was a secluded field away from town that was just flat piece of soft grass. It was great for fighting on during the summer when none of us wanted to go to the school. This was also where Corlissians dealt with their problems with one another.

Fighting other Corlissians was fun because we were all on the same skill level. We had been brought up the same and were trained all the same moves. The only difference was that some of us were better at hand-to-hand combat than others. Mason and I were nearly equal.

The sun was starting to set in the east and it would be nearly dark out before long. A few torches formed a circle around us and they were all lit and burning brightly.

Mason and I had deposited all of our weapons in our cars and were circling each other. We were both bare foot and wearing shorts and a tee shirt, things that wouldn't matter if they got bloody, because they were going to.

"You still want to do this, babe?"

I smiled and nodded my head. Training with Hotch, we had to keep things safe and couldn't do any real damage to each other. Out here, we could beat the shit out of each other and get all our frustrations out. There were only two rules to abide by: no weapons and no powers. It was fists and feet only.

"I'll try not to hit your face," he said with a massive grin on his face. That meant that he was going to try and seriously mess my face up. I had no issue because I wanted to do the same thing.

"How about I let you use one power against me just to even things up?" he suggested.

"Oh, I can handle you just fine, Mase. I have before."

"Kinky!" he said with a wink.

We continued walking in a slow circle, eyeing each other and waiting for the other to make the first move. Mason faked like he was going to make a move. I didn't even flinch because Mason always did that. He was too predictable.

The sun slunk below the horizon, throwing the area outside of us into total darkness. I wanted to get our fight over with and go home. Then I'd have to explain to Kate why I have bruises and cuts on me. That was all part of the fun.

Mason finally made a move. He dove and hit the ground on his hands and then pushed himself up and somehow managed to wrap his legs around my midsection. He had me pinned to the ground. Then he took a swing and I moved my head and he punched grass instead. That pissed him off and he swung again and made contact with my bottom lip. I knew it split open and I tasted blood in my mouth.

I brought my arm up and nailed his gut with my elbow. He let out a puff of air and rolled off me. I hopped up and kicked him in the stomach with my foot. He grabbed my ankle and twisted it. I hit the ground and he started crawling toward me. I brought my foot up and slammed my heel into his face. Blood started pouring from his nose.

"Nice shot, sweetheart," he muttered.

He grabbed my ankle again and flipped me over so I was on my stomach. He crawled on my back and punched me in the right eye. I brought my right elbow up and connected with his throat. He started coughing. I scrambled out from under him and kneed him in the forehead. He fell onto his back and just lay there for a moment.

He had a smile on his face. Any other guy would be crying and begging for it to stop. Corlissian boys weren't raised to be pussies though.

He hopped back up on his feet, and in one fluid motion, he kicked me in the stomach. I doubled over and he pounced. His fist caught me right in the chin. It rattled my teeth. I stood up and landed a blow to his nose for the second time.

This brutal assault on each other lasted a good fifteen minutes. When we'd called it quits, we both lay in the grass circle next to each other. We were breathing hard, and breathing itself was pretty damn difficult. I rolled my head over and saw how messed up Mason's face was and started laughing.

He rolled his head to the side and started laughing at me. I knew I looked just as bad as he did.

"Let's make a deal to go to school looking this messed up tomorrow," he suggested.

I sat up and looked back at him. "Deal," I replied.

He struggled to get to his feet, but once he did, he offered me a hand and I gladly accepted it. He hauled me to my feet. We walked around the circle and doused the torches. Then we walked to our cars that were parked up on the road not far away.

"I think if we would have done this when we were together, we might still be together."

"You mean something along the lines of every girl you slept with, I got to beat the fuck out of you?"

He chuckled. "Something like that." He paused and I waited for his next statement. I knew exactly what he was going to ask me. "Are you with the new guy or not?"

"I'm not."

"That's good."

"It shouldn't matter to you because we're not getting back together."

"You keeping telling me that, but I feel very differently."

"Keep dreaming, Mase."

"After rolling around with you on the ground, I've got plenty of dreams to occupy my wild imagination."

"Well, you have fun with your right hand," I said before getting in my car and shutting the door. I glanced over at Mason to see him humping the air. I started laughing, mostly because he looked ridiculous. He was covered in blood, standing on a dark road, humping air – not his finest moment.

I drove home and tried to think of excuses as to how I ended up like I did. Kate would see through it all. I figured I would just tell her the truth.

I parked the car and headed into the kitchen. Toby was sitting at the island. His mouth dropped open when I walked in the door.

"Who do Drew and I need to kill?" he said darkly as he took in my appearance.

"No one," I muttered. I was pretty sure I split my lip open again.

Then Kate and Drew rounded the corner.

"EMILY!" Kate shouted.

"Oh, you got fucked up," Drew laughed.

"Who did this?" Kate asked. Her eyes were darting all over my face, taking in all the damage. I didn't even know what I looked like. I avoided the mirrors on the drive home.

"Mason," I replied.

Drew stopped laughing and a shadow passed over his face. "He's dead."

"No need. He looks like this," I said, indicating my own face. "We decided to take care of our issues with each other at Culver's."

"Aww, man. Why didn't you call us? I would have loved to have seen that fight go down," Toby exclaimed.

"Sorry. I will next time."

"Oh no, young lady. There will not be a next time. Dammit, it's too late to call one of the healers here. You'll have to get fixed up before school tomorrow," Kate stated.

Obviously, Hotch hadn't called Kate and told her the wonderful news about her niece having four powers. I was grateful at the moment. I didn't want to be forced to heal myself. Plus, it was going to make school a whole lot more interesting tomorrow.

Kate gave me a once-over again and shook her head. "Go upstairs and clean up. And try not to get blood on the carpet!"

Chapter 13

I was standing next to Thea at the front of the hall, waiting for the bell to ring. Thea was gabbing about something that I was only half paying attention to. Thea could go on a twenty-minute rant about what could be considered the color mint.

"What the fuck?" I blurted out, cutting Thea off mid-sentence.

She turned her head to see what held my attention. Emily was walking down the hall towards us. She was dressed as wonderfully as always. Today, she had on dark gray pants that zipped up at the ankle, with black heels and a short-sleeved black sweater. Her wardrobe though wasn't what held my attention.

Her right eye was black, blue, and purple. Her bottom lip was swollen. There were bruises and cuts all over her face, neck, and arms. I couldn't imagine what the rest of her looked like.

Before I could say anything, Thea was already talking. "Come with me so we can try and fix this mess!"

"I'm fine, Thea," Emily replied in a bored tone. She clearly already had that conversation with her aunt this morning.

"No, you're not. What happened?"

By now, Sam, Tyler, Evan, and Micah had come closer. Emily didn't have to say a word about what happened. A moment later, Mason stepped up to the circle next to Emily looking like her twin. About the only difference between them was that Mason had two black eyes and his nose was broken.

A collective sigh went through the circle. The other Corlissians must have known what happened, but I was still utterly confused as to why Emily and Mason looked like they got jumped.

"I take it you two visited Culver's Field last night," Micah stated.

"What gave you that idea? Is it our pretty faces?" Mason teased.

"Well, I hope you got it out of your systems. Hotch is gonna be pissed when he sees you both," Sam said.

"After the beat-down she gave me last night, I think I can take anything from that old man," Mason replied.

"I hope you at least abided by traditional rules," Evan said.

They both nodded their heads. I wondered if Emily would tell me what this was all about. I thought I was finally understanding the Corlissian ways and then something like this happened and I was lost again.

"Why didn't you try and get patched up?" Thea asked. I noticed that they were all carefully choosing their words, since a simple human was standing in their presence. I found it kind of funny, since I had a good understanding of what they were talking about. It was just this whole fight thing had me puzzled.

Mason draped his arm over Emily's shoulder and pulled her into his side. "We made a little deal last night," he stated with a smile.

"Oh God, are you two back together?" Tyler asked.

"What would that have to do with them getting healed?" Micah asked, looking at Tyler. Tyler merely shrugged his shoulders. "You aren't together, are you?" Micah asked.

"No," Emily replied. She pushed Mason's arm off her shoulder. "We just took out our frustrations. That's it. Nothing more. Can we please drop it?"

"I'm saying one thing and that's it," Sam began. "I would have loved to have seen that fight."

Everyone else in the circle agreed with Sam.

The bell for school to begin rang out and the student body started to move towards their lockers and then to their homerooms.

I sat down in homeroom and waited for Emily to come in. There were a few murmurs in the classroom when she did enter. It wasn't normal for a girl to look like she did.

She sat down in the chair behind me. I turned around in my seat and looked at her. "I'll explain later," was all she said. It was nice that we had reached a point that I didn't even have to ask for an explanation from her; she was going to willingly give me one.

"Is this going to be another lake house explanation?" I asked.

She leaned back and that smirk of hers I was becoming familiar with curled up the corners of her mouth. "You enjoying our little lake house excursions?"

"Oh no. Not at all. Being alone with you in a secluded location is just the worst!" I said sarcastically.

"Well, being there with your fine-ass self is no picnic for me either," she teased. "But seriously, I'll just come by your apartment later. If that's all right?"

I tapped my chin and gazed off into the distance. "Will you be wearing that leather getup again?"

Emily started laughing. "Umm, not after last time. I don't particularly like being referred to as a stripper."

"I'm telling you, you could make some damn good money. Well, not right now, since your face looks like…" I trailed off when I saw the look on her face.

"Go ahead and finish that sentence, Lian."

"I'd rather not," I replied just as the bell rang.

Watkins walked in the room and his eyes immediately fell on Emily. He opened his mouth to say something and then snapped it closed again. He quickly averted his eyes from her.

"I guess you got your point across," I whispered.

Emily winked at me and I turned around in my seat.

Later that night, there was a knock on my door. I opened it to no one standing there. I stepped out in the hall to find Emily standing a few doors down, talking to someone. I leaned against the doorframe, crossed my arms over my chest, and waited. She walked towards me a moment later.

"What was that all about?" I asked as she just waltzed right into my apartment.

"That is your neighbor who thought I was a stripper. He asked me again where I worked. I just cleared it up for him that I am seventeen and he needs to stop asking me," she replied.

I shut the door. "How much did you threaten him?"

Emily put a hand on her chest and gasped. "Lian, I don't threaten people."

"Okay, what promise did you make to him?" I clarified. I remembered her little spiel to Watkins.

She leaned against the kitchen counter. "I told him that if he so much as looked at me again, I would separate him from his dearest body part."

"Now that sounds like the Emily I know."

"Sorry, I'm here a little later than planned. I had my final detention and then practice and Mason and I had to explain ourselves to our trainer. It was not pleasant. He was pissed."

"So, what did happen?" I asked. I sat down on the end of my bed and looked up at her.

"As you could tell yesterday, Mason and I sort of butt heads. Our little group has a way of dealing with our issues with one another. There is a field outside of town and we go there and beat the fuck out of each other."

I sat up straighter. "How do you resolve anything if you're just punching each other?" I asked.

"It gets the frustration you have out and on the person you're frustrated with. Trust me, it works. The thing is that none of our parents, guardians, nor our trainer approve of it. We usually get healed up before we go home, but Mason and I made a deal to go to school looking like we did."

"Why? I mean humans are not as stupid as you think. It was pretty clear what happened."

Emily shrugged her shoulders. "It's fun to let the humans start bizarre rumors."

"That's messed up. The whole thing is. And I can't believe that he would agree to fight you. I know you can hold your own self, but no guy in his right mind should do what he did to you."

She opened her mouth to say something, but I cut her off.

"Yes, I saw what he looked like and he seemed worse off than you. It still doesn't matter, Emily. A guy should never hit a girl… ever."

"We hit each other all the time in practice. How is what Mason and I did any different?" she asked.

"Because I've never seen you look like this after practice," I replied. She was being unbelievably stubborn about understanding the point I was trying to get across.

"That's because we always get healed after practice so you nosy humans won't notice anything."

I stood up and walked over to her. "I just don't understand one thing," I said.

"What's that?" she asked, looking up at me.

"How Mason seems hell bent on getting you back, but I just don't see how this would help his chances. I mean, to put even the slightest scratch on you is like destroying a priceless work of art."

Emily's eyes were wide and her mouth was slightly parted as she gazed at me. She blinked and shook her head. I closed the distance that separated us, put my hands on her hips, and lifted her up so she was sitting on the counter.

"Lian, don't," she whispered.

"I'm not going to do a thing," I replied. "I just like seeing you nervous for once. It's kind of cute."

I knew that she could easily get out of the position I had her in. She could shove me backwards or she could use one of her many powers on me. She didn't do a thing though.

Her eyes met mine. "I'm a healer," she muttered.

Okay, that was as far away from what I thought she was going to say. I was hoping for something a little different. I was shocked though.

"Do you have every Corlissian and Talyrian power, Emily?" I asked.

She shook her head no. "I don't have pyschokenisis, nor am I an aquamancer. Our trainer checked for those after practice."

"So, you could very well heal yourself now," I said.

"I very well could, but wouldn't it look a little weird to go to school tomorrow without a scratch on me?"

"Good point. You could say it was just makeup or something," I suggested.

"I'm not too keen on using my newfound powers. I've used pulso morsus like three times, pulso metus once, and I've healed once. I don't care about them. I'm a pyromancer, and that's what I'm going to continue focusing on being."

I took a step back so she could get off the counter if she wanted to. She didn't move though. She just sat there looking down at her hands. She had delicate hands too, with long skinny fingers. Those hands that looked so gentle were the most deadly things about her. I had seen flames dance around her fingers, I'd seen a man scream from her hand being on his arm, and I'd seen those hands throw a dagger at a man. And now she could do more with those hands. She could make someone see their worst fear and heal anything from a simple scratch to a gaping wound.

"I... I should probably go," she said. She hopped down from the counter and started for the door.

"Can I ask you one more thing?"

She paused and looked back at me. She nodded her head. "Sure."

"That first day I saw you at the beach, you were floating in the water away from everyone else. Then you stood in the water after all the others had left just to watch the sun set. Why?"

A small smile appeared on her face. "I'm a pyromancer and the sun is this massive ball of fiery energy. I lie in the water and just soak it up. Then at the end of the day, I give my thanks to it. I feel this sort of connection with it." She paused and shook her head. "I can't believe I just told you that. I've never told anybody before."

"Then why tell me?" I asked.

"I trust you," she whispered. Then she was gone.

I stood there for the longest time just staring at the door. No one had ever told me that they trusted me – not my sister, not my mother, and certainly not my father. Yet this girl I had known just over a week did.

It did make sense that she trusted me, I guess. I did know entirely too much about her. I suppose that a level of trust would be developed.

I had this feeling that outside of her family, Emily didn't trust many people either. I'm sure that she did trust the other Corlissians, but how many of them knew that she was a healer?

On Wednesday at school, Emily told me that we should study history that night. She said that she'd pick me up at six, but I decided to walk over to her house. It wasn't that far and I didn't mind getting some fresh air and exercise.

I rang the doorbell and heard a few voices yelling. The door was yanked open to Emily not looking at who was at the door, but looking upstairs while yelling, "You're an asshole, Drew!" She was pulling her hair up into another messy bun.

She turned her head and smiled at me. "Hey, Lian. I was getting ready to come pick you up. Are you that excited to see me?"

"Was I being that obvious?" I replied with a smile.

"WHO IS IT?!" Drew yelled down the stairs.

"THE FATHER OF MY FUTURE CHILDREN!" Emily hollered up to him.

That had Drew appearing on the top landing to see who it really was. "Oh, hey, Killian," he said. He completely didn't care at all what his sister had called me.

He trotted down the stairs and walked past us and into the kitchen. "Where are you going?" Emily asked. She nodded her head for me to come in and then shut the door.

"I have a date," he replied.

"What kind of people go out on a date on a Wednesday?"

"Apparently Bridgette and me."

"Are you seriously going out with that sea hag?" Emily blurted out. I bit back a laugh.

"She is not a sea hag. And yes, I am. What's the problem?"

"She's Mason's sister!"

"She's not Mason," Drew retorted. He grabbed his keys and left.

Emily turned to me with a look of disgust on her face. "Of all the females in this town, he has to go out with my ex's sister."

"I'm sorry, but when did you decide I was going to father your children?" I asked.

"Oh, you're not, because I'm not having any kids. It's just for shock value. Haven't you known me long enough to get that I do that sort of thing? Come on, let's go learn you some history!"

She started to head upstairs. "I thought we were studying in the kitchen?"

"Kate's not here, so we're doing it in my room," she replied with a wink. I shook my head as I followed her upstairs to her room.

We'd been studying for a while. We started studying in chairs and then we moved to the floor with our books and notebooks spread out in front of us.

"How exactly did you end up dating Mason for a year?" I asked.

"We're supposed to be studying U.S. history, not my relationship history," she muttered.

"Oh, come on. We need a break," I insisted.

"Are you really that interested?" she asked.

"Of course. I just cannot see you with someone like him."

"Like him?"

"Yeah, a douchebag!" I replied.

"Lian, he's not a… okay, yeah he is."

"Duh, now tell me the enthralling tale of how you fell for Captain Asshat." I got up and sat on her bed, since the floor was starting to hurt my butt. I got real comfortable by leaning back, cupping my hands behind my head, and crossing one ankle over the other. Emily just smirked at me.

"All right, so Mason had this reputation of being a…" she paused, searching for the right word.

"Man whore?" I added.

"Yeah, that works. He was a man whore. He'd date a girl for two weeks and would end it with them whether they'd sleep with him or not. Anyhow, last summer, Kate decided I'd been wearing glasses for too long and she let me get contacts. That same summer, these bad boys grew in," she said, grabbing her boobs. My eyebrows shot up and I knew I was grinning like a fool.

"A few days into school starting and he comes up to me and asks if I was new. We'd known each other since we were four, but I guess I looked a lot different. After that, he was walking with me between classes, hanging out at my locker, and just being a pest. Then one day, he asked me out."

"And you said?" I asked.

"No. He just stood there with his mouth hanging open, staring at me. I'm pretty sure he'd never been told 'no' before. I figured that would end it all, but I was mistaken by his highly competitive streak. He somehow got my cell number and started calling my phone and the house phone. Kate threatened to remove his manhood in a terrifyingly painful manner if he called the house again. That didn't stop him from calling my phone though. I finally became so tired of his general annoyance that I broke down and said yes to him."

"So, he annoyed you into dating him. Mental note taken!" I said.

"Well, that's how it all started," she finished.

"Okay, but you said that he'd date a girl for two weeks and be done. Why'd he stay with you for so long?"

"Why wouldn't he stay with me? Have you seen how hot I am?" she said with a laugh.

"Trust me, I've noticed," I muttered.

"Seriously, I'm not sure. I figured after two weeks he'd dump me and that would be that, but three weeks, then a month, then two months and we were still together."

"I want to take a stab at how your relationship ended. May I?"

"Of course," she said with a smile. Her eyes were saying, 'This should be interesting.'

"I think he finally talked you into sleeping with him and once he made that conquest, he broke up with you."

"And your theory is very wrong. Not that it's any of your business, but we slept together after we'd been dating for six months. We only dated for nine months, from when school started until school ended. I was the one who broke up with him."

"I knew that you dumped him, but I never heard why," I said.

"Micah told me that Mason had started doing the two-week thing again and that it had been going on for two months. Mason never told me, and if Micah hadn't, we might still be together."

"So, he cheated on you with roughly four girls?" I asked.

Emily nodded her head. "And now that school started back up, he wants us to get back together. He thought we were just taking a break for the summer. But we are done. Even if he can't get it through his head."

I sat up and folded my legs in Indian style as Emily got up and sat at the end of her bed. She leaned back against the footboard of her bed.

"I have a theory, one I think is actually true," I said after a moment's pause.

"Do tell."

"I think he truly loved you and he still loves you. He probably really enjoyed what he had going with you, but he had never been with someone for that long. He might have freaked himself out and maybe, just maybe, he was getting the cheating out of his system so he could be faithful to you in the long term."

"I don't think the last part is true. Yeah, he might have freaked himself out and fell back into his old comfortable habit. I just don't think he has it in himself to be faithful to someone for long term," she replied.

"And I don't think you two would have lasted for much longer anyways."

"Really? And why not?" she asked.

"It was from the first impressions I had of the two of you. Mason's the straight-laced, athletic, destined to get into an Ivy League school, and is just all around cocky."

Emily started to say something, but I held my hand up to stop her.

"This was *my* first impression of him. He is all those things, but there is more now that I kind of know him. Now, you. You were so far apart from your friends, floating in the water. You stayed behind to watch the sun set. I see in you a free spirit, a sort of bohemian soul, and someone who is very in tune with the world around them. The reason you wouldn't have lasted is because Mason would have tried to tie you down, and as a free spirit, you wouldn't have let that happen. You would have fought each other until it all crumbled. The life that he will lead is not meant for you."

Emily had tears in her eyes. Her lips were parted slightly. She was just staring at me with this look in her eyes that I hadn't ever seen before. I had a feeling that I had pegged her exactly like no one else had before. And that was after only knowing her a mere week and a half.

"What's more?" I continued. "You will be the one girl he will regret losing. I can imagine him as a middle-aged man working in some office with two kids and a wife at home that he doesn't really love. At nights, he'll lie awake trying to think of when his life started to turn down this path. It will come to him that it was the day he decided to cheat on you. He will know that you would have given him a life that was colorful, wonderful, and all around magical. But the thing is he will know that he never deserved you. Granted, I know that he won't work a typical job or live a typical life. That's just my thought on it all."

Emily closed her eyes and a few tears slid down her face and dripped off her chin.

"Shall I go on?" I whispered.

Emily shook her head no. She didn't want to hear any more of my predictions.

She had heard enough. I leaned forward and brushed away the trail of wetness the tears had left behind on her cheeks. She cracked her eyes open.

"I'm sorry. I didn't mean to make you cry, Em."

"You only have to apologize if you cause sad tears," she stated.

"These aren't exactly happy though," I said, staring at the tear on my thumb.

"You read me like no one else. I don't know how you do that," she whispered.

"That's because we are far more similar than either of us will ever realize," I said softly. I started to lean toward her just as her bedroom door opened.

"It's ten. Time to go," Kate said.

I leaned back with a grimace and got off her bed. "I'll see you tomorrow, Emily," I said before walking around Kate and out her door.

I heard the start of their conversation as I headed downstairs. "You know the rules. Your door cannot be closed if there are boys in your room," Kate stated.

"But there was only one boy in my room," Emily challenged.

I stifled a laugh as I walked out the front door. I was halfway down the block when I realized I'd forgotten my notebook. I turned around and went back to her house. The front door was still unlocked, so I just walked right in and went back upstairs. Kate was still talking to Emily and I stopped when I heard the topic of conversation: me.

"…much of a place to tell you who to be with, but if you do get involved with Killian, be careful. There is something about that boy and I just can't determine if it's good or bad. I know he guards himself in what he says around people and that's a good indication that he's hiding something. I just don't want you to get hurt and he's one that could seriously damage you."

"Why would you say that, Kate?" Emily asked.

"Because I saw what happened after you and Mason broke up. Mason may have hurt you, but Killian will destroy you," Kate said.

That fucking hurt. I could not believe I was hearing this from a woman who didn't know a damn thing about me. I had no intentions of ever hurting that girl in there, let alone damaging or destroying her.

I shoved off the wall and left Emily's house. The whole walk home, what Kate had said thundered in my brain and drove me insane.

I didn't sleep that night. I lay in bed and stared at the ceiling. I got up and paced a little while. I sat on the edge of my bed with my leg bouncing up and down.

How had it gone from me about to kiss Emily to her aunt saying that I would hurt her? I scrubbed my hands up and down my face as my alarm went off.

Chapter 14

"Toby, hurry up!" I yelled from the bottom of the stairs up to my brother. I knew he was messing with his hair like always. He spent more time on his hair than I did.

His bedroom door opened and he came strutting out a moment later. He was wearing a dark blue dress shirt with the sleeves rolled up and jeans. Toby never wore a dress shirt.

"What the hell are you wearing?" I asked.

"Today is the day, my dearest sister," he replied.

"For what?"

He winked at me as he walked past me towards the kitchen. Toby being cryptic was never a good thing. I had a gut feeling what was up, but I figured I'd hear about it later.

We hopped in the car and made it to school right as the first bell rang. "I swear your hair is gonna cause us to be late one day," I said.

"What matters is that my hair looks superb. Tardiness doesn't matter," he stated.

I was about to gag. Toby was starting to sound like Camilla. All she cared about was how she looked. School came in a distant second to her appearance.

I walked into homeroom right before the bell rang. Even if I was late, I doubted Watkins would count me tardy. That man was straight up frightened of me now. And all it took was a wee shock.

Lian had a ticked off look on his face as I passed him and he didn't even glance at me. Someone was in a wonderful mood this morning.

I tapped his shoulder and instead of turning completely around like he always did, he only turned his head.

"What's wrong with you?" I asked.

"Nothing," he said grumpily. He turned his head back around. Well, this was going to be a peachy day. I caught him as the rest of the student body was making their way to first period.

"Okay, seriously what's up?" I asked.

He averted his eyes from me. "It's nothing, Emily. I'm not obligated to tell you every fucking detail of my life. Leave it alone," he snapped.

He started to walk away, but I grabbed his arm and yanked him back so hard that his back slammed into a few lockers.

"You know very well that I will not leave it alone."

He took a deep breath and looked down at me. "Honestly, I just didn't get much sleep last night and I'm grouchy. I promise that's it," he replied.

He shoved off the lockers and walked away. I knew that he was lying, but clearly, he didn't want to tell me what was up.

The rest of the week went by as usual. Lian's attitude returned to near normal, but he still seemed like he was holding back something. I didn't ask him again what it was. If he wanted to, he'd tell me.

On Friday at lunch, Thea came bouncing into the lunchroom with a huge smile on her face. Lian leaned in close and asked, "What's with her?"

I shrugged my shoulders and waited for Thea to start blabbing, but she didn't say a thing. This was not normal Thea at all.

Everyone at the table looked at me. I guess as her best friend, it was my duty to ask the questions. I sighed.

"Okay, why the big goofy grin?" I asked.

She looked at me and her smile got even wider. I thought her face was going to split in two. "Your brother and I are going out tonight," she said.

"Which brother?" I asked.

Her smile disappeared. "Are you seriously asking me that? Why would I ever go out with Drew?"

I knew exactly which brother of mine she was going out with. Toby hadn't shut up about it since he asked her. Thea though hadn't said a thing to me.

I shrugged my shoulders. "I've been told that he has this hot, messy, unkempt thing going on. I don't see it though. So, what are you doing on your date with my little brother?" I asked.

"Just dinner and a movie," she said as that smile returned.

It was then that everyone's eyes at the table went above my head. I didn't need to turn around as my chair was spun around for me. Glaring down at me was Bridgette, Mason's older sister. Bridgette reminded me of Camilla. They both had blonde hair and blue eyes, though Bridgette's eyes were an icy blue and her hair was a dirty blonde. Bridgette didn't have the same reputation that my lovely sister had either.

Bridgette was wearing a dark blue dress with red polka dots and red heels. Her hair was falling around her face in loose curls and her makeup was done to perfection. She was also glaring at me with enough hate in her eyes to set fire to the room.

She leaned in close to me. "Stop messing around with my brother's emotions. I'm sick of hearing him talk about you and all the ways he has planned to win you back. Either get back with him or leave him alone," she spat.

I about started laughing. Bridgette and I rarely talked. The only reason we ever did was because we were both Corlissian. Our connection ended there.

She backed away from me a little and her eyes slid to my right where Lian was sitting. A devilish smiled slid onto her face. "You must be the new guy I've heard about. I'd heard rumors that you were delicious, but delicious doesn't do you justice," she said.

I stood up, shoved her to my left, grabbed her by the throat, and slammed her down on the table. I was leaning over her and could see the look of horror in her eyes. And in the refection of her eyes, I could see that mine were glowing violet.

"I don't want your brother. We broke up months ago. I had him and now it's over. I'm sick of having this same fucking conversation," I hissed.

"Emily, stop," Thea whispered behind me.

"If you come at me again like you just did, I will make your perfect little world a living hell. You know what I can do. Watch who you fuck with."

I let go of her throat and I saw her eyes go to Lian again. That's when I grabbed her throat a second time and slammed her head against the table.

I shoved off the table and walked to the door. The entire cafeteria was silent and everyone's eyes were on me. I could hear the soft whispers of the other students. A few students who were in my way quickly stepped away from me.

I let out a breath when I was out in the hallway. My hands were shaking violently. There was something seriously wrong with me and there was only one person I could talk to about it.

I grabbed the key that was always on me out of my pocket and headed for the door of the training center. I could hardly put the key in the lock; my hands were shaking so badly. I didn't even have the good sense to make sure no one was coming down the hall. I just stepped inside and shut the door behind me.

I walked down the long hallway, and in the massive room, Hotch was throwing daggers at several dummies that were hanging from the rafters.

"Emily? What brings you here?" Hotch loved when we showed up in the training center at random times of the day. This wouldn't make him happy though.

He noticed right off that something was off. It was probably my hands that would not stop shaking. "What's happened?" he asked in a harsh tone.

"You'll hear about it soon enough, but I attacked Bridgette in the lunchroom. She came at me first and I…"

"Just needed a little revenge?" Hotch finished for me.

I nodded my head. "I don't know why. I just felt so angry at her. I feel angry a lot lately and it's getting harder to keep under control. What is wrong with me?"

Hotch grabbed my hands. "First of all, you need to calm yourself down. You are a healer, so it will be easy. Just take a deep breath in and say the word *sanare*. Then breathe out. Let that power wash through you and soothe you."

I did as he said and I immediately felt better. My hands stopped shaking and my heart calmed its rapid beating in my chest to its normal rhythm. I nodded my head when I felt composed.

"Sit down," he said, indicating the blue mats that covered half of the concrete in the room. I did and he sat down across from me.

"I was wondering if this would happen and unfortunately it has," he started. "You have powers inside you that had been lying dormant. They had never been accessed before, so their energy wasn't alive inside you. Now that you have used them, their energy has awakened."

"I don't understand," I said.

"Do you remember when you first started using pyromancy?" he asked.

I nodded my head.

"Now, when you first started using it, there was that training period where you wouldn't use it for weeks at a time, right?"

I nodded my head again.

"Do you remember how you felt during that time?"

"I remember being really fidgety. I told Kate that I thought I had A.D.D."

"It was that energy inside you. You had started using it, so that power was alive. But it wasn't being expelled from you. It just built up and built up. After you used it, a sort of relief would come over you, correct?"

"So, that's what's going on again. The only thing is there is more power in me that I'm not using," I said.

"Exactly! The longer you go without using it, the more it will start to consume you. It will drive you to insanity if you withhold it. Your only choice is to use it, Emily."

I tipped myself back so I was lying on the mat. I covered my face with my hands. This was what I didn't want. Yet I knew that somehow I would be forced into using these powers in me, especially the one that I hated.

"I know that you have fought me on this, and at the time, I was okay with you not using them. Now that your health is at risk, you have no choice in the matter. My job is to make sure that no harm comes to you during the four years you train with me and I'll be damned if I let something happen to the only Corlissian with so many powers. You could be the one to end this centuries' long war we've had against all our enemies."

I pulled my hands away from my face and looked at Hotch like he was insane. He was staring at the wall that held all the weapons on it. I knew he wasn't looking at the weapons though. His eyes were sort of glazed over.

"Umm, I think you're getting way ahead of yourself," I muttered.

He blinked and smiled at me. "You are right. It is just a thought."

I heard the door to the training center open and voices carried to us down the hall. "And here comes the lynch squad," I mumbled.

Hotch chuckled and rose to his feet. I thought it was going to be Bridgette, Mason, Evan, and Micah, but it was Thea, Sam, and Tyler instead.

"Emily, we've been looking everywhere for you!" Thea said. There was exhaustion in her voice. She walked over and dropped down next to me. "What happened in there?"

"That was straight up disturbing, Em. Even for you," Sam said, walking over with Tyler beside him. They both sat down in front of me.

"Is Bridgette alright?" I asked. I really didn't give two flying fucks if she was, but the good-natured part of me thought I should show some concern for her.

"She was complaining about probably having a concussion, but other than her ego being severely assaulted, she's fine," Tyler stated with a smirk on his face.

"Blah, blah, blah. Now back to my original question: what happened?" Thea asked.

"I just snapped. I'm tired of the whole Mason-and-me thing. It's in the past, yet everyone keeps digging it up. Plus, she got in my face and I'm so not cool with that."

"Yeah, we all know about you and your attitude, Emily," Sam said. He flicked his tongue ring against the back of his teeth to make a clicking noise.

"I don't think it has a thing to do with your attitude. I think it's those powers inside of you. I don't want to sound mean, but you do have a Talyrian power and that could be causing you to hulk out on people. Just saying," Tyler suggested.

He wasn't far from the truth actually. I just nodded my head that I agreed with him.

"Hotch, is there really no way to remove even one of her powers?" Thea asked.

Hotch was shaking his head. "I have scoured countless books, but since this is the only case of this ever happening, there is no literature on it before. And you know very well that powers are permanent."

"Okay, don't get mad," Sam started. It was never good when that was the first thing your friend said to you. "But maybe a Talyrian got with your mom and created you."

"Come on, Sam!" Thea groaned. "Emily and Toby look like twins. There is no way that they didn't come from the same mother and father. And you know Toby only has one power."

"Well, if my mom did sleep around, that would explain Camilla," I chimed in.

Everyone started laughing, even Hotch. The bell to end lunch rang. It was hard to hear, since we were in a concrete room. Thea pulled me to my feet and had to practically drag me to where our lockers were. I was dreading the rest of the school day. I was glad that it was Friday and maybe by the time the weekend passed, everyone would forget that I slammed Bridgette Monroe's head into a lunch table. I would still have to deal with the whispers for the next few hours though.

I sat down in science. I could feel all the eyes on me, but I kept my attention on the fascinating cover of our science book. It was bright green grass with morning dew clung to the blades.

I heard the stool that Lian was sitting in scrape across the tile floor. I knew that he was right next to me. He folded his arms on the table and laid his head down so he could look up at me. "You okay?" he whispered.

"Nope."

"You wanna talk about it?"

"Not right now," I replied.

"Is there anything I can do to make you feel better?" he asked.

"Take me away from all of this," I said softly.

He smiled. "I would, but we would miss out on the wonderful world of weather. And I would not be a good friend if I kept you away from that!"

I tried to keep a stoic expression on my face, but that made me smile. Lian sat up suddenly and threw his hands up in the air, with fists raised high, and yelled, "SUCCESS!"

"Mr. Marlow, keep your voice down!" Mr. Evans said as he walked in the room.

I noticed that a few rows in front of me, Mason was turned around glaring at me. I figured he'd be pissed that I hurt his precious sister, but she shouldn't have confronted me about utter bullshit. I raised my middle finger at him. He smiled and turned around in his seat.

Lian wrapped his arm around my shoulder and pulled me into his side. "Don't let 'em get to you. You are far better than them," he whispered.

Toby and I walked in the backdoor. Kate was sitting at the island with her cellphone up to her ear. She mouthed, "Stay," while pointing at me.

Toby laughed. "Have fun!" he said, walking through the kitchen.

Kate ended the call and arched an eyebrow at me. "Emily, what am I going to do with you?" she sighed.

Of course, she had to ask me that right as Drew walked in the door. "I'm still for sending her to military school. They would whip her into shape in no time." I wiggled my fingers at him and he flinched away from me.

"Drew, can you please give us a few minutes?" Kate asked.

"Is this about Emily smashing Bridgette's head into the lunch table?" he giggled.

"Yes, now leave!" Kate watched as my brother left the kitchen and headed upstairs. "Talk," she stated bluntly.

I recounted exactly what happened at lunch to Kate. She listened carefully and grimaced a few times. Then I told her the conversation I had with Hotch.

"Well, then on Monday, you are going to be doing some extra training," Kate ordered. I didn't respond to her. "Emily, this is about you staying healthy. You're doing this for your own good."

"It feels like I'm doing it for everyone else's own good."

"I don't care who it feels like you're doing it for. On Monday, you are going to be learning all about pulso morsus, pulso metus, and being a healer. Yeah, thanks for telling me about that."

Oops. I had seriously just forgotten to tell her about me being a healer. I had some other things on my mind since then.

I sighed and rolled my eyes. It was my duty as a teenager to do that. And I knew Kate despised it when we did it.

"For assaulting Bridgette and for rolling your eyes, you're grounded tonight," Kate stated. She got up from the stool and walked to her room.

I stood there with my mouth hanging open. She had to be kidding, right? Clearly, grounding me wasn't working as it probably should. I didn't understand why she kept doing it.

I went up to my room and changed into my favorite pair of dark blue sweats and a white tank top. I decided to put my glasses on for the night. I really wanted to look like I didn't give a hell, and nothing said that more than my black-rimmed glasses. I pulled my hair up into my usual messy bun.

There was a knock on my door and Toby poked his head in. "I need the car keys," he said.

I grabbed them out of my bag and tossed them at him. "Aren't you going to wish me luck?" he asked.

"I'm not in the mood to wish anyone luck. Be nice to my best friend," I said.

I spent the night in my room. Even when Kate knocked on my door and told me to come down for dinner, I didn't leave. I wasn't about to spend any amount of time with her, not even if food was involved.

I ended up doing all my homework, rearranging my closet, and dusting all my furniture. Then I started reading *'On the Road'* again. It had been a little while since I'd last read it. It was shoved in between my bed and the wall.

At midnight, I heard the familiar sound of someone trying to sneak up the stairs. I popped my door open and watched as my little brother eased his door open. He smiled and tossed the car keys back to me.

I shut my door and leaned against it, the car keys still in my hand. An idea invaded my head and I went with it. I slid my black flip-flops on and opened my door. The hall was pitch-black. I crept across to Camilla's room. I shut the door behind me. I went over to her window and yanked it open. I was halfway out the window when the door opened.

I shut my eyes and waited to hear Kate yelling at me and grounding me for two weeks for attempting to sneak out of the house.

"I don't know where you're going, but be careful." I turned my head to see Toby standing in the doorway.

"I will." He shut the door and I used all the footings that Camilla had told me about. I never told Kate about them and I was glad I didn't. I could have gotten Camilla in trouble, but then I wouldn't be able to sneak out either.

I got in the car, put it in neutral, and pushed it out of the driveway. I couldn't start it with Kate's room right next to where the cars were parked. Once I had the A5 on the road, I slipped into the driver's seat and turned the engine over.

I parked around the back of the building and headed up to the second floor. I paused outside his door and hesitated for a moment before knocking. I didn't hear any movement on the other side. It dawned on me that he could be out. I knocked one more time and when no answer came, I started to walk away.

I was halfway down the hall when Lian called my name. He was standing in the hall outside his door in nothing but black boxers. His hair was a mess and he was rubbing one of his eyes. I walked back to where he stood.

"What are you doing here?" he asked through a yawn.

"I thought we could have that talk now," I replied.

"You pick the oddest times to have conversations, Emily Porter," he mumbled. He motioned his arm for me to enter his apartment. He shut and locked the door. "If you don't mind, I am going to get under the covers because I just realized I am standing in front of the hottest girl in school in my boxers. Plus, I am tired, but I won't fall asleep. Promise."

He walked over and slid under his blankets. He folded his pillow in half so his head was tilted up. I sat down on the corner of his bed.

"I don't know what is so important that we need to talk at," he picked up his cellphone to see what time it was. "Twelve thirty-eight, but I have to say that you look really cute in those glasses."

I laughed. "I look like a dork, but thanks."

"All right, let me hear it," he said.

"I don't know if you remember, but today, I sort of slammed a girl's head into our lunch table," I started.

"It's something I can barely recall," he said with a smirk.

"Well, I know why I did it."

"You mean it had nothing to do with the fact that she was in your face, talking about your ex, and that she was flirting with me?"

"I'm not saying those weren't factors, but not really. My trainer said that it's because I'm not using these other powers I have and their energy is starting to overpower me. If I don't use it, I will eventually go crazy."

"But you were pretty damn adamant about not using pulso metus."

"And therein lies my issue. I have no choice but to use it, but I really don't want to."

"What if you just used your other powers in excess? Would that drain the pulso metus power out of you?" he asked.

I shook my head. "The powers aren't connected, so the only way to release that energy is to use it."

"No choice then?"

"No choice."

"And I bet you just hate that."

"I'm not thrilled about it."

He pushed himself up on his elbows. "I don't mean to sound like an overprotective boyfriend or anything, but you having this extra protection isn't a bad thing. It just means that your enemies have less of a chance of hurting you."

"I guess you're right," I sighed.

"Of course, I am. That's why you came here. I'm not going to give you some bullshit answer like all your Corlissian friends and family."

"I know. It's why I tell you all this stuff," I said as I stood up.

"Where are you going?" he asked.

"Home. I'm technically grounded for the lunchroom fiasco."

"I don't care." He lifted his covers up and patted the spot next to him.

"Seriously?"

"I have not been more serious about anything in my life," he stated.

"Are you going to keep your hands off me?" I asked with a smile.

"Absolutely not. No one is here to stop me from finally kissing you. Now, get your ass over here. You're mine tonight."

Chapter 15

I rolled over in bed and expected to feel Emily beside me, but that side of the bed was cold and empty. I sat up quickly and let out a sigh of relief when I saw her sitting on the floor by the bed with my history textbook open in her lap.

"What the hell are you doing?" I asked.

She lifted her head up and furrowed her brows. "Hunting for platypuses," she said sarcastically. She dropped her head back down to continue reading.

"Am I really that boring that you have to read a textbook?" I asked.

"You were sleeping and I didn't want to wake you. I wanted to read and you don't have any normal books here. I thought it would be rude to sneak out while you slept."

I scooted over so I was on the other side of the bed, closer to where she was. "I would have been severely disappointed if you had snuck out."

She closed the book and sat it down beside her. "I would never want to disappoint you," she said with a smile. She stood up and stretched her back and yawned. "I better go. I'm sure I'm in for a lecture of epic proportions. I'll probably be grounded for a month."

"Just don't tell her where you were. She'd undoubtedly hunt me down," I muttered.

"I don't think she'd kill you for making out with me." She started to walk towards the door.

"If you're not grounded later, do you wanna hang out?" I asked.

She turned around and nodded her head with a smile on her face. "There's a party later at the beach. Or did you mean something else?" she asked.

"No, a beach party sounds awesome," I replied. "What time?"

She shrugged her shoulders. "Whenever."

"How about I meet you at your house at seven?"

She nodded her head. "I'll see you then," she said before leaving my apartment. As soon as that door closed behind her, I flopped back on my bed and stared at the ceiling. I could not believe that I just spent a night making out with and sleeping in the same bed as Emily Porter.

I spent the remainder of the day doing homework and running errands around town. I kept checking the clock throughout the day, driving myself crazier every time I realized it was nowhere near seven.

After hours spent wasting time watching some mindless shows on TV, it was finally 6:45 and time for me to leave. I shoved my cellphone, wallet, and keys in my pockets and headed out the door.

It was about a twenty-minute walk to Emily's house, so it was a little past seven when I knocked on the door. Kate answered the door. She glared at me for a moment and then opened the door wider so I could come in. I really didn't like that woman and she clearly didn't like me.

Kate hollered up the stairs. "Em, Killian's here." Then she walked into the kitchen where Emily's brothers were.

Emily came bounding down the steps a moment later. She was wearing dark purple shorts, black flip-flops, and a black bikini top. That was it. She smiled at me as she rounded the corner and walked into the kitchen.

"Emily, put a shirt on!" Kate snapped.

"I'm going to the beach. When have you ever seen me wear a shirt to the beach?" Emily retorted.

"Maybe now is a good time to start," Kate suggested.

Emily grabbed her bag off the counter and walked toward me without saying a thing to her aunt. "You ready?" she asked, rifling through her purse and pulling out her car keys.

"Yup," I said. I opened the door and we left the house. "So, I take it you're not grounded?" I asked once we were settled in the car.

"Oh, trust me, she tried to ground me even though I told her that I'd spent the night driving around trying to clear my head. I had to break out an oldie, but a goodie by yelling, 'You're not my mom!' and slamming my door shut. There's so much tension in that house that you could cut it like butter."

"Tension even from your brothers?" I asked.

"Yup. We had to have a family meeting this afternoon and Kate made me tell them about what's going on with my powers and how I'm going to have to start training with them. They weren't happy that I never told them that I was a healer. I'm getting so sick of the same bullshit that I'd rather just let these powers liquefy my brain and be done with it."

"You don't mean that," I said.

"I don't, but it's just aggravating having to deal with all this crap that no one else does. The rest of the Corlissians practice with their one power, do some weapons training, and then leave. Now, I'm going to be stuck in the training center for hours just to get the hang of using these new powers."

"You need to stop looking at these powers as a bad thing. There is a reason that you were given these powers and no one else was. You are strong enough to handle all the responsibility that comes with having them. You should look at having these things as a positive rather than a negative," I suggested.

"Look at you, Lian, getting all philosophical and motivational on me!" Emily teased.

"I'm being serious, Emily."

"I know you are."

"Can I ask you a question?"

"Yes," she replied.

"How did your parents really die?" I asked.

She was silent. For a moment, I didn't think she was going to answer me. "The drive to the beach isn't long enough for that story," she said.

"So I was right in thinking it wasn't a car wreck?"

She only nodded her head in reply. This was clearly not something that she liked to talk about. Not that I thought it would be. No kid wants to talk about how their parents died. God knew how long it took for her to finally move past their deaths and regain normalcy in her life.

We pulled into the parking lot where a handful of cars were. We headed down to the beach where a small group of people was sitting. Before we reached the group, Thea jumped up and ran towards us.

"Don't you answer your phone anymore?" she snapped at Emily.

"Not last night. I was grounded again, so I shut it off and I forgot to turn it back on," Emily replied.

"What were you grounded for last night?" Thea asked. She looped one of her arms through Emily's arm and her other arm through mine and tugged us along.

"I'm sorry, but did you forget that I hit Bridgette's head on the table yesterday? Hotch called Kate and I got grounded," Emily said.

"Oh, yeah! You should hear how that incident has gotten blown out of proportion. I heard some people last night saying that you hit her head so hard that it cracked the back of her skull. Someone else said that they were told that there was blood everywhere. It's ridiculous really."

"What did you call me for anyway?" Emily asked.

"Duh! You're my bestie and I always call you after a date," Thea replied.

"And normally I'm fine with discussing your dates, but not when they are with my brother. I don't want to know how long he held your hand or whether he's a good kisser or not. I'm cool with you two dating. I just don't want to hear about it."

Thea stopped and forced both Emily and me to stop too. "Who am I supposed to talk to then?"

Emily nodded her head at me. "Lian."

Thea glanced up at me and then back to Emily. She dropped our arms and then spun me around so I was facing her. I caught Emily trying to hide her smile, but she was enjoying this too much.

"Ask me how my date was," Thea ordered.

I cleared my throat. "So, ugh, Thea, how was your date?"

Thea's face had been hardened before, but it suddenly seemed to melt. Her eyes got wider and this goofy grin appeared on her face. "It was wonderful. Toby is just so sweet. We went and saw…"

Before Thea progressed any further into her date, Emily snuck away, leaving me to stand there and have all the details recounted to me. She was going to pay for it and from the devilish grin she gave me, she knew it too.

I watched Emily over the top of Thea's head. I just nodded my head every now and then to make it seem like I was listening to Thea, even though I didn't give a rat's ass about her date with Emily's little brother.

Emily was talking to Sam and Tyler when Mason approached her. "This isn't going to be good," I said, cutting Thea off. She turned her head to see what held my attention. She grabbed my arm and yanked me over to them.

"…could have seriously hurt her, Emily! She can't take a hit like most of us can. I just cannot believe you would do such a thing!" Mason shouted at Emily.

Emily was standing there with a bored expression on her face. She was just letting Mason get all his frustration out and I gave her props for standing there and taking it. Then again, this was a girl who decapitated a guy with her foot; listening to her ex go on a tirade was nothing.

Once he finally finished, everyone's eyes went to Emily. We were all expecting her to go off on him. Instead, she said, "Let's play some volleyball." Then she walked away. It took us all a moment to catch up to her, since we were standing there slack-jawed.

We split into teams and Emily was on the opposite side as I was. And of course, she played like a pro. I was pretty sure that anything she did, she was amazing at it.

We were taking a short break, since someone swatted the ball too hard and it went soaring towards the water. I was facing Emily with my hands gripping the net. She was glaring up at me on the other side.

"We are so going to beat you," I said.

"No, you're not. You're already losing horribly," she replied.

"We're just waiting for that spark," I stated.

She didn't say anything. She just stepped forward and wiggled her pointer at me. I pressed my face in between one of the squares of the net. She rose up on her tippy toes and kissed me softly before lowering herself and stepping back with a wicked grin on her face.

"Spark you say?" she whispered.

I smiled down at her. Then my eyes traveled over to where Mason stood. His eyes were slanted and he was scowling at me. I'm pretty sure he wanted nothing more than to kill me right then. And I was relishing in the fact that he was envious of me.

I looked back at Emily, but a dark shadow in the distance caught my attention. I squinted my eyes, but I couldn't tell what it was. Emily turned around when she saw I was looking over her head.

"Shit," she breathed. She took a step backward and slammed into me.

"What is it?" I asked.

"You mean what are they? Nexes." Emily turned around and looked up at me briefly. "THEA!" she yelled.

Thea ran over to where we stood. "Yes?"

"We have a problem," Emily stated, nodding her head down the beach.

"Fuck!" Thea exhaled. "ALRIGHT, GAME'S OVER!" Thea hollered. A few of the human students bitched about ending the game. They headed over to the bonfire where the other students were. The Corlissians though knew something was up.

Emily pulled me to the side as the other Corlissians gathered around Thea. "Stay here," she whispered.

"What are you planning on doing?" I asked.

"They'll follow us and leave everyone else alone. We'll head down the beach and fight them."

"You don't have any weapons on you though," I said.

Emily held her hands up and wiggled her fingers at me in response. She started to walk away, but I grabbed her arm. "Be careful."

Emily scrunched up her nose. "That phrase sounds familiar," she teased. Then she flounced over to the other Corlissians.

I walked back to where the other students were. I looked back and Emily blew me a kiss as they walked down the beach. This must be how military wives feel, that deep-in-your-gut feeling that you might not see them again. That helplessness of knowing you can't do a thing to aid in bringing them back home in one piece.

That was how I felt watching Emily and all the other Corlissians I had come to know over the past few weeks. They were leading a very dangerous threat away from innocent bystanders. And they knew that they were going to have to fight them with their powers, since not a single one of them had their weapons on them.

I sat down next to a guy named Alex who was in my math class. "Where'd all the populars go?" he asked.

I shrugged my shoulders. "Don't know," I lied.

"What are those lights down there?" he asked, nodding his head down the beach.

I turned my head and saw what was clearly fire. I saw a flash of blue and red sparks erupt.

"Someone is probably just letting off crappy fireworks," I muttered. My stomach instantly knotted knowing that somewhere in those flashes of light, Emily was fighting for her life and the life of her friends. I felt sick that I couldn't help.

Chapter 16

As we walked down the beach, I continually looked over my shoulder. Sure enough, the Nexes were following us. Our enemies were good about leaving humans alone so long as those humans weren't standing between us and them. That's when human casualties occurred. And human casualties drew attention, which was something we tried to avoid.

We walked quite a way down the beach, so far that the bonfire was a faint speck on the horizon. I'm sure people would see the light show, but hopefully they were smart enough to stay the hell away.

My hands kept instinctually going to my back, but my daggers were stashed away in every other place but not on me. I knew there were a number of weapons in my car, but a handful of Nexes stood between my weapons and me. I was just going to have to fight with my own powers. I suppose it was time to use those other powers. They were given to me for a reason after all.

The seven of us, Thea, Sam, Tyler, Evan, Micah, Mason, and myself, lined up down the beach and awaited the Nexes.

I had only ever fought the Nexes modules, never a real one. From what I'd seen of the modules, they were similar to the Midnight Brothers in that they wore all black. Unlike the Brothers, the Nexes didn't have their heads covered. They looked almost human. Their hair was cropped short to their scalps and they all had piercing green eyes and tattoos on parts of their faces and covering their entire hands. They may have had more, but because their cloaks covered them, I didn't know. I guess tonight I would get to see if Hotch's mods were accurate.

Mason stood next to me with his eyes fixed dead ahead. He was balling his hands up into fists and then flexing them over and over again. This was going to be the second time I'd fought with him. He glanced over at me and smiled. I didn't return the gesture.

My eyes traveled down the rest of the Corlissians who were standing there holding their gazes down the beach, waiting for the coming assault. I knew when the Nexes were close because half of their eyes turned to a glowing blue. It was known as our warrior eyes and only happened when we were fighting or really, really pissed off.

Our only light this night was from the waning moon overhead. It was about three-quarters full and putting out just enough light that we could see in the dark.

The Nexes came to a halt about fifteen feet in front of us. There were ten of them, so three of us were going to be fighting two of those bastards.

One of the Nexes in the middle looked at all of us in turn and started laughing. He had tattoos covering a good deal of his face. His head was shaved completely bald.

"You think you can fight us, young Corlissians?" he asked in a voice that sounded like gravel.

"I smell Talyrian blood in the air, sir," the Nex standing to the left of their apparent leader said.

Out of the corner of my eye, I saw Mason turn his head toward me. *Thanks a lot, asshole!*

The leader noticed this and broke rank to come closer to me. "Ah yes, I can smell both races in your blood. He will be very pleased to hear of this."

"Who is he?" I asked.

The leader smiled at me and showed a mouth full of sharpened teeth. "You'll find out soon enough, love," he replied in a sickly sweet voice. "I promise not to hurt you too bad. I can't say the same for your friends though."

I felt the blood inside me start to boil. I knew that my eyes had changed from the gasp he and the other Nexes let out. "Come at me, motherfucker!" I hissed.

He nodded his head and the Nexes advanced on us. The leader fell back and watched. The coward didn't want to fight apparently.

The Nexes drew their daggers from their cloaks. I saw one of the Nexes go up in the air and a burst of flame hit him. He cried out as his cloak went up in a blaze. He tried to struggle out of the cloak once he hit the ground. When the burned fabric wouldn't come off his skin, he took off for the water.

A few other Nexes had the same thing done to them. The leader didn't have a happy look on his face.

Sam grabbed the other Nex that was facing him and a scream ripped out of his throat when Sam used his pulso morsus on him. Mason hit the Nex with a blast of fire.

I looked straight in front of me. Two Nexes were standing there with creepy grins on their faces. The other Corlissians were helping one another with the remaining Nexes. I figured I would just deal with these two on my own.

I stepped forward and closed the distance between us. The smiles fell off their faces and they gave each other a brief, confused glance. They took a hesitant step backwards.

"Nexes never step back from an enemy. And she is a girl, you fools!" the leader snapped at them.

"I won't hurt you," I whispered.

They raised their daggers up and charged at me. I ducked and rolled between them. Then I hopped up and turned. I grabbed them both by the back of the neck and said two words: *dolor* and *timor.*

They started screaming and trying to claw my hands off their necks. I didn't let go. I kept a firm grip on them. I could feel the powers flowing out of me and into them. It was a wonderful release.

I heard the footsteps before I could react. I was tackled from the back. My grip broke and I saw blue and red sparks arc in the air from the sudden snap. I didn't know powers were visible like that.

A heavy body was lying on me. It was the leader who was sneering down at me. "What are you going to do now?"

I wiggled my arms free, slammed my hands on his face, and growled, "*Ignis.*" He ripped my hands off his face and there were two red handprints burned on his skin. He glanced back and only one other Nex was still standing.

He shoved himself up and off me and took off running down the beach with the other Nex in tow. I pulled myself up into sitting position. I saw that Micah, Tyler, and Thea all had cuts on them. Thea was healing Micah and Tyler was dealing with his own wounds.

Sam squatted down in front of me. "You used them both at the same time, didn't you?" he asked.

I nodded my head.

"You feel okay?"

"I'm a little tired," I replied.

Mason crouched down next to Sam. "We should get back before people start talking."

Sam nodded his head. Sam grabbed my wrists and pulled me to my feet. Then he hunched down in front of me. "Get on," he said.

I hopped on his back and wrapped my legs around his hips and my arms around his neck. He placed his hands under my thighs and the seven of us headed back down the beach to the bonfire.

The other students didn't even seem to realize that we had left. They had no idea that we had drawn deadly creatures away from them and destroyed all but two. Being a Corlissian was a thankless thing.

Sam set me on my feet and Lian was at my side in an instant. He crouched down so he was at eyelevel with me.

"Are you hurt? Did you kill them? What happened?" he whispered.

I shook my head. "Not here."

I walked passed him and through the crowd of people that surrounded the bonfire. I knew that Lian was behind me. I didn't even know where the other Corlissians were, but I could feel the presence of a guy I had known for such a short time.

I stopped at the front of the Audi and pulled my keys out of my bag. Lian stopped next to me. I looked up at him. "Do you have your license?" I asked. He nodded his head and I slapped my keys into his palm. "You drive."

I walked around to the passenger side, dropped into the seat, and leaned my head against the headrest. Lian got in the driver's seat and had to yank the seat back away, since he was taller than I was. He started the car and pulled out of the lot.

"Where to, ma'am?" he asked.

"Anywhere but home," I said sleepily.

I must have dozed off on the drive because Lian shook me awake. I cracked my eyes open and I couldn't even tell where we were.

"Is my place okay?" he asked.

I was too out of my mind to realize that he had parked in the parking lot at the back of the Domus. I nodded my head to let him know that I was fine with his choice. I really wanted to go to the lake house and sleep away everything that happened, but Lian probably didn't remember how to get there.

He hopped out of the car and came around to the passenger side. He opened the door and, without a word, he scooped me up in his arms. He used his hip to shut the door. Then he silently carried me upstairs to his apartment.

He didn't put me down until we reached his door and he had to fish his keys out of his pocket to unlock it. I leaned against the wall and gazed down the hall at nothing in particular. He grabbed my hand and pulled me into his apartment and shut and locked the door.

"Are you going to talk now?" he asked.

I had been staring at his bed, but when he spoke, I turned to face him. "What's there to talk about? We fought them and only two survived. And that was only because they ran away," I replied.

"You didn't get hurt?"

I shook my head no.

"What were those blue and red sparks?"

"Something I need to ask our trainer about. I was using both pulso morsus and pulso metus at the same time and when that connection broke, sparks flared up. I don't know why though."

"What happened when–"

"Can I please get in your bed? I'm about to fall over," I said, cutting him off.

Lian smiled and nodded his head. "I would never deny a girl access to my bed."

I crawled from the end of the bed to the head. His bed was unmade and I was able to wiggle under the covers. I turned on my side, curled into a ball, and yawned.

"I'll be back. I need to take a shower," Lian muttered. He headed into the bathroom and I heard the shower running. I pulled the covers tighter around me and closed my eyes.

I opened my eyes when I heard a noise and Lian was standing at his dresser rummaging through his drawers with nothing but a towel on.

"Sorry," he whispered. "I forgot to grab clean clothes." He then headed back to the bathroom.

A few minutes later, he came out again and shut off the main lights to the apartment. I felt the other side of the bed dip from his weight. I flipped over so I was facing him instead of having my back to him. It was quiet in the room.

"Emily, how did your parents really die?" he asked. I had a gut feeling he was going to ask me some question. My parents' deaths was not my favorite thing to talk about.

"Car wreck," I muttered.

"Don't lie to me."

"Talyrian raid."

"Care to expand on that?"

I sighed. "My parents were the two best pyromancers in the Corlissian ranks. My dad was the best."

"Seriously?" he asked.

"Corlissians don't joke about being the best with their powers. Now, don't interrupt me." I paused. "A couple of nights before, word was sent through our community that a group of Talyrians was getting close to town. For some reason, the higher-ups decided that my parents should be the ones to go and do some scouting to see if they were just passing by or if they were going to attack us."

"I'm interrupting you. Why would the higher-ups decide to send out two people who are married with four kids?"

"Great question. It's one that we never got an answer to. Anyways, Mom and Dad left, and that night, someone came to our door saying they were killed by the Talyrians. I mean, that morning, Mom was talking about what she was going to make us for dinner when they got back. We never thought that was going to be the last time we saw them. It was just supposed to be a scouting mission and they weren't supposed to get close enough to attack. No one even knows what happened because the only Corlissians there died and the Talyrians sure didn't own up to it."

"I'm sure you've all got assumptions about what happened," Lian stated.

"Maybe everyone else does, but I don't. It's not something I think about. I just try to remember Mom and Dad and the little quirks about them. Now can we talk about something other than my dead parents?"

Lian made a weird noise beside me. "Umm, yeah, sure," he muttered.

"OH! I'm sure you haven't heard that homecoming is in four weeks," I said to change the topic.

"Shouldn't homecoming be sooner?" he asked.

"In Autumn Falls, we take our time with this sort of thing. And homecoming here takes weeks of planning."

"So, what happens during homecoming?"

"Well, throughout the week, everyone dresses up. Like Monday is Pajama Day and Tuesday is Eighties Day and so on. Friday is Class Colors Day. Then Friday night is the football game and Saturday is the dance."

"A dance? Is this one of those towns where the guys ask the girls in a very elaborate way?"

"For homecoming? No. For Prom? Yes."

"And are you wanting me to ask you to homecoming?" he asked.

"God, no! I'm not going with anyone. If you go with someone, then you feel obligated to be with them the whole night, and if you go dance, one dance with a guy you have known since you were four, then you get the skunk eye the whole time and then you get berated with questions about why you were dancing with Sam and not with–"

"OKAY! I won't ask you. But I do want one dance with you."

"Just one," I whispered. I yawned loudly.

I felt the bed move and Lian's arms wrapped around me and pulled me towards him. My forehead was pressed up against his chest, his chin was resting on top of my head, and our legs were tangled up together.

It wasn't right – this weird relationship we had developed in a few weeks. I shouldn't have trusted him more than I trusted people I had known my whole life. I knew so little about him and he knew way too much about me.

I knew that I was putting us both in danger the more I told him, but my heart said to trust him. My gut told me to stab him in the heart and dump his ass in the lake. I never knew which to follow. I'd had people tell me to always trust my heart and others told me to only trust my gut.

I didn't know what drew me to him. From that day he had approached me on the beach, I felt a connection to him. Us Corlissians associated with other students, of course, but we didn't let any into our tightknit group. Lian was the first one to be a part of our circle.

I knew he had fallen asleep when his breaths became steady and even. His arms tightened around me and he mumbled something about leaving Zoë in his sleep.

Sleep was one thing I was not going to get tonight. I was tired as hell from the fight, but my mind wouldn't shut up. It kept replaying the fight over and every detail about the Nexes was at the forefront of my head.

What had the leader meant about some guy being interested in me? Who was this person? The Nexes would only share this information about me with Avids and Midnight Brothers. It wasn't Talyrians I was worried about. I was worried about there being a bounty on my head in our enemies' ranks. To kill a Corlissian with Talyrian blood would probably be wonderful for them.

And that led into a whole other issue. Where did this Talyrian blood come from? I wasn't adopted and I wasn't another man's daughter. I was the daughter of Allan and Charlotte Porter, just like my sister and brothers. I was no different from them.

But I was different. I had four powers coursing through my body and they were only blessed with being pyromancers, just like our parents were.

It made me feel like somehow someone had turned me into a science– experiment-gone-wrong… or maybe right. There was this excitement that burned in my veins right before a fight, even the one I had with Mason. It was this sick joy that went through me at the very thought of bringing harm to someone. I always chalked that up to the warrior in me, but I suppose it was really the Talyrian in my blood.

Lian muttered something else about a piano. I closed my eyes and let the endless chatter quiet in my head. I somehow fell asleep with Lian holding me tight.

Chapter 17

Unlike yesterday morning, I didn't have to reach my arms out to attempt to find Emily. This time, she was still wrapped up against me. I pulled my head back to see that she was still asleep. Her right arm was folded under her head and her left arm was draped over my waist.

She looked so small and delicate when she slept, but I knew she was anything but delicate. She was born to be a fighter and had grown up surrounded by fighters. Both of her parents were killed when she was so young. She had to carry on without them and train to carry on what legacy they left behind.

She moved slightly and I felt her palm open up and splay across my back. She whispered something and then it felt like an explosion ripped through to the front of my brain. My vision went white and then an image appeared. I was standing in a massive room with floor-to-ceiling windows on two walls and dark-colored drapes hung open, letting a bit of light streak across the hardwood floors. The room had a few paintings and mirrors on its walls. But nothing about the room itself was what held my attention. It was the dark-haired girl lying on the hardwood floor in a pool of blood that was growing larger.

She twisted her face and stood up with blood covering the front of her and one side of her face. Her dark hair was matted in blood. "See what happens when you leave those you confess to love," she said darkly.

I reached out for her and she was gone. It was my worst fear. It was my little sister… dead. I could hear some far off screaming, but didn't know where it was coming from.

My vision returned to normal and I was in my bed. It was like I hadn't just witnessed the most dreadful thing in the world to me. I sat up and Emily was standing at the foot of the bed, staring at me with a horrified look on her face. One of her hands was covering her mouth and she had tears in her eyes.

She pulled her hand away slightly and said, "I am so sorry, Lian."

Then I realized what she was apologizing for. She had used pulso metus on me in her sleep. She did it without even knowing.

I shoved the covers back and crawled toward her. She backed away from me and held her hands out. "Please, don't touch me," she whispered.

I ignored her plea, snagged her wrist, and yanked her toward me. She tried to shove away from me, but I was stronger than she was and I was able to pull her against my chest. I felt her wet tears running down my torso.

"Emily, you didn't hurt me," I whispered.

"You were screaming," she muttered into my chest. Oh, so that was me then. I had no idea that was coming out of my mouth. Then again, I did just see my little sister in a puddle of blood.

I pulled her away so she could look me in the eyes. "Emily, look at me. I'm fine. There is not a scratch or burn or anything on me." I stretched my arms out to the side so she could see that I really was okay.

Emily walked to the side of the bed and glanced at my back, since that was where her hand had been. A brief moment of relief passed over her face which was quickly replaced with a look of disgust.

"I… I used pulso metus on you?" Her voice quivered when she spoke.

I nodded my head and she started to back away from me again. "It didn't hurt or anything, I promise."

"Of course, it didn't hurt physically! God, what did you see?"

I swallowed down the lump that was in my throat. "My sister," I whispered. "She was dead, I guess."

I reached out for Emily, but she was quicker this time. She slid on her flip-flops. "Where are you going?" I asked.

"Where are my keys?"

I nodded my head at the countertop in the kitchen. She grabbed her keys off the counter and headed for the door. I caught her before she could leave.

"Where are you going?" I asked again.

"I have to get this under control. I could have seriously hurt you, Lian."

"But you didn't."

"What if I would have used pulso morsus on you and I didn't let go? What if I would have set the bed on fire? I wouldn't have gotten burned, but you would be a pile of ash right now. I have to get these powers under control." And then she was gone.

I walked back to my bed and sat on the edge with my elbows resting on my knees. There hadn't been a dull moment in my life since I met Emily Porter. Her mood swings were enough to make any sane person's head spin around. And her personality was a whole other story. I honestly didn't know how her friends kept up with her. I even found myself wondering how Mason dealt with her for so long. Then again, she was just a simple pyromancer back then. Now she had three more powers and didn't know how to properly use them all.

I lay back on my bed and stared up at the white ceiling. I had so many thoughts ricocheting around my head that I couldn't even grasp one. I just saw images flash past my vision: my sister dead, Emily walking out my door, looking down at the beach, my first day in Autumn Falls, Emily tapping my shoulder on the first day of class, standing on Emily's stairs listening to her aunt talk about me, Emily killing that computer-generated Midnight Brother on the first day of school, my father whacking my knuckles with his yard stick when I missed a key on the piano, my mother smiling at me and kissing my forehead, Emily kissing me through the volleyball net, watching her walk down the beach, us at the lake house, in her car, in my bed, in her room, Emily, Emily, Emily…

I woke up suddenly to my alarm clock on my cellphone blaring. I fumbled for it on my nightstand and managed to shut it off. I glanced at the screen and then had to do a double take. It was Monday morning. I had slept nearly all day Sunday. The only time I had been awake was when Emily had woken me up by accidentally using pulso metus on me.

I had fallen asleep lying across my bed, but I was under the covers and lying in my bed properly. I didn't even remember scooting around. Then again, the body does weird things when we're sleeping.

I shoved the covers back and stood up. I felt dizzy and I had to sit back down again until my head stopped spinning. Was that from sleeping too long or the pulso metus?

Once I took a few deep breaths, I felt okay again and stood back up. I pulled on my clothes – dark gray tee shirt, jeans, and black boots. I grabbed my bag, cellphone, and keys and left.

I was walking up the front steps just as the first bell rang. Emily's younger brother fell into step next to me as I was walking down the main hall.

"Hey, Killian!"

"Hi, Toby," I replied. This was weird. I had never said more than a few words to Toby, yet here he was walking beside me like we were the best of friends. "Umm, is Emily okay?" I asked.

At this question, Toby smiled and then started laughing. "Dude, my sister is never okay. She was seriously messed up yesterday. I thought Kate was going to take her to a mental institution. Then she just left and didn't come back until late. I heard her and Kate having a yelling match at like two in the morning."

"About what?"

"I heard something about Kate wanting to know where she was. I think Kate thought she was with you. Emily said she was with… umm, someone else…" He paused and cleared his throat. "So, I take it she wasn't lying?"

"I saw her Sunday morning, but not for long."

Toby grabbed my forearm and forced me to stop. He was like his sister – small but strong. I was sure he could bring down someone twice his size. It was definitely all that training they went through.

He looked around before he spoke. "I'm worried about her. There are things going on in her life that I can't tell you about, but she is really freaking me out. I swear everything just hit the fan at once with her and it's been all downhill since. She's constantly sneaking out of the house and I rarely see her anymore. I'm afraid to talk to her because she's been so moody lately. I just don't know what to do."

"Why are you telling me this?" I asked. It was strange for him to confide in me when he didn't even know me.

"Because she talks to you. And she seems to listen to you. I was hoping you might talk to her and see what's up."

I knew exactly what was up with Emily. The thing was I couldn't tell Toby without giving it away that I knew about them being Corlissians. If he was anything like Emily, he would drag me out of the school to the woods and slit my throat without a second thought.

"I think you should just be honest with her. Tell her what you told me. She's your sister and she cares about you. She probably doesn't even know that she's freaking you out with her behavior."

"Whose behavior?" We both turned our heads to see Emily standing there with a smirk on her face. "You boys wouldn't be talking about me, now would you?" She still had that smirk on her face, but there was an iciness to her voice. She stared her brother down and her eyes turned that glowing violet color I had seen once before when she was about to murder Watkins.

"Em, your eyes," Toby whispered. He glanced up at me nervously.

She blinked and it was gone. She walked around us and we both watched her go for different reasons. Toby was scared for and of his sister. I was just gawking at her ass in the leather skirt she was wearing. She had a dark purple tank top on and black heels that made her legs look longer than they were.

Toby looked up at me. "See what I mean," he stated before following in his sister's wake. I knew what he meant. Emily was frightening sometimes. But there were other times, like Saturday night, when she was so vulnerable. With Emily, you just had to deal with whatever temperament she was in at that particular time.

I sat down in homeroom, but Emily wasn't there yet. She walked in right as the bell rang, with a book open in her hands that she was thoroughly engrossed in. Watkins looked at her for a moment, like he was thinking about marking her tardy, but thought better of it. I'm sure his brain could conjure up that pain she put him in rather quickly.

She slid into her seat and laid the book flat on her desk. I turned in my seat. "What are you reading?" I asked.

She responded by lifting the book up so I could see the cover. "Latin, Seventh Edition." She dropped the book back on the desk. I knew that the Corlissians used Latin words to invoke their powers, but she knew all the words she needed to. I didn't know what she was looking up and I thought it best not to ask.

"Killian?" Watkins said. I raised my hand to let him know that I was here. I was pretty sure that after being in the same seats for four weeks, he could just look around the room to see who was here and who wasn't.

He called off a few more names before coming to Emily. She raised her hand in the air with her middle finger pointed at him. Then she lowered it. She never took her eyes off the book. A few students snickered. Mr. Watkins opened his mouth, then closed it, and then opened it again. He looked like a fish out of water. Emily raised her eyes and stared at him for a moment. He moved on to the next student without a word to her.

When the bell rang, I was up and out the door with the rest of the students. Emily grabbed the back of my shirt and pulled me to the side of the hallway.

"What were you talking about with Toby this morning?" she asked.

"The fact that he is scared of you," I stated rather bluntly.

Emily cracked a smile like I was joking. "I'm not scary," she said.

"Emily, you just flipped off a teacher in class and he didn't say a word to you. Yeah, you kind of are."

"Are you scared of me too?" she asked.

"Sometimes you do frighten me. But I think you need to talk to your brother and let him know that you're okay even if you're not." Then I walked away from her. It was slightly gratifying to be the one to walk away for a change, since it was usually her walking away from me.

I sat down at the lunch table. Everyone was there except for Emily. I asked Thea where she was.

"She's busy." Thea then leaned closer to me. "Did I see you two kiss on Saturday night or did my eyes deceive me?" she asked with a wicked grin.

"I think you need an eye exam because I have no idea what you're talking about," I replied.

She swatted my arm. "Ooooh, I knew you two would get together!"

"We're not together. It was just a kiss," I said.

"Pssshhh, it's never just a kiss," she said before leaning back in her seat. I honestly had no idea what Thea meant by that. We had slept in my bed together two nights in a row and that was it. It never went further than sleep.

I was talking to Tyler when Sam let out a whistle. "Damn, Emily Porter! You look fine as hell today!"

Emily slid into the seat next to mine and smiled at Sam. "Thank you, my dear," she replied.

"No, I'm serious. I kind of want to throw you on the table and have my way with you. I totally would if I didn't think your boy would snap my neck," Sam said, glancing at me.

Emily started laughing. She turned to me with a smile on her face. It was one of those rare smiles that lit up her whole face. She patted me on the chest. "Awww, you're my boy, Lian," she said.

"Sweet. What does that get me?" I asked.

"One ass grab," Tyler joked.

"No, no, no," Sam started. "There needs to be more."

Emily leaned back in her chair with a grin on her face. She was clearly enjoying watching her two guy friends let me know what I deserved for being known as her boy.

"But she's wearing a leather skirt. Do you know how amazing an ass grab would feel?" Tyler argued.

"Do you want to grab my ass, Tyler?" Emily asked.

Tyler's eyebrows shot up his forehead. Sam, Thea, and I started laughing. Tyler was just gaping at her. I was waiting for drool to start dripping from his mouth.

"Maybe later," he muttered just as the bell rang. We all rose from our seats and headed for the main hall.

Sam threw an arm around my shoulder as we followed Thea and Emily. He was just a few inches shorter than I was. "I would love to do that brotherly thing where I get to tell you that if you hurt her, I'll hurt you, but I think Emily could cause you enough damage on her own."

"Sam, we're not together," I said… for the second time that day.

"Maybe not right now, but it's inevitable." He patted my shoulder and headed the other way.

I sat down next to Emily in science. I stared at the front of the room for a moment before turning to her. "Are we in a relationship that I'm not aware of?" I asked.

Emily furrowed her brows. "No. Why?"

"Because both Sam and Thea seem to think we are."

Emily rolled her eyes. "Let them think what they want," she replied in a bored tone. She eyed me for a moment. "Do you want to be with me?" she asked.

"No… kinda… I don't know," I muttered.

"Having zero confidence is an unattractive trait, Lian. You need to say, 'No, I think we should just be friends.' Or say, 'YES!'" she slammed her hand down on the table, "'I want you here and now on this table, dammit!'"

It was at that time that Mr. Evans walked in. "Ms. Porter, this is not sexual education. Please refrain from such remarks in my classroom."

"Sorry, Mr. Evans," Emily said with smile.

"I think the leather from that skirt has seeped into your brain," I whispered.

"Speaking of my leather skirt, you have made no mention of it. Do you not like it?" she asked.

"Oh, I like it all right. I've been too busy ogling you in it that I forgot to say anything."

A note skidded to a stop in front of Emily. She turned her head at the table across from ours. The student who threw it nodded up to where Mason was sitting.

"Well, the last time he gave me a note, I ended up slamming him on this table, going to the principal's office, then having a grand ole time fighting him," she muttered while opening the note up.

I read it out of the corner of my eye because I was being nosy. It said, *"Can we talk after class?"*

Emily grabbed my pen and replied, "No, but you can talk to me after school." She tossed the note back to the guy across from us and waited until Mason read her reply. He turned around and nodded his head that he was okay with that.

I kind of wanted to know what he needed to talk to her about. The last time that he did talk to her, he was yelling because Emily had slammed his sister's head into the lunch table.

Emily opened her science book and pulled two white slips of paper out of them. She slid one to me. "Don't go to study hall today. Meet me in the library so we can study history."

I held the slip up. It had Watkins' handwriting and signature on them, stating that we were allowed to use the library during our study-hall hour. "How'd you get this?" I asked.

"I asked Watkins and he had those slips signed and in my hand in an instant. It's fun having a teacher terrified of me," she said.

I met Emily outside of the school's library. I followed her inside the spacious room. This was the first time I had set foot in the library. Emily handed her slip to the librarian and I did the same. She was a classic librarian too. She had white, short, and curly hair, glasses that were attached to that string that went around the back of the neck, and her nose had a permanent crinkle to it like all of us disgusted her. She was wearing a button-up dark blue shirt that was buttoned clear up to her throat and a long skirt.

The librarian nodded her head that we were okay. I followed Emily to one of the corners of the library. There was a desk and four chairs around a table that was next to the window. The window looked out onto the football field and to the woods just beyond.

Emily slid her history book across the table to me as we sat down. She opened up the Latin book that was in her possession once again. She dropped her cellphone on the table too. There were headphones wrapped around the phone.

"What do you need to know?" Emily asked, leaning back in her chair.

We had been studying for half an hour when Emily hopped up and excused herself to go to the bathroom. While she was gone, I pulled her cellphone towards me and slid my finger across the screen. The song she had been listening to appeared on the screen and I hit the PLAY button.

A song I had never heard started. I read the screen to see who it was and what song was playing: *Harper Simon, The Shine.* I didn't know what kind of music Emily listened to. If I had to guess, I would have said death metal, but she actually listened to chill and calming music. At least she had been. She might have had one of those eclectic tastes in music where she listened to everything.

I hit the PAUSE button and slid her cellphone back to where it had been. I didn't think she would care if I was listening to her music, but I didn't want to be caught seemingly snooping on her phone.

Emily sat back down a few minutes later and looked at me. I thought she knew what I had been doing. "I just remembered that you never forgave me."

I furrowed my brows. "For what?"

Emily looked at me like I had lost my damn mind. "For Sunday morning."

"What do I need to forgive you for? I already told you that you didn't hurt me," I said, dropping my voice.

"I caused you to see your worst fear. And it felt like reality, didn't it? I don't think I can tell you how sorry I am for that."

"Emily, it's okay, but if you need my forgiveness, then I forgive you," I replied. I scrunched up my nose. "Is this going to end our sleeping arrangement? I was kind of getting used to you being there."

Emily scratched the back of her neck. "I think it's best that I only sleep in my bed from now on. Sorry."

"Now that I am not forgiving you for!" Emily and I started laughing. The librarian let out a loud, "Sssshhhhhh," telling us to quiet down.

Chapter 18

I went to the training center right after school was over. I had spent Sunday afternoon and went into the night with Hotch at Culver's Field to practice using my other powers. After I had accidentally used pulso metus on Lian, I freaked out. He was lucky that it was pulso metus and not one of the other two that are far more deadly.

Kate didn't believe me when I told her where I was. She had some issue with Lian and I didn't know why. He had never been anything but nice to her, so I didn't know what she had against him. She was convinced that I was with him, even after I made her call Hotch who confirmed that we had been practicing nearly all day.

Sunday's long practice gave me a little more confidence in using these powers. I wasn't a pro at them like I was with pyromancy, but I was better.

I was the first one to walk in the training center that day. Hotch shook his head when he saw me. "In all my life, I never thought I'd see the day when you were the first one here. I know something bad happened that scared you into getting serious about these powers and I know you will never tell me what it was, but I'm glad it happened."

I sure as hell wasn't glad it happened. Even if Lian said I didn't hurt him and even though he did forgive me, it didn't stop me from feeling like shit. I had made him see his little sister dead. That was his worst fear – her dying.

"There's something I need to talk to you about after practice is over," I said. Hotch nodded his head as Micah and Sam walked in.

"Please let me have fight time with Emily today," Sam pleaded to Hotch.

Hotch gave him a funny look. "You never want to fight with Emily," Hotch stated, which was true. Sam was scared he might hurt me.

"I know you're not blind, old man. Look at that skirt and how it clings. I'm gonna try and cop a feel. If you know what I mean," Sam said, winking at me and making me laugh.

"You're definitely not having fight time with Emily then. Perv."

The rest of the Corlissians began filing in after that and I was partnered up with Mason, since he begged Hotch to pair us up and promised not to feel me up. I knew he wanted to talk to me, even though I didn't really want to hear what he had to say. Last time he spoke to me was when he was yelling at me on the beach.

Mason grabbed two swords off the rack that held all the weapons. He tossed me one and then bent his knees in sparring position. I stood where I was. He moved toward me and I knocked the sword out of his hand and sent it skidding across the floor. Micah and Evan had to hop over it.

"Damn, Em," Mason muttered before retrieving his sword.

"What did you want to talk about?" I asked. I figured we might as well get it over with. It was kind of like pulling a Band-Aid off. Get it over with and it hurts less.

He lunged at me again and I knocked it out of his hand again. "Fuck," he breathed. He grabbed his sword again but instead of lunging at me, he had the blade pointed against the floor and leaned against it like a crutch.

"What are you doing Friday?" he asked.

"Probably coming to school," I stated.

He rolled his eyes. "Friday night, smart-ass."

"I don't know yet. Why?" I didn't like where this was going.

"Will you have dinner with me?" he asked. And there it was.

"No."

"No?"

"No."

"But it's just dinner. That's all. I just want to take you out to dinner as friends," he said.

"But we're not friends. And I can't think of anything worse than spending even a half hour in a restaurant with you. I don't want to make small talk with you and pretend like I'm having a good time when in fact I seriously doubt I would."

I snapped my sword out at his and knocked it out from under him. He lost his balance and fell over.

"Can I practice with someone else?" I stated loudly as Mason got to his feet. Sam jogged over to me instantly. He lunged at me and we actually sparred properly for a while until Hotch yelled at us all to stop and practice our powers.

Sam grabbed my sword to put it back, and as he walked by me, he grabbed my ass. "VICTORY!" he shouted, throwing his fists in the air. I started laughing again.

Everyone grouped off into whatever power they had. The pyromancers were in one corner of the room, as were those with pyschokenisis. Sam and

Micah were the only Corlissians in our group to have pulso morsus besides me, so they worked together.

Since I was the weirdo with four powers, I had to work with Hotch. I didn't mind because he knew more about all the powers than I did and he was a good teacher even if he did get on my nerves.

As the evening wore on, people began to trickle out. The pyromancers always left first and then those with pyschokenisis. Sam and Micah were always the last to leave, but now that was me. I was only about halfway through my training when Sam and Micah left. Sam gave me one last wink on his way out.

"Well, now that everyone is gone, what did you want to speak about?" Hotch asked.

"Two things, actually. First, on Saturday night when we were fighting the Nexes, I was able to use both pulso morsus and pulso metus at the same time, but when my connection was broken, blue and red sparks flew up in the air. Why?"

Hotch had a wrinkle form between his eyebrows. "Our powers don't have colors, nor are they visible, aside from the fire thing. I honestly don't know why colored sparks appeared. This is something else I'll have to look into."

"Okay, ummm, you know how when we get mad or before we fight, our eyes turn to that glowing blue?"

Hotch nodded his head. Of course, he knew about it. He was a Corlissian.

"Well, the thing is that my eyes glow violet, not blue," I said.

Hotch's mouth fell open. "Show me," he muttered.

"Ugh…"

He shook his head and went to his computer. A moment later, six Nexes and six Brothers surrounded me. I knew that they were mods, but my instincts kicked in and I immediately palmed the twins that were at my back. I knew that my eyes turned when Hotch let out a gasp.

"Dear child!" he said.

He killed the mods, and the twelve enemies that had been surrounding me disappeared. He came over to me and held my face in his hands. I blinked and I knew the violet was gone.

"Can you explain that one to me?" I asked. He dropped his hands from my face and shook his head no, as I expected.

"The only thing I can think of is all your powers have changed the color of your warrior eyes."

"Wait!" I said, holding my hand up even though he had stopped talking. "Blue and red make purple when mixed together, right? So, maybe our powers do have colors, but we can't see them. Those other powers mixing changed my warrior-eye color," I said.

Hotch was rubbing his chin and nodding his head. "I think you're on to something with that theory." It wasn't a theory. It had to be the truth.

He clapped his hands together. "All right, you can leave for the night. Tomorrow we'll be sure to practice your healing abilities and pyromancy. You can't slack on that because of these other powers. It is still your primary power. Off with you!"

I grabbed my bag and headed out of the training center to the parking lot where my car was waiting and someone was leaning against the driver's side door. I knew it was Mason before I was even near him.

I sighed. I just wanted to go home, eat something, do my homework, and go to bed. But nooooo, I had to have another 'talk' with Mason in the dark parking lot of the school.

"Get off my car or you'll scratch it," I said when I got near him. He shoved off and stood right in front of the door so I couldn't get in.

"Long practice," he stated.

"Well spotted. I do have all these lovely powers I have to train into my brain now. Shall I test one on you?"

He smiled at me, but didn't move.

"What do you want?" I asked.

He puckered his lips, squinted his eyes, and looked up at the clear starry sky overhead. "There is just one thing I want, but she keeps refusing me. I don't know how I'm supposed to get her back if she seems to despise me so much."

"Maybe you're not supposed to get her back. And maybe she wouldn't despise you if you hadn't been a lying, cheating asshole. Just a theory though. Or were you talking about one those other girls you dated before me?"

"There was never anyone before you."

"You mean your two-week trollops don't count?"

"Why can't you just get back with me and pretend that I was never with anyone else? I haven't been with anyone since you broke up with me, Emily. Four months of being with no one. I've been good and I'm trying to show you that I am deserving of you."

"Why can't you pursue someone else?" I asked.

"Because they're not you. God, what do I have to say and do? I want you back, Emily!"

"Mason, I really can't deal with this anymore. I have a lot going on and," I couldn't believe what I was about to say to him, "I'm not saying we'll never get back together, but just now is a really bad time for me to be with anyone."

A smile broke across his face. I hadn't seen that smile for a long time now and I felt bad that I was the reason that he hadn't smiled like that in a while.

"You're saying there is a chance then?"

"Just back off for a while, please."

"Anything… of course." He stepped aside and opened my car door for me. I slid into the driver's seat and he closed the door for me. He walked across the lot to his shiny, cherry-red Lexus LF-LC. I pulled out of the lot with him right behind me. He headed right out of the lot towards his house and I headed left.

I didn't head home though. I went to Lian's because I needed to talk to someone who wasn't a Corlissian and didn't have opinions that benefited them. I pulled into the lot behind the building and headed up to the second floor.

I, of course, passed a group of guys heading downstairs who were saying things they'd like to do to me. Note to self: never wear the leather skirt again. I smiled as they passed because I knew that if one of them so much as attempted to grab me, I would have him on the floor in an instant with a dagger against his throat.

I knocked on Lian's door and he opened it just as one of the guys ran up to me. "Do you think I could get your number?" he asked. He was cute, but he had no idea that I was in high school.

Lian stood in the doorway and folded his arms across his chest. Lian stood a head-and-a-half taller than the guy and had more muscle than him. The guy looked up at Lian and then at me.

"I suggest you run along and not talk to my girl ever again," Lian said in a deep tone.

The guy blushed and nodded his head, made a quick apology, and took off to catch up with his friends.

"I can take care of myself," I said.

"I know. Trust me, I know," he breathed. "What's up?"

"I know why my eyes glow purple instead of blue."

"Geesh, come inside. I swear you Corlissians just run your mouth out in public now!" he teased. I ducked under his arm and went into his apartment that was beginning to feel like a second home. I glanced at the bed, and the memory of waking up to him screaming popped into the front of my brain. It was something I would never forget.

He sat down on the end of his bed and patted the spot next to him, but I shook my head no. He shook his head in disappointment. I didn't trust myself to sleep in the same room as anyone else, let alone the same bed. And that bed held a very bad memory. I didn't even want to sit on it.

"So, why do your eyes glow violet?" he asked.

"Remember when you were asking about those sparks?"

"The red and blue ones on Saturday night? OH! Duh! Red and blue make purple," he said, suddenly remembering his elementary lesson on primary and secondary colors.

"The thing is my trainer doesn't know why there were colored sparks. He said he'd have to look into it."

"And that means that he won't find a thing, since you are a one of kind."

"Pretty much."

"Did you and Mason have that talk he was so eager for?" Lian asked.

"Yeah, he wants to have dinner with me on Friday night," I replied.

"And what did you say?" There was an edge to his voice.

"Yes. Free food!" I lied.

He stood up from the bed and glared down at me. "Well, I hope you two have fun." He definitely didn't try to hide the anger in his tone.

"Seriously? You really don't know me that well, do you? You think I'd actually go out with him?"

His face softened. "You're not?"

I shook my head. "Jealous much."

"I'd say a tad possessive."

"Just a tad?"

My cellphone started ringing in my back pocket. I plucked it out and saw Kate on the display. "The warden is calling," I muttered before sliding my finger over the screen to answer it.

"Yes?"

"You're late," Kate said.

"I was told by you that I had to start practicing with my other powers starting today. And that is what I'm doing."

Kate sighed. "How much longer?"

"As long as it takes for me to master these powers and become the greatest motherfucking Corlissian ever, then I'm going to use these badass powers of mine and defeat all Talyrians so we can live in a world of peace and beauty."

Lian had a hand covering his mouth, trying to subdue the laughter.

"I want you home in ten minutes."

"Or you'll call the cops?"

"Ten minutes, Emily." The call ended.

"All Talyrians, huh?" Lian asked.

"All of them." I stretched up on my toes and kissed his cheek. "I better go. I'm already gonna get a stern talking too."

"You missed my lips, Ms. Porter," he said.

"I'm a tease, Mr. Marlow."

"That ain't no lie. That skirt..." He made a noise in his throat that sounded like a growl.

"Which is why I'm not wearing it again." I turned around and wiggled my butt at him. His hand connected with it. I turned back around with a look of mock appall.

He shrugged his shoulders. "If you're not wearing it again, I would never get a chance to collect on being your boy."

"And what do I get for being your girl?" I asked.

"I'll think of something," he stated. "Now get out before Kate sends out a search party. And she'll have to, because I'm close to keeping you here for the night."

I smiled and backed toward the door. He followed me, and when I got outside his door, I strutted down the hallway, making Lian groan. "Dammit, Emily!" I heard behind me.

I pulled in the driveway about fifteen minutes later. Right when I walked in the backdoor, Kate was on me. "Have you no concept of time? I said ten minutes, not fifteen."

I had a smartass remark on the end of my tongue, but instead, I just replied with a simple, "Sorry."

Kate looked a little taken aback that I had apologized rather than arguing with her. "Umm, it's alright. Just head upstairs and clean up before dinner, okay?"

I nodded my head and went up to my room. I grabbed some clean clothes out of my closet and then went across the hall to the bathroom. I took a long hot shower and felt better. My arms ached a little. It was probably because I was sparring with Sam who doesn't show any mercy even in training.

I went back to my room and pulled my cellphone out of my bag and sat down on my bed. I needed to talk to someone who probably understood me better than I knew: my sister.

Camilla picked up on the third ring. "Em?!" she yelled into the phone. I could hear loud music and laughter in the background. "Hang on a sec!" she yelled again. I heard a door close and the music and voices died down considerably. "Em?" she said again.

"Hey, Cami,"

"Oh my gosh! How are you? I haven't talked to you since, well, since that day I came home. What's up?" she asked.

"Umm, I know this is kind of weird for me to ask, but do you think you could head down sometime this week so we can talk in person?"

There was a pause and I was half expecting her to say no and hang up on me. "My last class on Thursday ends at ten, and I could catch the ten-thirty train. That would put me in Autumn Falls at eleven thirty. Yeah, I can do that. Pick me up at the station?" she asked.

I let out a sigh of relief. "Of course. Thanks, Cami." I would have to skip a class and lunch, which didn't matter. And Camilla didn't even think about me having class at that time, since she skipped school more than anyone. I still wasn't sure how she graduated or got into college.

The rest of the week flew by, and before I knew it, I was slipping out the side door during the transition time between third period and lunch. I hopped in my car and drove out of the lot towards the station that was on the far edge of town. The train was just pulling away when I drove up. Camilla walked out of the station and slid into the passenger seat.

"I can't tell you how much I miss this place," she said. She sucked in a big breath of air and slowly let it out. One thing about Autumn Falls was there was fresh air. There were no factories or industries near us. Plus we had the ocean on one side of us. The salt seemed to cleanse the air of our town.

I pulled out of the train station lot and drove to a small coffee shop that wasn't but a few blocks from the station. We walked in, placed our orders, and sat down at a small table.

"I know this must be serious or else you wouldn't be calling me for help. So, spill it, little sister."

There was one thing I really loved about Camilla. She didn't beat around. She got right to the point and she was brutally honest.

"How did you deal with Kate?" I asked.

Camilla started laughing. "Ugh, oh. She's on to you now that I've moved out."

I nodded my head. "Even before I found out about these new powers, she's been on my case. Hell, it started even before you moved out. Remember how I was grounded for two weeks?"

"You did break into the school, Em."

"No, I didn't actually. And don't get off topic. How did you deal with her? I can't do this for two more years!"

"Okay, what is she on your case about more than anything?"

"It varies between me never being at home and practicing these newies I got," I said.

"Why are you never at home?"

"How many times did you sneak out in the middle of the night? Did I ever ask where you were?"

"Point taken. What I did when she was on my case was to do as she asked. Don't look at me like that. It's that simple. For a few weeks, I would do everything that she wanted. I stayed at home through the night. I went home right after practice, and on the weekends, I was home at a decent time. Then she saw I was doing what she wanted and she was happy and was off my back. Then I'd fall back into my old routine. It was a back-and-forth game that I had to play with her that was really tiring."

"That seems really tedious."

"And it might not work on you. You can try my method, but what always got you into trouble was that you have a really bad attitude problem. Even when Mom and Dad were still alive, you would lip off to them. It's just who you are. But I think that if you were home at a proper time and kept your mouth closed, she would probably lay off you for a while."

The male barista brought our coffees over and smiled at Camilla who winked at him. She popped the lid off her drink and blew on it.

"So, did you ever get with that fine-ass boy who was at the house last time I was home?"

"No."

"Damn, Emily, get on that or some other skank is going to get him first. And this advice is coming from the biggest skank Autumn Falls High has ever seen. I swear if I was there this year, I would have already screwed him."

I rolled my eyes, even though there was no doubt in my mind that it was true. What Camilla wanted, Camilla got.

"Anyhow, Mason is still trying to get back together," I said to change the subject.

"Ugh, I still don't know why you ever dated that douchebag." Mason and Camilla never liked each other. It started in elementary school. Mason was playing with a basketball and Camilla walked up to him and pushed him over and stole the ball. Mason jumped up and tackled her and took the ball back. That started them just laying punches into each other. They haven't liked each other since.

"He was different when it was just the two of us."

"Well, of course he was. All guys are different when they're not around their friends. How are the new powers?" she asked.

"Oh, they are just wonderful. I feel so blessed to have them," I muttered sarcastically.

"Okay, that's what everyone wants you to say, but how do you feel?"

"Like a science experiment. I just want an explanation as to why I have them and you, Drew, and Toby don't. I'm not trying to sound like a whiner, but it's not fair."

"I have a feeling you'll get an answer as to why. The thing that worries me is that it's going to be bad. Is there any way that Talyrians have something to do with it?" she asked.

"I've never met an actual Talyrian and I don't think Mom and Dad would have willingly given me to one when I was a baby to somehow give me more powers."

She shrugged her shoulders. "Just a thought," she muttered.

She glanced at her watch. "Anything else, dear?" she asked.

"No. I really just wanted to talk to you about Kate. I knew that you would understand and give me some advice."

"I'm glad you called. And if you ever need to talk again, let me know. I don't mind coming down here. Especially for you."

We stood up and threw our arms around each other. "I actually like having you gone, Camilla," I said.

She pulled me back and scowled at me. "Why?"

"Because I get to sneak out of your room."

"Just be careful, Emily. I don't like hearing about these random Nexes and Midnight Brothers being in town. I know you're powerful and very capable of taking care of yourself, but I do still worry about you."

"I'm always careful." I grabbed my coffee off the table.

Camilla looked at me for a moment. "You know what you need?"

"What?"

"I think you need a weekend at the lake house to just chill."

"I doubt Kate would allow that."

"She might. Just tell her you need some time to clear your head, and use some other bullshit words she likes to hear. Go up there and chill out and practice your powers. It would be good for you."

I nodded my head. "I'll think about it. Ready?"

"Actually, I'm going to hang around here for a bit," she said, eyeing the barista.

"Well, you have fun," I muttered on my way out. I didn't look back. I didn't need to see my sister flirting with the guy who she would probably lure into the bathroom.

I walked into science just as the bell rang. I sat down in my seat next to Lian. "Where were you?" he asked.

"Stop being nosy."

"No! Where were you?" he asked again.

"I was with my sister."

"Why?"

"Because I needed to talk to her."

"I thought you only talked to me."

I sighed. "There are some things that I can't discuss with you. My sister may be a loud-mouthed whore, but she is honest with me."

"Were you talking to her about me?" he asked.

"No. Well, she did bring you up."

"What did she say?"

"Sister's code of silence. I cannot tell you or I would be betraying my sister." I glanced at the front of the room and Mason was staring at me. He gave me a brief smile before turning around. "What are you doing this weekend?" I asked.

"Oh, there's some big end of summer party at the beach. Why?"

"I'm thinking about spending the weekend at the lake."

"Are you asking me to join you?"

I nodded my head.

"Hmm, a party at the beach or a whole weekend at the lake with you? Yeah, I think I'll hit up the beach," he teased.

"I guess I'll ask Mason. He won't say no," I said with a straight face.

"Fuck that guy! I'm going!" he stated a little too loudly, earning us a dirty look from Mr. Evans.

Chapter 19

"Just so you know, you're sleeping in my brother's room. You can have either Drew's or Toby's," Emily said as soon as we walked in the door of the lake house.

"Damn, Em, you're taking all the fun out of this," I said.

"Sorry, but I've only been training with these new powers for a week. I'm not staying in a bed with anyone." She walked down the long hall, with her shiny-red weekend bag in her hands. She disappeared into her room. "OH, my babies! I forgot you were all up here!" she stated.

I had no idea what she was talking about until she walked out of her room twirling one of the daggers around her fingers. I didn't know how she wasn't cutting herself. I had seen people do that with pencils before, but never with a very sharp dagger. She tossed it up in the air, caught the tip of the blade, and sent it careening across the room until it buried itself, hilt deep, into the wall.

"Yeah, you're totally not scary," I muttered, making Emily laugh. "So, how did you convince Kate to let you come up here for the whole weekend?" I asked.

Emily nodded her head for me to follow her. "Oh, it took a lot of begging and pleading. I told her that I needed some time to clear my head and to practice my powers with no distractions."

"And I'm guessing she doesn't know I'm here?"

"Definitely not. She'd castrate you!"

I followed Emily down the hall and peeked my head in her room as I passed. It was similar to the room at her house in that it was light and airy. It was light purple and everything else in the room was white – the furniture, bedding, doors, and trim. Dividing the room was a row of bookshelves that did not have many books on them. There were mostly weapons laid on the shelves. On the other side of the shelves were her bed, a dresser, and a door that I was guessing was the bathroom. A large window with sheer white curtains looked out over the lake.

Emily stopped in front of one door. "This is Toby's room." It was a light blue and had a nautical theme with pictures of boats and anchors. The bed was directly under the window that had dark blue curtains. The bedspread was made out of an off-white material that looked similar to a sailboat's sail.

Emily nudged my arm and walked down to the next door. "Or this is Drew's room." It was dark as hell even with the light on. The walls were black and the curtains blocking the window were black too. The covers on the bed were dark gray. "Drew loves to sleep in a pitch-black room," Emily muttered.

"I like this one. It's more my style," I said, dropping my bag just inside the door.

"I figured. That door in the corner is for the bathroom," she said, indicating the only other door in the room.

She stepped around me and walked back down to her room. She wiggled her finger and I dutifully followed. She was unzipping her bag and dumping the contents on to her bed. I walked around the weapons' shelves and leaned against the wall. "What do you want to do today?" she asked.

I shrugged my shoulders.

"Umm, we can swim or lay on the docks or you can watch me practice my powers. Whatever you want, I'm game for."

I felt the corners of my mouth tug up into a smile. Emily glanced at me and shook her head. "Do guys think of anything else other than sex?" she asked.

"Of course, we do. Hell, I slept in a bed with you for two nights and I was a perfect gentleman. You, on the other hand…" I trailed off.

"I said I was sorry," she mumbled as her cheeks turned bright red.

"And I forgave you. That doesn't mean I'm not going to tease you about it."

She started rooting around the pile of clothes on her bed. She snagged a pair of bikini bottoms and tossed them to the side. I walked over and glanced at the few books that were on her shelves: *'Walden' by Thoreau, 'Persuasion' by Austen, 'The Catcher in the Rye' by Salinger, and 'The Iliad' by Homer.*

I heard a door shut, and when I turned around, Emily was gone. She walked out of the bathroom a few minutes later in a dark purple bikini. She was twisting her hair up into a knot on the top of her head.

"I'm going to the docks," she said, walking past me.

Emily Porter was a tease – plain and simple. No sane girl walked around in front of a guy in a tiny swimsuit. It was just not right. I shook my head as she walked by me and out the door.

I went and put on a pair of swim trunks and was heading outside when a phone on the dining-room table chimed. I picked mine up and checked it, but there was nothing. I craned my neck to see Emily jump in the lake and I picked hers up and checked it. There was a message from Mason, reading, *'Please, think about dinner tonight.'* For some reason, my finger started scrolling through their correspondence. There were a lot of texts from Mason begging Emily to take him back and her just replying with a simple, *"No."* I hit a few buttons to get her phone back to the main screen.

I saw the camera-roll icon in the top corner and pushed it. I found myself scrolling through pictures of her and Mason. They looked so damn happy together and that fool had to go and ruin it. There were pictures of them on the beach. He had his arms wrapped around her so tightly and her head was resting on his chest. There were others of him giving her a piggyback ride. There was one of him holding her up in the air and they were just looking at each other. In the next picture, he had lowered her down and was kissing her. I shut the phone off and tossed it on the table.

I took a deep breath before stepping outside and onto the porch. I saw Emily down below floating in the water. She was a good distance out in the water. I sat down on the end of the dock that she had dropped a towel on. I just sat there and watched her. She seemed so at peace floating in the water. She didn't have a care in the world. She wasn't thinking about her powers and all the pressure on her. It was just her, the water, and the sun.

She popped her head up, noticed that she was far away from shore, and started swimming back. And of course, she swam with grace and power. Every Corlissian I had met was good at everything they did. There was probably a reason that none of them were in sports because they would absolutely dominate. No human student at that school could match even the weakest Corlissian. They were all powerful. It came with being trained since they were born.

Emily swam up to the dock I was sitting on. She stretched her arms up and pulled herself up onto the dock with ease. Her arm muscles bulged a little when she did that. I didn't think she had a single ounce of fat on her. Her stomach was flat and her legs were thin, yet they were muscular too, just like her arms. She bent sideways until her head was over the water and wrung her hair out. She took her hair out of the knot, ran her fingers through it, and then braided it.

"Scared of the water?" she asked as she twisted the band around the base of her braid to hold it in place.

"I'm not exactly fond of it." It was the truth. I never had swimming lessons, nor did I grow up next to an ocean or lake. We didn't even have a pool at our house.

"Then why come to a town that sits on the edge of the ocean?" she asked.

"I liked the view," I said, smiling up at her.

"It is nice at sunset," she said, wrapping the towel around her dripping body.

"That's not the view I was talking about. I was thinking of you floating in the water."

Emily caught her bottom lip between her teeth and knelt down in front of me. She placed a hand on my chest, and with a shove, I was lying on my back staring up at the pale blue above me. I felt a few drops of water on my stomach and her hip grazed my right leg. She was hovering over me a moment later. She lowered herself down until her full weight was on me, which wasn't a lot. She was as light as a feather.

"You can't say things like that to me," she whispered. She stretched her hands up and ran them through my hair. Her fingertips grazed my scalp and it felt so good.

"It's the truth," I murmured. "I felt drawn to you."

Emily giggled. "You make me sound like a siren. Only I'm not luring sailors into wrecking their ships with my voice."

"I thought you liked history, not mythology," I said.

She lowered her chin onto my chest and I tucked my hands behind my head to prop it up so I could see her better.

"I can make fire appear at my fingertips with one word. I can bring a full-grown man to his knees screaming in pain with a touch and a word. I can make anyone see their worst fear with a touch and word. And I can heal nearly any wound anyone can sustain. I wonder why I find mythology so fascinating. I feel like I'm part of it sometimes only. This is not stuff made up by ancient poets; this is really my life."

She dropped her hands from caressing my head and placed them on my chest. She brought her legs forward and shoved herself up so she was straddling my stomach. She went to stand up, but I grabbed her wrists and held her in place.

"Stay," I whispered.

She looked down at me for a moment before lowering herself back down. She laid her cheek against my chest and I wrapped my arms around her back.

It was nearly silent. The only noise was made by Mother Nature herself – the birds chirping in their high perches in the trees, the breeze blowing, and the sound of the water lapping against the shore.

"You were happy with him, weren't you?" I blurted out. Ever since I saw those photos on her phone, I couldn't get the image of them together out of my head. I wondered why she didn't delete them.

She didn't say anything for a while. I thought she was either asleep or choosing to ignore my question. "Of course I was," she replied softly.

"Do you still love him?"

She was quiet again. The fact that she was carefully gauging her responses bothered me for some reason.

"No. I do care about him though as I care about most of the other Corlissians."

"You know he's never going to stop trying to get you back, don't you?"

"I think he'll get tired after a while. Part of me is just so sick of it." She stopped there. I knew there was more though.

"But?"

"But in a weird way, it is kind of flattering."

"How in the hell is being constantly pursued by your ex flattering? That's just not normal to think like that."

"Nothing about my life is normal, Lian," she replied.

"How do you deal with it?"

"With what?"

"Having powers."

She sat up and looked at me. "I don't deal with it. I've known all my life what I am and what I'm capable of. We learn what we are at a young age and we learn to keep quiet about it. We are taught to fight from a very early age. I got my first dagger on my third birthday. We access our powers when we're thirteen. When you grow up around this sort of thing, it just becomes your normal."

"But how do you deal with being the most powerful Corlissian?" I asked.

She snorted and rose to her feet. "That is something I don't even think about." She stepped over me and walked back up to the house.

I went back inside a few hours later. I had fallen asleep on the dock and woke up when the sun was just below the tree line. Emily was lying on one of the couches in the living room, talking on her phone. Her back was on the couch and her feet were propped up on the back of the couch.

She lifted her head up and smiled at me before dropping her head back down. "I told you I don't want to hear about it. I don't care that you're dating my brother. I just... ugh."

She was clearly talking to Thea. I grabbed a drink out of the fridge and leaned against the kitchen counter.

"No." *Pause.* She sighed. "Of course!" *Pause.* "Oh, every last juicy detail," she laughed. "I promise." *Pause.* "Yes, yes, yes." *Pause.* "Okay, bye, love." The call ended.

Emily sat up on the couch and looked at me. "So, I was scouring this place trying to find a few movies and my brothers must have taken most of them home because all I found was…" She leaned over and picked up two DVD cases off the floor – *'The Notebook'* and *'Pride and Prejudice.'* "Now, I know what you're thinking. These are not guy-friendly movies, but you are so wrong, my friend. This movie," she said, tapping the case of *'The Notebook,'* "is, well, I suppose most guys watch it just to get laid, but you also get to see Rachel McAdams in a bikini and… yeah, that's about it. BUT," she stated, tapping the cover of *'Pride and Prejudice,'* "the other is about a guy who is kind of a prick and a strong-willed girl who hate each other at first and then… okay, so neither of these are manly movies. Blame my brothers!"

I was laughing at Emily at this point and her wonderful description of each movie. "Which one did you say would get me laid?"

She wrinkled her nose and dropped both movies on the couch. "Neither. I am not that kind of girl!" She hopped off the couch and went to her room. She came out wearing dark gray sweats and a white tee shirt. Her purple bikini was still on underneath. She had her black-rimmed glasses on too.

"How can you look equally attractive in a leather skirt and sweatpants?" I asked.

"It is one of my many gifts," she said, hopping up on the counter across from me. She stared out the massive windows that looked across the lake.

Suddenly, her hands start shaking. She looked down at them with curiosity for a moment.

"Emily?"

Her eyes darted around the room for a moment. "Fuck," she said rather casually. "It's been well over a week since I've used pyromancy."

She twisted her shaking hands until they were palm-up and she whispered, *"Ignis,"* and flames appeared dancing across her fingers and hands. She let out her breath and closed her eyes.

It was fascinating watching her hands still themselves as the flames continued lapping at her skin and leaving not a single burn. After a few minutes of letting her pyromancy out, she whispered, "Intereo," and the flames immediately went out.

She opened her eyes and glanced down at her hands to see that they were still. "Mmm, better," she mumbled.

"Can a pyromancer ever burn themselves?" I asked.

Emily started laughing. "No. I could turn this burner on high and put my hand on it and it wouldn't leave a single mark," she said, indicating the stovetop to her right. "Do you want me to prove it?" she asked, arching an eyebrow.

"No!"

She turned her head and looked over at the dining-room table and sighed. "It took me the longest time to come back here," she said.

"Huh?"

"After my parents died. We spent so much time here when they were alive. My dad would have Toby and Drew down at the lake fishing and Camilla and I would be with Mom having a dress-up party in Mom's closet. We'd always eat dinner as a family there." She nodded her head at the table. "After they were killed, Kate tried to get us all to come up here for even a day. I would always stay at home. I didn't want to be in a place that they were once so happy in."

"When did you finally come back?" I asked.

"Last year," she said, turning her head to face me. "Two days after I got my license, Kate pulls up in front of the house in that car," she said, nodding her head towards the black A5. "She handed me the keys and told me that with having the car, I had to drive Toby around and that when he got his license, we'd have to share it. Anyhow, I had to take it on a test drive and I came here. I hadn't been here in eight years."

A tear ran down her cheek and dripped onto her gray sweats. I set my drink on the counter behind me and walked over to where she sat on the counter. I pulled her glasses off and used my thumb to wipe the wetness off her cheek.

"I'm sorry," she breathed.

"Don't be. I like this side of you. It proves that you can let your guard down."

"You're the only one I've ever told that to."

I smiled. "I told you once that we are more similar than you will ever realize. You feel a sort of kindred spirit in me."

She wrapped her legs around my waist and yanked me up against the counter. She sat up a little straighter and draped her arms around the back of my neck. "Stop talking for once," she whispered before softly pressing her lips against mine.

I wrapped my arms around her lower back and pulled her closer to me while kissing her a little more roughly. I moved my hands up her back, and when I did, her tee shirt came up too. I slid one of my hands under and felt her warm, soft skin. The muscles in her back moved slightly under my touch.

She moved her hands up to my head and tangled her fingers in my hair. Then she leaned back and pulled me with her. I had to crawl up on the counter, keep my balance, and not tear my lips away from hers. It was so worth it though.

I moved my hands around to her sides so they wouldn't be trapped underneath her. One of my hands started moving up her stomach under her shirt, but she smacked my hand and pulled her mouth away from mine.

"We should stop," she breathed before running her tongue across her lower lip.

"We probably should," I replied. I started to lower my head back to hers when she placed a hand on my chest, halting me.

"I'm serious."

I sighed. "You are such a tease, Emily," I said a little rougher than intended. I scooted back and hopped off the counter. Emily sat up and put her glasses back on.

"I've only known you for five weeks," she snapped.

"And yet you tell me things that you've never even told your best friend. I know you better than people you have known your whole life."

She slid off the counter and glared up at me. "Yet I know nothing about you," she hissed. She walked away from me and into her bedroom, slamming her door behind her.

I ran my hands through my hair roughly and groaned. She was the most aggravating person in the world sometimes. But she was right. She had spilled so much to me about her family and past and she knew near nothing about mine. It was really for the best that I kept her in the dark. The less she knew, the less hurt she would be in the end.

The next morning, I woke up at six forty-five a.m. I hadn't slept that much because what Emily had said to me rang in my head. We hadn't spoken since she stormed off. I didn't think she even came out of her room again.

I shoved the covers back and pulled a pair of black sweatpants on and a dark gray tee shirt. I crept down the hall and into the kitchen. I unlocked the door and headed down to the dock.

I completely understood why Emily came up here to clear her head. It was a place with zero distractions and no one to bother you if you were alone. The early morning was even more silent than it had been yesterday afternoon. No birds were chirping yet, and there wasn't even a breeze blowing.

My eyes sort of glazed over as I stared out across the expansive lake and the early sun glittering over its surface. Thoughts of times with my family entered my head. We never had the kind of family time that Emily did. We spent little time together. The only time we did occasionally come together was when my mom would force us all to do something as a family. We would hardly speak to one another. It was awkward and not pleasant for any of us.

I don't know how long I'd been sitting there thinking about how Emily and I came from such different backgrounds. She came from a loving and supportive family and I came from one that was fractured by my verbally abusive father.

I didn't even hear her walk up behind me. I had been so lost in my thoughts. I felt her hands on my shoulders, her legs against my sides as she crouched down behind me, and her warm breath on my ear.

I smiled and closed my eyes. I wanted this moment and all the senses attached to it forever stamped on my brain – the way she smelled like strawberries, the feel of her lips gently touching the outer part of my ear, how the sunshine sparkled on the water, and the way her voice whispered softly, "Where are you?"

I opened my eyes and turned my head so I could see her. I had no idea what she was asking, since I was clearly sitting right in front of her. She reached out and ran her fingers along the crinkle that appeared on my forehead when I was thinking.

She rose back up from her crouched position. "You were in your thoughts and I wanted to know where those thoughts took you," she explained.

"Emily, why don't you speak like everyone else?" I asked.

That smile of hers stretched across her face. "Because being like them is no fun."

She turned to walk away, but I reached out and grabbed her hand. "I thought you wanted to know where I was?"

That smile of hers disappeared. "I never expect you to tell me anything about your past, Lian." I dropped her hand and she just stood there looking down at me. Her eyes traveled up and she nodded her head. "It's gonna rain," she stated.

I turned my head and saw the sun had disappeared and you could see the rain racing towards us across the lake.

I stood up and grabbed her hand again. We didn't make it to the end of dock before it hit us. Emily started laughing. I looked over at her as we jogged up toward the house. She wasn't even looking where she was going. Her face was tilted up toward the rain and her eyes were closed. It made me smile because it was just a typical Emily thing to do.

I pulled us inside and shut the door behind us. We stood on the hardwood floor between the kitchen and dining room in dripping-wet clothes.

She reached up and cupped her palm against my cheek. "I'm sorry about snapping on you yesterday."

I placed my hand on top of hers. "I'm sorry for calling you a tease."

Emily smiled again. "That was just you being honest. I kind of am," she stated. "I promise I won't tease you again," she whispered.

Then she hooked her fingers under the hem of my shirt and yanked it up and over my head. Then she tugged on the waistband of my sweats until they were around my ankles. I stepped out of them and stood there in nothing but my black boxers.

"You just said you weren't going to tease me anymore," I said kind of rudely. I didn't see how undressing me was not categorized as teasing.

"I'm not," she said before pulling her shirt off and dropping it on the floor next to my clothes. She kicked her shorts off and stared up at me. Then she sort of hopped up into my arms. She wrapped her legs around my hips and I cupped her thighs in my hands to hold her up. "My room," she whispered in my ear.

I rolled over and lay down beside her. "I'm glad we did that. Now all that sexual tension is gone and we can focus on just being friends."

I turned my head because I thought she was looking at me, but she wasn't. She was staring at the ceiling. She sat up suddenly, but didn't say anything. I reached out to touch her back, but before my fingertips even grazed her skin, she slid off the side of the bed and went into the bathroom. She slammed the door hard behind her.

I sat up and gazed at the door. I had no idea what just happened. I waited quietly, listening for any sound, but I never heard a thing. A moment later, the shower turned on. I normally loved listening to the shower while I was sleeping. It was a carefully controlled rainfall inside your house and I loved the sound of rain. This shower sound did not comfort me at all.

I rolled out of bed and slowly made my way around the bed and to the bathroom door. I placed my ear on it, but the pounding of the water on the porcelain tub drowned out all other noises.

I knocked on the door, but like I expected, there was no answer. I turned the doorknob and stepped inside the steam-filled room.

"Emily?"

She still didn't respond. I was starting to freak out a little. I didn't know what caused this reaction from her. I went from having one of the most pleasurable experiences of my life to being almost frightened to pull back a shower curtain, afraid of what I might find.

I found the courage and strode over to the curtain and peeked inside. She was sitting down under the spray. Her arms were wrapped around her legs and her chin was resting on her knees. I could see her elvish tattoo with perfect clarity.

"Emily?" I asked again.

She slowly picked her head up off her knees and turned to look at me. Her eyes were rimmed in red. She had either accidentally gotten shampoo in her eyes or she had been crying. I knew it was the latter. I had, for the first time and I hoped the last time, made her cry sad tears.

She didn't say a thing. She simply turned her head back around and rested it on her knees again. I grinded my teeth together and opened the curtain wider so I could step in.

"Leave me alone," Emily muttered.

"I will as soon as you tell me what's wrong."

"There is just so much that's wrong that I don't even know where to start. I mean, the war is still going on. In some countries, women are still treated as second-class citizens…"

"You know that's not what I meant," I growled. She could be so frustrating sometimes. "What is going on here and now with you and me?" I asked again, rephrasing the question.

She stood up, shut the water off, and stepped outside of the tub. I yanked the curtain open. She pulled a towel off the shelf and flicked her wrist to unfold it before wrapping it around herself. I climbed out after her and grabbed a towel myself, securing it around my waist.

I followed the trail of wet feet prints through her room, down the hall, through the living room, and out the door that led to the porch. She was sitting on the bottom step with her head in her hands.

I opened the door and heard her sigh. "I really don't know how I can be any more clear that I do not want to talk to you," she said.

I walked down the steps and stood in front of her. "Em, I have no idea what's going on. You're confusing the hell out of me," I confessed.

She caught her bottom lip between her teeth. I knew she was going to tell me. "You really just want to be friends?" she asked, looking up at me.

I opened my mouth to reply when it dawned on me what she was really asking me. "Emily, you have to know by now that I really want to be with you. But it is stupid for us to get involved when I'm only staying in this town until December. After that, I'll be gone. It's just not a good idea to be more than friends with a guy like me."

She nodded her head and brushed away a few tears that had run down her face. She stood up and stared at me for a moment. "Can you just wait out here for a few minutes?" she asked.

I nodded my head and she walked back in the house. As nice as it felt that she seemed okay with what I said, I knew something wasn't right. Emily was born a fighter. She fought for what she wanted. This time, she wasn't fighting, and that scared the shit out of me.

A few minutes later, I heard a noise at the side of the house. I ran across the porch and peeked around the corner to see all my clothes scattered across the lawn. Then Emily strode out of the house with her bag in her hands.

"What the fuck?" I breathed.

She didn't respond. She just walked toward her car. I grabbed her arm to stop her, and that was a huge fucking mistake.

She dropped her bag on the ground and in turn gripped my forearm. I knew it was going to be painful before the words even left her lips. I hit the ground and couldn't stop the scream that ripped out of my throat. She breathed another word and I felt the burn on my arm.

She let go of me, picked her bag up, and got in her car. Then she was gone. I was left holding my blistering forearm in nothing but a towel. I had a ten-mile walk back to town too. And it decided to start raining again. Fucking perfect!

Chapter 20

I didn't feel the least bit sad about what I did to him. If he knew all along that he only wanted to be friends, then he should have been upfront about it and told me, not waited until after we had sex to do so.

Even though I didn't like using my powers on people who weren't trying to kill me, Lian was just an asshole, so he deserved it. Big difference!

I drove towards town, but the last place I wanted to be was at home. I knew Kate or my brothers would be able to tell something was wrong with me and they would pester me until I told them half the truth just to get them off my back. As far as Kate knew, I was going to be at the lake house until later today.

I had three quarters of a tank of gas and that gave me plenty of time to just drive and drive and drive until I had to go home. It also gave me plenty of time to replay that damn conversation over in my head again and again, and then to remind me again and again at what I did to him.

The night started to fall over Autumn Falls and I only felt worse about burning him. I only meant to use pulso morsus on him. I didn't really mean to burn him. It just sort of slipped out of my mouth and I did nothing to stop it.

That had to be the Talyrian in me – that evilness that seemed to come out. It was probably why I had an attitude problem. But the Corlissian in me was whispering in the back of my head to do the right thing – to go to his place and at the very least heal his arm.

That Corlissian part of me got louder and louder until I finally gave in and parked in front of the Domus. I got out and walked into the building. I knew that if I slowed for even a second, I would lose my will and I would go back.

I headed up to the second floor and when I came to his door, I didn't knock. I just reached for the doorknob and turned. I thanked every star in the sky that it wasn't locked.

When I walked in, Lian was sitting on the edge of his bed with a wet washcloth pressed up against his arm. That made me feel horrible. I walked over to where he sat and crouched down in front of him. I carefully peeled the washcloth off his arm and got to see just how bad it was. He probably should have gone to the hospital.

I heard him take a breath and I knew he was going to say something. "Don't," I said.

I held my hand just above his burned arm and whispered, "Sanare." I could feel the power flowing out of me and into him. The burn on his arm turned from a blistered, vicious red to a smooth pink, though you could hardly see it through his tattoos.

He reached out his free hand and tried to brush the hair behind my ear, but I yanked my head away from him. I stopped the flow of the healing power and stood up. I glanced down at my work. I was satisfied. I turned and headed for the door.

"Emily," he said.

"Don't."

I managed to keep it together. I was quite proud of myself. I was hurting inside so fucking bad too. But I managed to have a conversation with Kate and even sat through dinner without a single tear running down my face. I even sat and listened to Toby tell me about his date with Thea. And Drew told me about getting admittance letters to three colleges he applied to.

I held it all together until I was up in my room. It was then that I let my body take over. I lay on the floor and just sobbed into the carpet until I was pretty sure it was leaking through the floorboards and down onto the main floor. I was waiting for Kate to come upstairs and find out what was going on. And then she would say, "What did I tell you? I said he'd destroy you, but did you listen to me?"

That thought alone made the tears subside. I turned my head to the side and saw the Latin book I'd borrowed from Mr. Foreman, the Latin teacher. I pulled it toward me and opened it to where a piece of paper stuck up out of the top. I was never one to dog-ear pages in books. It felt like defacing them. I would always just stick a scrap of paper in my place instead.

I scanned the page that I had stopped on, and my eyes fell on a word that immediately caught my eye. I used the scrap of paper and scribbled the word down. I tossed the book on my desk and shoved the paper in my backpack. I was determined to test it out tomorrow.

Toby knocked on my door about six times before I finally crawled out of bed and yanked the door open.

His face said it all. "Fuck, Emily. You look like hell!" He stuck his head downstairs and yelled for Kate. She was in front of me in no time. She did the motherly thing and had the back of her hand to my forehead. Then she was ushering me back to bed.

The thing was I was fine. I just had no desire to go to school. I didn't want to see anyone today, anyone being Lian.

Lack of sleep can give you bags under your eyes, and if you hold a flame to your forehead, it does tend to get kind of warm. I knew exactly what I was doing, but since I rarely got sick, I knew Kate wouldn't suspect a thing. Plus, I knew she would leave for work after Drew and Toby were gone. Toby would get a ride with Drew and I would have my car at the ready. My plan was pretty much flawless.

I waited around a while. I didn't start to get ready until well after an hour after Kate left. I showered and dressed and even ate breakfast. Then I ran back upstairs to get my backpack and my car keys. I drove out to Culver's Field.

I stood leaning against the passenger side of my car, staring out at the field for a long time. I knew that using other Latin words in place of the ones we normally used could turn out really bad. Hotch had forced us all to read about things going wrong when Corlissians meddled with the old ways. He had said that the words we used were chosen for a reason and it was so that no harm would befall us.

The thing was that the old ways didn't seem to apply to me. It was hard to convince me anymore that things were done for a reason when no one could explain to me why I was the way I was. I wasn't like the rest of them, so my thought was that the same rules didn't apply to me.

I opened the passenger door and dug around in my backpack until I pulled out the piece of paper I had shoved in there last night. I studied the word several times before shoving it in my back pocket. I glanced at my watch and saw that it was lunchtime at Autumn Falls High School.

I imagined my friends sitting around the lunch table trying to figure out where I was. And Lian would be sitting there knowing the reason I didn't come to school today. Even if he heard that I was sick, he wouldn't believe it. He had to know that I did not want to see him again.

I walked down the ditch and a little way into the main part of the field. I kept away from where us Corlissians fought. Not that long ago, Mason and I had it out there by kicking each other's asses quite badly.

I had the good sense to put my cellphone on the ground behind me. It would be easier to use if it was already out of my back pocket, just in case there was an emergency.

I let out a big breath and flexed my fingers several times. As much as I hated to admit it, I was nervous. I knew very well that things could go very wrong. But I just had to suck it up and deal with the consequences.

I muttered, "*Ignis,*" and the flames popped up in my hands. I watched as they twisted and coiled around my fingers. I watched them weave themselves up my arm too. I blew at the flames when they edged too close to my shirtsleeve. They immediately obeyed and went right back to my hand.

I sucked in a breath and slowly let it out. I held my hands out away from me so my palms were facing the tree line on the other side of the field. The flames circled around my fingers.

Then I whispered the word, "*Incendia.*" I can't say what I was expecting, but it certainly wasn't what I got. It was like twin flamethrowers had been attached to my arms. The flames extended out so far. I was half expecting to see the trees go up and they were a solid mile away from where I stood. The field in front of me was absolutely scorched bare.

I breathed, "*Intereo,*" and the flames instantly died at my command. Then I looked at my hands. Pieces of my skin were hanging off and they were so red. Blood was oozing out here and there. It was utterly disgusting and I was shocked. I had never in my life been burned before. I was a pyromancer. It just didn't happen to us. Yet, here I stood with at least second-degree burns on my hands.

I bent down and used my elbow to unlock the screen on my cellphone. I managed to get to that annoying woman's voice that always asked how she could help me. This was the first time I had ever used that component on my phone.

"Call Thea," I stated clearly.

"Do you want me to call Thea?" she asked in that voice that made my skin crawl.

"Yes!"

"Calling Thea for you."

The phone started ringing and Thea picked up. "Oh my God, I am so pissed off at you. Where the hell are you? I know you're not sick, even though Toby said you looked horrible this morning. You never get sick. So?"

"I really need you right now," I said.

"Where are you?" she asked without a pause.

"Culver's."

"I'll be there in seven minutes."

She ended the call, and so I didn't have to. I tipped back until my butt hit the ground. Then I kept going until I was lying on my back and staring up at the clear blue sky. I held my hands up above me and studied the damage that I had done to them.

I heard tires crunching over gravel and Thea was at my side a moment later. I glanced up at her, but she wasn't looking at me. She was staring at the scorched field instead.

"What happened here?" she asked.

I cleared my throat and she looked down at me. Then she saw the mess that was my hands. Her hand flew to her mouth. It took her a moment to compose herself. "I need…" was all she said before running back to her car. She came back a few minutes later with some gauze and ointment.

"What are you doing? Just heal me," I said. I didn't know why she was using those archaic human medicines on me.

She swallowed. "I can't."

"Why not?"

"I don't know how to heal burns that bad! I can only heal minor burns. What the fuck did you do, Em?"

It was then that another car pulled up behind Thea's. I knew that car well. She had called Hotch. So, my best friend had betrayed me to get a stern lecture from Hotch. I was glaring at her while he walked toward us. His eyes were focused on us and he didn't see the wasteland that I had made.

"What is the meaning of this? Why weren't you at school?" he snapped at the both of us.

Thea tugged his sleeve and pointed at what was once a beautiful field. Hotch's mouth dropped open. It was really hard to shock that old man, yet I kept managing to do so. It made me inwardly smile.

"What… who… how?"

Thea then directed his attention to me sitting on the ground. Hotch crouched down next to me and placed his hands carefully under my own. He studied the burns very carefully before turning to Thea.

"You should go back to school. I'll take care of this," he stated.

Thea shot me an apologetic look as she went, but I wasn't mad at her. She only did what she thought was right in this situation.

I knew Hotch wasn't a healer, so I was kind of expecting him to tell me some word that I could use on myself. But he started unwrapping the gauze instead. He must have known what I was thinking.

"There is no word that healers have to deal with burns of this severity. Why? Because pyromancers don't burn themselves… ever. Yet, here you are with very brutal burns on your hands. You will heal quite fast, but you will not be able to use pyromancy for at least a week. Dear child, you won't be able to use any of your powers, since they all require the use of your hands. I hope you are able to deal with the consequences for these actions. You are in for one hell of a week."

I nodded my head and watched as he plucked a few of the bigger chucks of skin off and tossed them on the ground. Then he applied a generous amount of ointment before wrapping both my hands in gauze.

He sat down next to me once he was done. "What word did you use?" he asked.

"Incendia."

"Oh, I never thought to try that one. I did try *flamma* when I was a little younger than you. It only made the flames a little higher, but it didn't do any damage to me. I never thought about *incendia*. I figured it would have the same results."

"I just thought…"

"That it wouldn't affect you because of how powerful you are? And I think you're right that it wouldn't, had you used the proper precautions."

"What do you mean?" I asked.

"You need to use your healing power when you use *incendia* again. It will heal your skin so this doesn't happen and still allow you to… well," he nodded his head at the charred field.

"What do you mean by *when I use it again*? I figured you'd put your foot down and not let me do this again."

Hotch let out a low laugh. "I know I can't stop you from trying things. You are a lot more powerful than your peers, Emily, so it's natural you're going to push your body to do more. All I can do is make sure you do it without doing something like this again. You could have hurt yourself a whole lot more than you did."

"So, you're not mad at me?" I asked.

"I'm not happy with you at the moment, but I do admire your tenacity to try new things. Just promise me you'll talk with me about it first."

I nodded my head. "I promise."

"Good."

Hotch helped me to my feet and guided me back to where the cars were parked. I knew it would be tricky, but I assured him that I would be able to drive home just fine. And tricky it was. It took me a couple of tries before I managed to get the hang of using my forearms and legs to drive.

When I got home, I went straight up to my room and crashed in my bed. I just lay there with my gauzed hands resting on my stomach. I heard my cellphone ringing nearly nonstop in my backpack that I had dropped just inside my bedroom door.

I didn't even move when I heard Kate come home. I didn't try and hide my hands from her. There was no way I would be able to keep this from her.

She opened my bedroom door slowly. "How are feeling?" she asked before stepping inside all the way.

I didn't reply. I didn't need to. She saw my hands as soon as she stood at my side. There was worry in her eyes as she sat down next to me and carefully picked my right hand up in her own.

"What happened? Did you cut yourself? Did you break something? I should call one of the healers," she said rapidly.

"There is nothing the healers can do. My hands are burned."

And then Kate did something I did not expect. She started laughing. "Emily, for heaven's sake, don't joke around. What really happened?"

I didn't say anything. I just lay there and stared at her. Then her face fell and she knew I wasn't lying to her.

"But…but you're a pyromancer, just like the rest of us. How did you burn yourself?" she asked.

"I wanted to try a different word."

"Emily, you know there are rules set in place about the words we use. They are there so…"

"So we don't hurt ourselves. Yes, I am very aware of that. But tell me, Kate, where is it in the rules that one person can have four powers?"

She opened her mouth, but no words came out. She knew I was right. "Okay. I should call Hotch though."

"He already knows. He did this," I said, holding up my hands. "We had a nice little talk too. He said I can't use any of my powers for a week."

Kate's mouth dropped open. "How are you going to be able to survive that? Hell, how are the rest of us going to survive that?"

That made me smile. Kate smiled too. "I say you put her in a convent until she heals," Drew said, leaning against my doorframe. I hadn't even heard him. "I mean those nuns will keep her in check."

"So, who all knows?" I asked. I knew that news spread like wildfire in a Corlissian community.

"Well, Thea told Toby, then Toby told me, and I told Bridgette, who told Mason, who told Micah, who told Evan, and he told Tyler, who told Sam," Drew said. I knew that he was making it seem like a joke, but that little line of who told who was probably really accurate.

Chapter 21

Emily didn't show up to school that Monday. Thea had told me that she was sick, but I seriously doubted that was true. She didn't want to see me. And I couldn't say I blamed her.

What I had said was so stupid and so not true. I had grown to love this town and all the people in it. I was honestly planning on staying in Autumn Falls for a while. That reasoning was all because of one girl who now more than likely wanted nothing more than to see me dead.

I truly wanted to be with her more than anything, but for some reason, what her aunt had said about me destroying her played a major role in what I ended up saying to her. There was going to be no take-backs with that.

I was leaning against the lockers just like the first day of school when I saw Emily and Toby walking down the hall. The first thing my eyes landed on was Emily's hands wrapped in gauze.

She and Toby were arguing with each other.

"I said I can carry it," she said angrily.

"How? With your hands? I'll just give it to Thea and she can put it in your locker. Fucking invalid." Toby was carrying Emily's backpack, since she couldn't exactly use her hands.

As soon as she reached the group of Corlissians, Mason was in front of her. "What the hell happened? Thea wouldn't tell us what you did. So, spill," he said deeply.

Emily's back was to me, so I didn't hear her response. If she had been facing me, I would have been able to read her lips. But there was no need to. I was able to read what Mason whispered to her with perfect clarity.

"Pyromancers don't burn."

She had just told me a few days before that she could hold her hand over a red-hot stovetop and it wouldn't make a mark on her skin. Yet, the gauze on her hand stated otherwise. I wanted to know so bad what she had done to do that. It was a fat chance that I would ever find out the truth. It wasn't like another Corlissian was going to tell me, and she sure as hell wasn't speaking to me.

I sat down in homeroom and my foot wouldn't stop bouncing up and down. Then Emily walked in, looking as beautiful as she always did. Her hair was up in her trademark messy bun. She had on ripped jeans, a white tank top, and teal high heels.

As she walked by without even looking at me, I died on the inside. It absolutely killed me that I could have had her and I thought by keeping her at a distance, I would be protecting her.

I think I actually understood Mason and why he was so desperate to get her back. On the other side, it seemed like he was just an obsessive asshole, but really he knew what it was like to have her and then for her to not even acknowledge that he existed. It really fucking sucked.

Mason and I were far more similar than I cared to admit. We both fucked up with her. And what Sam had said to me on my first day popped in my head. He had said that if you piss her off, she will make you wish that you never met her. That was partially true. I did regret pissing her off because she had wicked and painful powers. But I would never wish that I didn't meet her.

Emily sat down in her usual seat behind me. It took a lot of willpower to not turn around in that chair like I always did. Out of the corner of my eye, I saw Nelson Hagan, who sat directly across from her, leaning towards her.

"What happened to your hands, Em?" he asked.

"I burned them," she replied.

"On what?" he asked.

"Umm, I was reaching up into the cabinet over the stove and I didn't know the burner had just been turned off. I had both my hands on it." I knew that was a straight-up lie.

"Damn, that sucks. Do you need help carrying anything? Or is, umm, Killian helping you?"

"Thanks, but I'm fine on my own." Ouch! If that wasn't an obvious smack in the face, I didn't know what was.

As soon as the bell rang, Emily scooted her books into her arms and strode around me and out the door.

She ignored me the entire week – not a word, not even a glance. She wanted absolutely nothing to do with me anymore.

By Friday, I was sick of it. As she was leaving homeroom, I caught up to her in the hallway. I pulled her to a stop by grabbing the top of her arms, since both her hands were still wrapped in gauze. I didn't know it took a whole week for a Corlissian to heal. She must have done quite a bit of damage to herself.

"WHAT?" she snapped at me.

"Are you ever going to speak to me again?" I asked in much more civilized tone than she did.

"I'd rather not. Is that all or was there something else you wanted from me?"

"Else? Emily, I don't want anything from you. I just want..." She arched her eyebrows at my use of the word. "I just... wish we could be friends again. Like we were before last weekend."

"Ah, so you wish to pretend like last weekend never happened?" she asked.

I let out a grumble and slammed my fist into the locker beside me. Sometimes, she was so irritable and just said things to get on my nerves. Now was one of those times.

"That is not what I said. I would never wish last weekend never happened. All I'm asking for is to go back to how things were before."

She turned her body and faced me. She tilted her chin up in a defiant manner. "Fine. We can be friends again. But there are going to be some rules. I will not come to your apartment ever again. I will continue to tutor you in history so long as it is done on school property. I will not take to you to the lake house again. And I will certainly never tell you anything about Corlissians again. So don't ask."

"So, basically we see each other in school only and we can't talk about anything Corlissian. That really sucks, Em."

"Well, you're the one who only wants to be friends. I mean, you're leaving soon, right? So it would be stupid to be anything more than friends. And there really is no point in you knowing anything else about my other life."

So she was throwing back in my face what I had said to her at the lake house. She knew exactly what she was doing, and it was working. I was standing there getting more and more pissed off.

"Emily, it's not that–" I didn't get any more than that out before she turned and walked away from me. Just like that, mid-sentence.

I slammed my fist into the locker a second time before heading to my first class. I should have just skipped it. I sure as hell couldn't concentrate on anything. The only thing going through my head was what Emily said.

I didn't see Emily at lunch that day. I was pretty sure she was avoiding me again. I was hoping that maybe we could have moved past that, but clearly, she didn't want to be just friends with me.

I sat down in study hall feeling like crap. This week had completely defeated me. And it was all because of Emily. Not having her acknowledge my existence was brutal. I just wanted to get through this last class and go home and crawl into bed.

I heard someone slide into the seat behind me and just assumed it was Emily. Even though she seemed to hate me, she still sat in her same seat. Even in science, we were still lab partners.

Then I felt a tap on my shoulder. I couldn't keep the smile off my face. It felt like that same tap I'd received on my first day of school when Emily asked if Killian was really my name.

I turned around with a big goofy grin on my face that fell off when I saw that it was not Emily. It was Heather Weston, the girl who Emily had told to move on my first day. She was always staring at me and giving Emily dirty looks. If she only knew how badly Emily could hurt her, she would have stopped.

"Umm, I'm sorry to bother you… but, umm, well, I was wondering if maybe you wanted to get together and study sometime?" she stuttered out.

"Do we even have a class in common that we could study?" I asked.

Her mouth opened a little, forming an *o*. She clearly hadn't taken that into consideration.

"Ugh, crap. I guess I didn't think this through all the way. Okay, I really don't care about studying. I really just want to go out with you."

It was then that Emily arrived. She was standing in the aisle looking down at Heather. Heather looked up at Emily.

"I'm not moving. Killian and I are having–"

"I don't give a fuck what you're doing. And I don't give a fuck where you sit. I just want to get by, and since your tree-trunk-sized legs are in my way, I can't," Emily said rather calmly.

Heather's mouth popped open at what Emily said about the size of her legs, which she wasn't exactly wrong about. Emily arched an eyebrow and Heather sneered at her while pulling her legs under the desk.

Emily walked by and sat down in the seat in front of me. She didn't even make a show of it. Normally, she would have stuck her butt out and wiggled it or she would have been tormenting Heather. This time, she just sat down.

I turned back to Heather who was glaring at the back of Emily's head. "Are you and her together?" she asked me rather loudly.

I knew I took way too long to respond to her. It was hard forming that simple word in my mouth. And saying it out loud this time made it all the more true to me.

"No."

"So, can we?"

"Can we what?" I asked.

"Go out?"

"Oh, yeah, I guess."

A huge smile spread onto Heather's face. "Really? Oh, this is awesome. Should we do it tonight or tomorrow?" she asked.

"Tonight is fine," I replied as the bell rang.

Emily stood up and walked to Watkins' desk. She bent forward and whispered something to him. He signed a slip and she walked out the door.

After the final bell rang, I headed upstairs to where Emily and Thea's lockers were. Emily, as I had figured, wasn't there, but Thea was. She was the one I wanted to talk to anyways.

"Hey, Killian!" Thea said when I walked around the corner. "Don't ask because I have no idea where she is. She has been off this week and I don't know why. Actually, I do know why."

"You know why?" I asked. Thea was Emily's best friend, so I didn't know exactly what Emily had told her.

Thea shut her locker and leaned against it. "It's kind of hard to explain, but let's just say that Emily needs to release built up… energy and with her hands being all injured, she hasn't been able to do that, so she's really grouchy right now. Well, grouchier than she normally is."

"Oh," I said. I had totally forgotten about what Emily told me. She said that once a power has been accessed, it has to be used and released or else it would start eating away and driving the person crazy. She couldn't use any of her powers because her hands were damaged.

"What has been going on with you two lately anyways? I mean, normally you two are all flirty and this week you haven't even said a word to each other."

"Umm, we just had an argument last weekend and it has spilled over into this week. Hey, I've gotta get going. I'll see you later."

"Bye," Thea murmured as I left.

Heather and I had decided to meet at Two Pisces Coffee at seven. I suggested a coffee date, since they were less intimidating than a dinner date. She just nodded her head that it was fine.

At six forty-five, my cellphone starting ringing. I picked it up off my kitchen counter and saw the display read *'Heather.'* Every time my cellphone rang, I hoped to see one name pop up, but it never did.

I hit the green answer button. "Yeah?"

"Oh, ugh, hi. I was just wanting to make sure we were still on for meeting at seven?"

I rolled my eyes. I had gotten so used to Emily's assertiveness that someone this unsure of themselves was kind of annoying. "Yeah, I was just about to head out," I replied.

"Oh, right. Okay. See you soon!"

From the chatter in the background, I had a feeling that she was already at the coffee house. I was seriously regretting saying yes to her at all. I should have been wherever Emily was, begging for her to forgive me and telling her that there was no one I would rather be with.

I was an idiot.

I was a fool.

I finished getting ready and headed to the café. It was two minutes past seven when I walked in. And as I figured, Heather was already there. The place was fairly crowded for a Friday night.

I walked over and sat down at the table with Heather. She had her strawberry- blonde hair curled all over and she wore a dark blue dress that was a few sizes too small. She smiled at me as I sat down.

"You look really nice, Killian," she said brightly.

I glanced down. I was wearing the same black tee shirt and jeans that I had worn to school. The only thing I did was pull my leather jacket on over it all, which I took off and draped over the back of the chair.

"Thanks," I muttered. "You too," I added, even though I didn't mean it.

"I already ordered for you," she said, pushing a white mug with two fish on the outside towards me.

"Oh, you didn't have to," I said. A frown formed on her face. "But it was very nice of you," I said, picking the mug up and taking a sip. It was ice-cold. "I didn't know you ordered ice coffee," I said.

"I didn't," she muttered.

"You know what? It's fine. I'll be right back," I said, getting up and heading to the counter.

On my way, the front door opened. Thea strode in with Emily right behind her. Emily froze when she saw me. Then her head turned and she saw Heather sitting at the table I had just came from. She then glanced back at me and rolled her eyes before walking out of the café.

Thea let out a deep breath and shook her head. "You and I need to have a very long talk later."

"What did she tell you?" I asked.

"Like I said, we'll talk later. Call me after your..." she glanced over at Heather, "date is over," she finished dryly. Then she followed in Emily's wake.

I had no idea what that was about, and frankly, I was kind of scared of what we needed to talk about. Thea wasn't nearly as frightening as Emily was, but I knew that Thea was just as deadly as her best friend.

I ordered another coffee that was actually hot and returned to the table. "What was that all about?" Heather asked.

"Umm, nothing," I muttered before taking a sip of coffee.

"What is going on with you and Emily anyways?" she asked.

"She's just a friend. Why?"

Heather turned her head and stared out the window. "I hate Emily Porter. We have been in school together since kindergarten. She was so nice for a long time. She got along with everyone. Everybody wanted to be Emily's friend. She was just so welcoming to everyone. But once high school started, she changed. She started walking around with this air of superiority. Like she was better than everyone else. Last year, she got worse. She got contacts and started looking more womanly. Now she's just a bitch who needs to be shown some humility."

"I know Emily well enough to know not to cross her. If I were you, I would just stay out of her way. She's not having a good week and I don't think you should be so hard on her."

"What do you mean?" she asked.

"Are both your parents still alive?"

"Yeah… oh, hers aren't."

"Exactly. You should probably just ignore her. I think that's for the best." I was really only saying that because if Heather started to annoy Emily, then Emily would most definitely make Heather wish she had stayed the hell away from her. Emily was a violent creature.

"You like Emily though, don't you?"

"Yeah, I do. It's just complicated right now. I sort of screwed things up last weekend," I stated.

"What happened last weekend?" Heather asked.

Oh, we had sex and I told her that we should only be friends. Yeah, not the thing I was really wanting to share with anyone at the moment… or ever for that matter.

"We just had an argument. I was being a typical guy who said the wrong thing at the worst time. Don't worry about it," I said.

"You do know that dating her is like a death sentence, right?"

"A death sentence?"

"Yeah, Mason is her ex and it's well known that he desperately wants her back. They were like high-school royalty last year. All the guys were jealous of Mason for being with her and all the girls were jealous of Emily for getting Mason. All the students just gawked at them in the halls. They were like the king and queen of this school until Mason started… Well, I'm sure you've heard."

"Yeah, I heard. And Mason doesn't bother me. I know he hates me, but so does Emily right now." It dawned on me at how different Heather was from Emily, and not just in their outer appearances. That was obvious. Heather had blonde hair, was rather pale for living in a beach town, and was a little on the chubby side. She probably had zero athletic ability either. Emily had dark brown hair, she was tan, and was fit. I was pretty sure she didn't have any fat on her body. Actually, I was very sure. Under her skin was all muscle.

But it was how they both spoke that really got to me. Emily didn't have much of a filter and would say anything. She did not care what anyone thought of what she said. And she would talk about anything and everything. Heather was more reserved in what she said. And she kept her words very PG… meaning: she was a bit prudish.

"I do understand why you like her. She is really pretty. It makes me sick to even say that about someone like her. Most of the guys thought her sister was hot, and Camilla was, but Emily has this natural beauty about her that seems to go unnoticed."

"It's not as unnoticeable as you think," I paused. "I'm sorry. I don't mean to be rude, but you talk about her an awful lot. Especially since, as you said, you hate her."

Heather's cheeks turned bright pink. "I'm sorry. It's just that you should know what you could be getting yourself into with her."

I stood up and looked down at her. "I don't think that's the issue at all. I think you're just jealous of her. And that is really sad, Heather. You would be a nice person if you stopped talking about her for more than a second." I grabbed my jacket off the back of the chair and walked out of the café.

As soon as I was outside, I pulled my cell out and called Thea. She didn't say hi like a normal person. All she said was, "Meet me at the beach." I shoved my phone in my pocket and headed for the beach.

Thea was sitting in between the water and the massive pile of charred wood where the bonfire always was. There was a tiny piece of wood in front of her that was hovering in the air. I had a feeling she didn't hear me walking up or else she wouldn't have been doing that.

I sat down next to her, but she didn't drop the wood or act surprised to see me. She turned her head.

"So I thought," she murmured before letting the wood drop back to the sand, "a normal human would have taken off running, yelling that there is a freak on the beach, but you just sit down like it's nothing that there is a piece of wood floating in the air."

"Maybe I'm just really open-minded," I replied.

"Or maybe Emily told you about us."

"Or that," I whispered.

"Stupid girl! What the hell was she thinking? She knows it is forbidden for a human to know anything about us. What do you know?"

"Ugh, I know that you are called Corlissians and you all have certain powers. I know that your enemies are called Talyrians and you have other enemies too. Umm, I know that Emily has more powers than anyone and no one knows why. I think that's about it."

"By rights, I should kill you now and dump you in the ocean."

"I would prefer you didn't. I promised Emily that I wouldn't say anything and I won't. I know we're not on good terms right now, but I will still keep my mouth closed," I said. I really didn't feel like being murdered by Thea.

"Not on good terms you say? THAT is something entirely different I need to yell at you about." She stood up and was standing in front of me. "What the hell is wrong with you? You must have some sort of brain malfunction, Killian."

"I'm taking it Emily told you about last weekend," I grunted.

"She is my best friend. She is having the worst week of her… the second worst week of her life. I pretty much forced her to tell me what was going on with her. So, why in the hell did you say what you did to her?"

"Thea, I know that you're trying to smooth things over between us, but this is something that I would rather talk with Emily about. I don't know if she will ever speak with me again though."

Thea crouched down so she was at eyelevel with me. "She talked about you and she made it sound like you put all the stars in the sky. It was kind of sickening, but cute in a weird way. So, do you like her?" she asked.

"Yes," I admitted.

"Then do something about it, you idiot!"

"What? What am I supposed to do when she won't talk to me?"

Thea tapped her chin and pursed her lips. "Timing is everything. I know it's two weeks away, but I think you should tell her at homecoming."

"You want me to wait two weeks to tell Emily that I like her?" I asked just for clarification.

"Yes. That would give her time to cool off. You know how she is," Thea said, standing up.

Chapter 22

My life seemed to be finally returning to normal. Hotch had taken the gauze off my hands and they were both healed perfectly. There wasn't a scar left behind. I was finally able to use my powers. I spent four hours at practice that night, just releasing all that energy from my body that had built up.

Thea had forced me to go shopping with her so we could pick out dresses for homecoming. I was actually planning on not going, but I sort of gotten roped in. I'd had eight guys ask me before Mason did. Then Mason asked me and asked me and asked me and asked me until I finally said yes. It was the same way he had gotten me to go out with him. I made it very clear though that this didn't mean anything and nothing would come of it.

I hadn't spoken to Lian for two whole weeks. After that Friday, he asked if we could be friends and I was a massive bitch to him. I wasn't expecting him to ever speak to me again.

I wasn't so mad at him anymore. I still wasn't happy with him though. What he had said hurt and I wanted to distance myself from that. It was hard to do when I saw him every day in school and even sat next to him in every class we had together.

On the Saturday of homecoming, I was in the bathroom leaning against the counter, putting eyeliner on when Toby leaned up against the doorframe. He was in black pin-striped pants and a dark gray dress shirt with the sleeves rolled half way up.

"You look hot," I said with a smile.

"And you're not ready yet," he replied.

"Please, Mason is always late, so it doesn't matter," I said.

"I still cannot believe you're going with him."

"It doesn't mean anything."

"Maybe not to you, but I'm sure he isn't thinking like that," Toby stated before pushing off the doorframe and heading downstairs.

I was just finishing up with my makeup when Drew walked out of his bedroom that was directly across from the bathroom. He was buttoning up his vest that was over his blood-red dress shirt. He glanced up at me and smiled.

"If Mason touches you in any way I don't like, I will kill him. Have a good night, sis!"

I shook my head and went to my room to put my dress on. It was a solid black, strapless, floor-length gown. The back was like a corset that ended right above my butt. Kate didn't like how far down the lacing went, but I didn't care.

I pulled the dress on and then stuck my feet in my purple Chuck Taylors. If I was going to be on my feet all night, I was not going to be in heels. Then I headed downstairs with the back of my dress flopping open.

Kate was in the kitchen making a cup of coffee when I walked in and turned around pointing at my back. She laughed. "It's good that you still need me for some things," she said before she started lacing the back of my dress up.

Drew walked around the corner and shielded his eyes. "Dress before coming downstairs!" he snapped.

"You are such a prude, Andrew Allan Porter," I teased.

Drew stuck his tongue out as he walked through the kitchen. He grabbed his keys off the counter and headed out the backdoor.

"You know things worked out well this year. I figured I'd be letting someone use my car tonight. But with Mason picking you up, Toby was able to use the A5 to get Thea. Even though you know I'm not thrilled that you are going with Mason."

Kate gave one last final tug before tying off the lace in a bow. She fluffed it out and stood back to admire her work.

"I have to admit you look amazing, Emily." Then her eyes filled with tears.

"Kate, what's wrong?" I said, stepping forward.

"You look so much like her right now," she muttered.

"Mom?" I asked.

Kate nodded her head just as the doorbell rang. "Crap!" she said, grabbing a napkin and dabbing under her eyes.

"It's just Mason. No need to get your panties in a bunch."

"And there is no need for your panties to come off tonight."

"I'd actually have to be wearing them for that to mean anything," I said.

Kate yanked the door open. "Go put some on then!"

Mason was standing on the porch with a confused look on his face. He was wearing a white dress shirt with a vest, a black-and-white-striped tie, and black pants. He looked good.

I walked over to Kate. I leaned in and whispered, "You need to remember that I tease you relentlessly." Then I kissed her on the cheek and stepped outside.

Mason held his elbow out and I slid my arm through his. "You look incredible, Em," he said.

"You don't look so bad yourself," I replied.

Mason opened up the passenger door of his red Lexus and helped me in. He more so just stuffed the bottom of my dress in. He hopped in the driver's seat and headed to the Perlinian Hotel. That was where all school dances were held. It was far nicer than the school's gymnasium. Plus, the fact that Mason's dad owned the place helped. He gave the school a deal on it.

It was quiet in the car and I was glad the drive to the Perlinian wasn't far from my house.

"Why did you finally say yes to me?" he asked.

I laughed. "Because I just wanted to stop you from asking me anymore."

A small smile appeared on his face. "How many guys asked you before I did?"

"Eight," I replied.

"That many? Hmm," he muttered to himself.

He turned into the parking lot that was behind the Perlinian that was reserved for employees. The main parking lot was across the street. He pulled into a spot that was marked: *'Reserved for M. Monroe.'* Beside his was one that read: *'Reserved for B. Monroe.'*

Mason jumped out and came around to open the door for me. He offered me his elbow again and we walked around the side of the building and to the front where a few late arrivers were still trickling in.

He pulled me to a stop before we reached the front doors. "Thank you for coming with me tonight."

"You're welcome." He smiled and tugged me along and into the hotel.

Two hours went by in a flash. I had danced with all my guy friends at least twice and with Mason for rest of the night. When we weren't dancing, he was standing off to the side with his monogrammed flask to his lips. Every time he came over to me, his breath became more and more potent.

I was talking to Thea for a while to take a breath. She looked beautiful in a strapless light pink dress. It fell down in ruffles to the floor.

"Oh wow!" Thea stated.

"What?" I asked.

"Killian just walked in and he looks fine!"

"Umm, I'm going to head up to the roof for some air. It's kind of warm in here," I said.

"Yeah, it got warm after his hot ass walked in," Thea said.

I shook my head and made for where the elevators were. I pushed the button that read *'Roof'* and felt that familiar jerk all elevators made as they began their accent or decent. I never liked that feeling.

The doors opened to a wide canopy overhead to protect the doors from the elements. Roof access was cut off during the winter months. I stepped onto the roof. A few couples were already up there making out in the darkened corners. White lights were strung around, giving an ethereal glow to the top of the building.

I walked over to the ledge and leaned my arms on the top of it. From that vantage point, if you leaned forward enough, you could peer over the edge and look down to the sidewalk that ran in front of the building.

I let the cool night air seep into my lungs. I didn't lie to Thea. I was getting hot. All those bodies dancing in that one room made it warm. I just wanted to cool off. And I didn't really want to see how good Lian looked, not at this moment at least.

I let my gaze drift from the sidewalk below to above. The dark sky was littered with stars, but only a few could be seen, since the lights of the town drowned them out. The lake house was prefect for stargazing.

I felt a few fingers trace the back of my arm. I turned around expecting it to be Mason. But it was Lian standing there. He didn't say anything. He shoved a small black box in my hand and walked away.

I stood there confused. It wasn't like him not to say anything. I turned around and leaned against the ledge again. I clutched the box tightly in my hand. I didn't want to open it up here.

It was then that two arms wrapped around my midsection and his lips pressed to my exposed shoulder blade. I could smell the alcohol on his breath even in the open.

"I love you, Emily," he whispered against my skin.

"Stop, Mason."

"You wanna go to the room?" he asked.

I nodded my head and he pulled me towards the elevator. All the students' rooms were reserved on the third floor.

Mason nuzzled my neck the whole way down. I just made sure to keep the box in my hand hidden from him. He was drunk and I knew him well enough to know that when he was drunk, it was best just to keep him happy. The smallest thing could make him blow up.

I let him lead me off the elevator and down the various halls to Room 380. He let go of me to unlock the door. As soon as he stepped inside, the vest he'd been wearing came off.

"Come here, baby," he stated.

"Umm, I need to use the bathroom," I muttered.

I stepped into the all-white bathroom and shut and locked the door behind me. I sat down on the edge of the bathtub and gazed down at the small black box in my hand. I had no idea what I was going to find in there. My mind didn't even dare come up with any suggestions.

I popped the top off and inside was a gold key with a tag attached, reading: *418*. I didn't pull it out of the box. I put the lid back on instead. I stood up and walked out of the bathroom.

More of Mason's clothes littered the floor. He was lying on the bed with just his boxers on.

"Come on, Em," he mumbled.

"I left my purse downstairs. I'm just gonna grab it and I'll be right back," I lied.

"Call Thea and tell her to hold on to it for you," he suggested.

"I'll be right back," I insisted before walking out the door to him groaning.

I made my way back to the elevators and hit the button to take me up one floor. I headed for the room that was printed on the key tag.

When I reached Room 418, I took the key out of the box and unlocked the door. I shoved the door open with my hip and shoved the key back in the box. I slowly walked in the room, letting the door close by itself behind me.

There was no one in the room. All the lights were on, but no one was in there. It was then that I noticed the sliding door was open to the porch. A figure was leaning just to the side of the door.

"I wasn't sure if you'd come or not," Lian said.

"I just wanted to return your key," I stated, placing the black box on the desk.

He turned his body so he was leaning against the doorframe and facing inside the room. Thea was right. He looked hot. He was wearing a black dress shirt, black pants, a black belt, and black shoes. Most guys wouldn't have been able to pull off the all-black look, but Lian did… so well.

"I thought you said you weren't coming with anyone."

"I decided I didn't want to be alone," I said.

"So, of all the guys who you could have come with, you decided on Mason?"

"Yeah, you can stop with the accusatory tone right there."

He held his hands up. "Sorry." He took a few steps into the room. "Forgive me for not saying sooner how gorgeous you are."

"I should go," I muttered.

"Emily, please wait," he requested.

I hadn't moved, but he reached out to stop me from going.

"Will you please just hear me out, please?" His green eyes were pleading for me to stay.

I folded my arms across my chest and leaned my hip against the desk. He scrubbed his hands up and down his face and groaned.

"I have practiced what I wanted to say to you a thousand times in my head and in front of my medicine-cabinet mirror. And I can never seem to get it right. And in my head, you always walk out and never speak to me again," he said. "But you're still here right now and that's a good sign." He let out a shaky breath.

"I lied to you, Emily. That day at the lake house, I lied. What I said to you that has made you hate me for three weeks was a lie."

"What?" I whispered.

"I didn't mean what I said. I was trying to push you away from me. I thought if there was distance between us, it would be better for everyone."

I was standing there with my mouth parted, staring at him. I was trying to process what he just said. He was gracious enough to keep quiet and let me speak.

"Why would you lie to me and who exactly was it better for?"

He let out another breath. "You remember that night we were studying in your room and your aunt busted in and said it was time for me to leave?" he asked.

I nodded my head.

"I left in a bit of a hurry and I realized that my notebook was still in your room. I went back to your house and I was at the top of the landing when I heard your aunt say my name. I stopped and I listened to what she was saying about me. She said that I would destroy you. Every time the two of us were together, her voice saying that would weasel its way into my head. So, I guess it was better for everyone else but us."

I felt this anger rising up in me. I walked forward and punched him in the chest with the side of my fist, and then I hit him again with the side of my other fist. I continued doing it again and again, and the whole time he just stood there and took it.

"YOU FUCKING DUMBASS!" I yelled at him. "You really hurt me, Lian."

"Emily, I am so sorry. If I could take back what I said, I would in an instant."

"Then take it back," I said.

"What?"

"Take back what you said."

"I take back saying that I was glad we did that so we could focus on being friends. And I would like to replace that with this instead. Emily, you are the most beautiful person I know and I am so in love with you."

I swallowed down the lump in my throat and said what I knew to be true. "I love you too."

"Now you know that I'm not letting you go back to Mason, right? You're mine," he said as a devilish grin appeared on his face.

He picked me up and placed his hands around my ass to hold me up. I draped up arms around the back of his neck. Then our lips met. It was soft and slow at first. Then it turned a bit rougher.

Lian pulled his head back suddenly. "No. We're not doing anything tonight. I just want to lie in bed with you. That's all," he said.

He turned and carefully set me down on the bed. Then he started laughing. "Are you seriously rocking purple Chucks at homecoming?" he asked.

"Obviously," I said, wiggling my feet.

"You are one of a kind, Emily." He knelt with his legs on either side of mine and walked himself forward. He sort of forced me down on the bed as he went.

"I thought we were just going to lie together."

"I think I want my lips on yours again for a while. I haven't kissed you in three weeks and well, I'm kind of addicted to you now," he whispered.

He started to lower himself toward me when his cellphone rang. He groaned as he pulled it out of his pocket and held it to his ear without checking who it was.

"What?" he snapped.

"Ugh, yeah she is."

"Yup." He then held his phone out to me. "It's Thea."

I took the phone from him. "Yes?"

"What is going on? You come with Mason and end up with Killian? You are such a slut, Emily."

"Is that all you called for?"

"No. It was just that Mason called to see if I had seen you. I had a feeling I knew where to find you. So, I was just… OH MY GOD!"

I shoved Lian off me and sat up. "THEA?"

"Brothers are flooding in here! What do I do?"

"Get the other Corlissians in the elevator and get up to the fourth floor now!"

"Okay… right. Sam, get him… yes… Come on…" There were feet pounding on marble. Then Thea sighed. "We're in. What now?"

"Come to Room 418. We'll plan something once you get here."

"Okay," Thea whispered before she ended the call.

"What is going on?" Lian asked.

"Midnight Brothers are crashing homecoming. We're going to have company." A moment later, there was pounding on the door. I hopped off the bed and opened the door. Sam, Thea, Tyler, Toby, Drew, Bridgette, Micah, and Evan streamed into the room.

"What's he doing here?" Evan snapped.

"He's with me," I said.

"And? What? Does he know about us too?"

I nodded my head. "Emily, are you trying to get us all killed?" Drew groaned.

"Where's my brother?" Bridgette asked. Her eyes fell on me. "WHERE IS MY BROTHER?!" she screamed.

"He's down a floor. Someone put a fucking sock in her mouth before she lets the Brothers know where we are and I'll go get Mason," I said.

"Here, Em," Sam said, pulling a dagger off his back holster and handing it to me. "Keep safe."

I cracked the door open and peeked out into the hall. I could hear screams from a distance away. I hoped the Brothers weren't hurting the humans. They normally left innocents alone unless they thought the humans were protecting us.

I went the opposite way of the elevator and made my way down the stairs instead. I listened carefully before opening the door that led to the third floor. I opened it slowly and then I slipped through the door. I didn't hear a thing as I crept down the halls of the third floor.

I peeked my head around the corner to where Mason's room was and saw three Brothers moving down the hall. Their noses were in the air and I could hear them sniffing from where I was. I knew that they were close to Mason and they could probably smell him.

I swung my body out into their line of vision. They immediately stopped sniffing the air. They saw the dagger in my hand and knew I wasn't a human. They all whipped out their swords and started toward me.

The hall wasn't wide enough for them all to stand next to one another and fight me, so two of them fell back as they advanced. One came at me swinging his sword wildly. I ducked under his blade and spun around, sinking the dagger into his back. He fell to the ground twitching. I scooped his sword up just as the second Brother lunged toward me. I blocked his blow with the blade in my hand and reached up and wrapped my free hand around his wrist. I whispered, *"Dolor,"* and the blade fell out of his hand. He dropped to his knees and a weird hissing sound escaped his mouth.

The last Brother grabbed me from behind. I felt the cold metal blade press against my neck. "I will enjoy killing you. You are a mutant freak of both races, an abomination. You should not live."

I pulled my leg forward and brought it back with enough force to hear his kneecap snap. He fell to the ground, but as he went, his sword sliced the bottom of my chin. I turned around and drove the sword into his heart. I heard a gurgling noise and then it was quiet.

I stood up and took a deep breath. I pounded on the door for Room 380. Mason opened the door a few minutes later. He was rubbing his eyes.

"Hey, there you are!" he said sleepily.

"We need to go," I said, grabbing his arm and pulling him out into the hall littered with bodies.

"What is going on? Are those Brothers?" he asked, stepping over the one with the sword sticking out of his chest.

"Yes. We're under attack and you're drunk and nearly naked."

"Did you save me, Em?" he asked.

"Did I keep those Brothers from killing you? Yes. Now, come on. We need to get to the others."

We made it to the main hallway and the door for the stairs was in sight when it opened up, and at least ten Brothers spilled into the hall. Neither of us had a weapon on us. We were utterly fucked.

The Brothers advanced toward us and Mason's bitch ass pushed me in front of him. Chivalry is dead apparently.

I held my hands out in front of me. "STOP!" I yelled. I really didn't expect that to work, but they all actually did stop.

"Umm, look around you," I said. The Brothers did look around them. I had no idea why they were doing what I told them. "This is a beautiful building and there is so much history here. I know you guys just love archaic things. You don't want to see this building damaged, do you?"

The Brothers all shook their heads no. "Right, so how about we convene at another location and kill one another there?"

The Brother that was at the head of the pack nodded his head. "The empty warehouse down one block in twenty minutes. If you are not there, we will come back and ransack this place of beauty."

"Deal!" I said. I really couldn't believe I was making a deal with a Brother in the first place.

"I look forward to seeing your lifeless eyes soon, child of both races," he said. The group of Brothers turned and went back to the stairwell.

"I cannot believe that worked," Mason breathed.

"And I cannot believe you shoved me in front of you. Asshole!" I smacked him on the side of the head.

Mason followed behind me as we headed upstairs to Room 418 to let the other Corlissians know what was going on. We would all have time to change into proper fighting clothes and meet the Brothers at the warehouse.

Who said homecoming wasn't a good time?

Chapter 23

After Emily came back to the room with Mason and told us all what was going on, that she had somehow talked the Brothers into fighting elsewhere, did we all leave the hotel room. We, as one massive group, crept down the hallways to the stairwell.

We walked through the ballroom that had once been filled with well-dressed teenagers dancing to crappy music. It was now abandoned and trashed. Tables were flipped over, punch was spilled everywhere, banners and balloons were lying on the floor, and the song that had been playing when the Brothers entered was skipping. The good news was that no one was there. There were no Brothers lingering and no humans were injured or dead.

We split up at that point to get into cars. Mason was parked at the back of the hotel and with him went Bridgette, Micah, and Evan. Drew and Emily's cars were parked next to each other. Drew had Toby, Tyler, Sam, and Thea in his car. That left just Emily and me in her car.

"So, what's the plan?" I asked.

"Well, first we're going to the school to put our fighting gear on and to get some weapons. Then we're heading to the warehouse to kill some Brothers."

Emily was the last one to pull into the school parking lot. She didn't get out and follow the rest of the Corlissians into the building though. Once they were all inside did she get out and walk to the back of her car and pop the trunk.

I slid out of the car to see what she was doing. In the back was a black duffel bag that she yanked out and dropped onto the ground. She bent down, unzipped it, pulled out a set of leather fighting clothes, and draped them over the back of the car.

Then she turned to me. "Can you undo this for me?"

"Of course. I didn't know that me giving you the key to my room would result in getting you out of that dress," I stated while pulling the ribbon out of the corset and loosening the dress.

"And it's all for naught," she replied, holding the front against her.

I stepped back when I was done, and Emily tugged the dress down and kicked it to the side. She was standing in the parking lot of the school in her underwear.

"What?" she asked, pulling her leather pants on.

"Nothing," I muttered.

She snorted under her breath. "You have seen me in less than this."

"Yeah, but not on school grounds in the middle of the night," I replied as she tugged a tank top on and pulled her leather jacket on over it.

She bent down and started pulling weapons out of her bag and strapping them on herself. She glanced up at me.

"You should head home before the others come out."

"Emily…"

"You're not coming with us. You'd just be a liability and all of us need our attention focused on one thing tonight. I promise I'll call you once it's all done." She stood up and yanked me to her. "You look so damn good tonight," she whispered.

"Thea might have told me that your dress was black and I might have picked this out to match you."

She looked up at me with sad eyes, those eyes that only a moment ago were bright and ready for a fight. "I wish you had been honest with me. I spent three weeks hating you," she said. She still had a grip on the front of my shirt.

"Don't think about us right now and the mistakes that were made. I want your head in the right place for this fight. And just so you know, I'm going to be freaking out until I get a call from you." I bent down and kissed her briefly. She let go of my shirt and I turned and left the parking lot and headed up the street.

For some reason, I turned left instead of right. Rather than heading to my apartment, I made my way to the warehouse where the Brothers were waiting on the Corlissians.

I saw a few of the Brothers headed into a building and figured it was the right one. I snuck along the side and around the back. None of the Brothers were lingering around outside.

There were three abandoned loading docks at the back of the building. Trash and debris littered the area where the trucks would back in. Along the concrete platform, I noticed a rusted door that was propped open.

I hopped up on the docks and made my way to the door. It was open far enough that I was able to squeeze through without having to touch the door. Inside it was pitch-black. I didn't know if I was in a small room, a hallway, or a massive room with Brothers standing around.

I pulled my cellphone out of my pocket and turned it on so it illuminated a good distance around me. I was in a hall, a very long hall actually. I slowly made my way down, keeping my eyes peeled for any movement and my ears listening very closely for any noise.

I came to the end of the hall without seeing or hearing anything. I peered in both directions and still didn't see anything or anyone. This was a massive building though.

I walked down the hall that intersected the other and tried to make my way towards the front part of the building.

Then I heard voices that brought me to a halt. I shut my cellphone off and slipped it into my pocket. I stepped back against the wall, but when I did, I kept going. I stumbled back through double doors I didn't even know were there.

I fumbled for my cell again, and when the light turned on, I saw that I had fallen into a massive room. Three rows of long wooden tables were set up in the center of the room. There were two pillars in the back corners of the room, and that was it. There was nothing on the walls and nothing on the floors, just bare concrete.

I heard voices drawing near me again. I ran and hid myself behind one of the pillars in the back and pocketed my cell just as three bodies ran in the room. They all had flaming torches in their hands.

"We need to draw them in here. We'll have our back protected this way." That was Mason. I knew his voice well enough by this point. I peered around the pillar and saw Thea and Evan were with him.

Evan made a quick phone call, and a few minutes later, the rest of the Corlissians showed up – all of them except Emily.

I didn't have much time to think about where she was and why she was clearly on her own when about a dozen Brothers swarmed into the room. My ears were filled with the clash of metal on metal and the screams caused by the Corlissians using their deadly powers on their powerless enemies.

I watched the carnage from my vantage point behind the pillar. I just made sure to keep out of view of both the Brothers and the Corlissians.

Through the open double doors I had stumbled through, more Midnight Brothers streamed in. By this time, every Corlissian in the room was fighting three Brothers.

And then, Emily strode through the doorway twirling a dagger between her fingers. I had seen her do that at the lake house and it still amazed me that she was not cutting her fingers up by doing that.

She paused just inside the doors and her eyes darted across the room, surveying what was going on. Since I had left her, she had put on black boots that came up to her knees, and the twin leg holsters that were attached to her thighs were lined with daggers and throwing stars. She was the epitome of a badass.

A Brother who was close to where she was standing lunged at her from the right. I held my breath. She didn't turn to fight him; she simply tilted her body back enough that he flew right past her. He crumpled to the ground and didn't move.

Another Brother was sneaking up behind her. She stopped twirling the dagger and let it fall into her palm where she tossed it up in the air, caught it by the tip of the blade, spun her body around, and sent the blade flying. It slammed into the Brother's forehead.

Emily turned back around and her eyes locked on a Brother standing at the end of one of the long tables. He lifted a gloved hand and pointed it at her. A smile spread onto her face. She enjoyed this way too much. She was scary beautiful.

She unsheathed two daggers from her back and took off running. She did a front flip and landed with both feet hitting the table. Without a second's pause, she was running down the length of the table.

The Brother pulled himself up in a less graceful manner than Emily did. When Emily was close enough to him, he drew his long sword and swung it towards her. She ducked and he barely missed hitting her.

She pulled both her daggers up to where the left dagger was above her right elbow and her right dagger was under her left elbow. When she was a breath away from him, she ripped the daggers in either direction.

There was a pause where they both stood motionless. I held my breath. I didn't know if she had cut him or he had stabbed her. Then Emily pulled her head back and quickly snapped it forward, landing a loud head-butt on his forehead. His head tipped back and back and back until it landed with a thud on the table and then casually rolled off the side and onto the floor. The body of the Brother crumpled on the table.

Emily took a quick look around the room and saw that one of the Brothers was latched onto Mason's back and he could not get free. She hopped off the table and then jumped on the Brother's back. The force of her weight made the three of them fall backwards.

The Brother let go of Mason and Emily kept him subdued while Mason scrambled to his feet. A moment later, he was standing over the Brother and Emily with a sword in his hands. He drove the sword down just as Emily shoved herself out from under the Brother. If she wouldn't have moved, that sword would have impaled her too.

Mason winked at her and went back to fighting. I was sure that was a move they'd practiced plenty of times before.

Just as Emily stood up, Thea raced to her side. "There are too many, and more just keep coming. Emily, you need to end them."

Emily sighed as her eyes danced around the room. "I haven't used that since I roasted my hands," Emily replied.

"Well, I have talked to Hotch, so I have a plan. Trust me," Thea said. Then she cupped her hands around her mouth and yelled, "FALL BACK!"

And that they did. Within a minute, all the Corlissians were standing behind Emily and Thea.

"No one is to come near me," Emily hissed.

The Midnight Brothers were regrouping at the other end of the room as more were filing in.

Emily muttered, "*Ignis,*" and two flames flared up in her palms. She lifted her hands so that her palms were facing away from her.

"Everyone, get down," she said quietly, but loud enough that the Corlissians behind her heard. And every Corlissian slowly lowered themselves down into a crouched position. All the Corlissians were armed with a dagger in each hand.

Emily took a deep breath. "I hope you're sure about this, Thea," Emily whispered to her best friend who was kneeling directly behind her.

"I am."

With that, Emily whispered a word so softly that I couldn't hear, but as soon as that word passed her lips, twin flames burst forward from her palms to the other end of the room. The flames were licking up the walls and spread across the floor.

The three tables were incinerated in seconds and the Brothers didn't stand a chance either. They all turned to ash as quickly as those wooden tables.

Thea turned her head and her eyes locked on mine. She pointed for me to move over next to her. I shook my head no. Thea arched an eyebrow and a felt my body being moved. I had forgotten that Thea had pyschokenisis and could move whatever the hell she wanted. I stopped right next to Thea.

More Brothers could be seen in the hall, not daring to enter the room. Emily twisted her hands and the flames extended out the double doors and into the hall, wiping those Brothers out.

Emily whispered, "*Intereo,*" and the flames went out. I could tell from my point of view that Emily was examining her hands.

"Em, get ready for round two. I got you," Thea said.

Emily's head popped up, and sure enough the room was once again filling up with more Brothers. You'd think they wouldn't want to come in a room where their Brothers were just turned to dust.

Emily brought her hands up and again whispered the word too quietly for me to hear. Those flames shot out from her palms again.

"Thea," Emily grunted.

Thea scrambled to unzip Emily's boot and pull her pant leg up. Thea wrapped her hand around Emily's calf and started whispering so quickly under her breath that I couldn't understand anything she was saying. The fact that she was speaking in Latin wasn't helping either.

Emily let forth another quick blast of the flames, whispered the word to stop them, and then tilted back until her butt hit the floor. She pulled her knees up, rested her forearms on them, and let her hands dangle in front.

Thea scrambled around to examine the damage. "They're not as bad. Either you're getting used to it or my sending healing energies through you helped."

Emily nodded her head but didn't respond.

Thea dug around in her pockets as the other Corlissians were rising to their feet. Every single one of them, save for Emily and Thea, were gaping open-mouthed at the sheer carnage Emily had done with one little word.

Thea pulled out a wad of gauze just as Tyler knelt down on the other side and started helping Thea wrap Emily's hands up.

Emily turned her head and her eyes met mine. She looked straight up, exhausted. "Hey, Lian! What brings you here?"

"Oh, it seemed like a fine day to watch your scary ass turn some dudes to dust," I remarked.

A lazy smile spread onto her face. I scooted over and sat behind her with my legs on either side of hers. My chest was against her back and I felt her put all of her weight on me and sink back.

"We need to get out of here now. I hear sirens coming this way," Sam said from where the double doors used to be. They were now a pile of ash on the floor.

"What? Why?" Mason asked.

"Because Emily's flames are going down the halls, catching things on fire. I'm pretty sure this whole building is going to go. So, unless there is an aquamancer here, we need to roll," Sam stated.

The Corlissians made quick work of going around the room and picking up daggers and the throwing stars that littered the ground. I was guessing they had been protruding from the Brothers, but since they were all dust now, the daggers were just lying on the ground, untouched by the flames.

Emily struggled to get to her feet, so instead, I scooped her up in my arms. Of course, she had to complain about it.

"I can walk, Lian," she replied.

"Oh, I'm sure you can, but we need to get out of here quickly," I stated. She let out a grunt and draped her right arm around the back of my neck.

The Corlissians filed out of the room, with Emily and me bringing up the rear. Sam and Mason were leading the group and they were going the same way that I had come in from. The pyromancers of the group – Mason, Bridgette, Drew, and Toby – all were walking along with the flames glowing in their hands. They did act as a wonderful source of light. Who needed a flashlight when you hung out with pyromancers?

We made it to where the loading docks were and we hit the stairs that ran down the opposite side that I had come in on. A wide alley stretched out in front of us and we hauled down that alley just as we heard the fire trucks nearing the building.

Our group stopped and turned around to watch, since we were far enough away to not be noticed. Emily sat up in my arms and let out a breath. "GET DOWN!" she screamed. We all looked at her like she was crazy. And then we were forced to our knees anyway. A massive explosion rocked the ground we were standing on. The building blew up, sending chunks of bricks and debris flying across the area.

I covered Emily with my body as the other guys did with Thea and Bridgette. Debris rained down around and on us. I was sure we were going to have cuts and bruises.

Then it all became eerily quiet. There was no sound – no cars, fire trucks, or people's voices.

Evan's voice broke through the silence. "We need to go. This place is going to be crawling with police and firefighters."

We all stood up and dusted ourselves off the best we could. The three-story brick building that we had been inside only minutes before was completely gone. A massive pile of bricks was scattered around the property, and a small section of the west wall still stood.

I scooped Emily back up in my arms, and this time, she didn't protest. We ran down alleys and streets and more alleys, weaving our way around the main part of downtown until we finally came to the school's parking lot. The warehouse was a five-minute walk from the school, but our detour was a good half an hour.

The other Corlissians got back into the two cars they had come in and drove off, leaving Emily and me standing there.

"Can you drive?" I asked.

"Not well," she said, rubbing at her forehead with her arm.

"Where are your keys?"

She turned around and stuck her butt out towards me. "Back pocket," she muttered.

"You like torturing me, don't you?" I asked before sticking my hand in her pocket to fish her keys out.

"It is my favorite way to pass the time," she replied.

I opened the passenger door for her and she dropped in. I got in the driver's seat. I glanced over at her. "You want to go home?" I asked.

She leaned her head back against the headrest and turned to look at me. "Can we go to your place?" she whispered.

"Are you going to use pulso metus on me again?" I asked with a smile.

She didn't smile. She just shook her head no.

"I was kidding, Em."

"I know. I'm just really tired and I sleep better when you're next to me."

"Well, I can't say no to that logic." I started the car up and drove the short distance from the school to the Domus parking lot.

Emily got out of the car on her own and she quietly followed me up to my apartment. I unlocked the door and let her in. She yanked her leather jacket off and laid it on the couch. Then she turned and looked at me.

"Would you mind if I took a quick shower?"

I shook my head no. She walked over to me and held her hands out. "Need some help?" I asked.

"Yes, please."

I unwrapped the gauze on her hands and got to see what they looked like. They were both red from the burns, and in a few places, skin was peeling off. But they didn't look too bad. I imagined that the first burns she had were ten times worse.

"What word did you use?" I asked.

She looked up at me. "I prefer to keep some things a secret." With that, she turned and headed into the bathroom.

I took my clothes off while she was in the shower. My clothes that were only a few days old were now ruined. There was a fine white powder coating them and a few rips in the shirt. Then again, I wasn't expecting to be near an exploding building tonight.

Emily emerged from the bathroom with a towel around her. "Umm, do you have a shirt I could borrow for tonight?"

I went to my closet and tossed her a dark gray tee shirt. Then we switched places, with me heading into the shower and her staying out in the room.

When I came out a few minutes later, she was sitting on the end of the bed, staring at her hands. The skin had pretty much come off in the shower and they didn't seem to be as red.

"I healed them a bit," she stated.

"Can I ask you something?"

"Sure," she replied as I pulled the covers back on the bed.

"How did you know that building was going to blow?" I asked as I got in bed and patted the spot next to me. She got up, came around, and lay down.

"Honestly, I have no idea. I just had this feeling. Maybe because it was my flames doing all the damage. I just knew it was going to happen." She yawned.

I looked over at her lying beside me. Since the day I met her, she had been nothing but honest with me. She told me what she was and what she was capable of. Even when she was going through finding out about the new powers, she had told me about it. What was more? Even when she was mad at me, I always knew what she was mad at me for. She wasn't one of those girls that when you ask what was wrong and the reply you get was: "Nothing." She had no problem telling you what she was pissed at you for.

But I couldn't say the same. I had not been honest with her at all. In fact, she knew so little about me. I knew that it bothered her, but I figured that at this point, she just didn't care anymore. What could a guy who wanders around be hiding anyway? She deserved to know the truth though. What killed me was I knew the consequences I was to endure after I told her. She would hate me more than she did the past three weeks. I would have to leave Autumn Falls and I would never see her again. But she was the only girl I had ever loved and to leave her would destroy a piece of me.

"Emily."

"Hmm?" she mumbled.

"I need to tell you something." I sat up and glanced down at her. Her eyes were starting to close. "Please, don't fall asleep."

"Okay," she breathed as her eyes fluttered shut and she was gone.

"Emily?" I whispered, but she did not stir. "Dammit," I exhaled. I knew that I would not have the strength to tell her now. I had lost my nerve.

I lay in bed and stared at the ceiling. Then I rolled to my side and stared at the wall, and then I rolled to my other side and stared at Emily sleeping soundlessly next to me. I gave up and sat on the edge of the bed, cradling my head in my hands.

Even as the sun streamed in through the window, I didn't move. I almost felt like I couldn't face her. She didn't deserve it.

I felt her warm hand on my lower back. Then I felt the bed move. Her hand moved up my back to my shoulder. She rested her chin on my other shoulder. Her chest was pressed into my back.

"Where are you?" she asked. I smiled. I remembered the last time she asked me that was at the lake house.

"I'm torn between two places: far away with my family and here with you."

"And where would you rather be?"

I turned my body around to look at her. She sat back on her heels and looked up at me. Her hair was a mess from it drying naturally. Her gray eyes were wide and well rested. And to top it off, she was sitting there in my shirt. She was so damn beautiful.

"I'm right where I want to be," I whispered. I grabbed her around the waist and pulled her to me. "I hope you don't have any plans because you'd have to cancel them. You're mine today," I whispered.

Chapter 24

I drove back home late in the afternoon. I had to put my leathers back on, since I had no other clothes, and walking in the house with Lian's shirt on would have gotten me grounded for life.

As soon as I shut the backdoor, Kate came running into the kitchen. Kate was one of those people who was always ready for the day. She was an early riser and she always looked flawless when the rest of us rolled out of bed. Her clothes were on and her hair and make-up were perfect.

The Kate who came in the kitchen was not what I expected. Her hair looked like a rat had styled it, black streaks ran down her cheeks from her mascara running, and she still had her jammies on. She just ran up to me, threw her arms around me, and hugged me tightly to her.

I was momentarily shocked. I was kind of expecting her to start yelling at me. I put my arms around her and hugged her back.

She pulled me away from her after a few minutes of us just standing there hugging each other. She looked at me up and down. I was wearing my fighting leathers. I knew Kate had never seen me in them.

"You really look like Charlotte now," Kate said. She wiped at her eyes quickly. "I was so worried, Emily. I heard the explosion from here and to think that you were all right there next to that building. Your brothers told me everything that happened with the Midnight Brothers crashing homecoming, and you all fighting them, and the way you incinerated them all. I am so proud of you and I know that your parents would be too. You are all shaping up to be a lethal crop of Corlissians."

"So, you're not mad at me?"

"Dear, what would I be mad at you for? Fighting? Doing your duty as a Corlissian?"

"Ugh, staying out so long. That's usually what I get in trouble for," I stated.

"Come here," she said as she grabbed me around the wrist and led me to the couch in the living room. "I remember being a young Corlissian like you are now. I remember getting into fights with Nexes and Brothers. I remember at how your adrenaline starts flowing through you and just doesn't want to stop. I remember that feeling, Emily. I know it takes a while to come down from that high. I would walk around town for hours and hours just to calm my body down. I have a feeling you were doing the same thing."

I was totally not doing that. But I still just nodded my head to appease Kate. She really didn't want to hear what I had been doing or who I had been doing it with.

"Why don't you head upstairs, take a shower, and rest for a while? When you all wake up, I'll make a nice meal. Okay?"

"Okay," I replied. I stood up and headed upstairs. I went to my room first to grab some clothes before heading to the bathroom. I stripped my leathers off and hung them on the back of the door. I was going to have to clean them. They still had brick dust and a fine powder all over.

I hopped in the shower and let the hot water run down my back as I inspected my hands. They were completely healed. I knew they were. Lian had watched as I finished healing them. Then he picked up one of my hands and said, "It amazes me at how dangerous these delicate hands are." Then he kissed my palm.

I finished showering and I put my clothes on – a pair of jeans and a white tee shirt. I put my hair up in a bun instead of drying it. My brothers would have killed me if I had turned the blow dryer on.

I grabbed my leathers from the back of the door and went to my room. I didn't need to sleep or rest, since I wasn't tired at all. I spent the next few hours cleaning my leathers and all the weapons that had been on me last night.

There was one thing I remembered my dad telling me. He said that it was vital to keep your weapons clean because they would hold up a lot longer. He also said that any little thing could cause the balance to be off. The balance in a blade was essential to throwing it straight and true. And when I was six years old, I sat next to him on the floor of the living room as he taught me how to properly clean daggers.

He was also the one who taught me how to twirl a blade around my fingers without it cutting me. That was something none of my brothers or sister managed to accomplish. They would always cut themselves and run to Mom, screaming about Dad being 'a meany head.'

I was lying with my back on the floor and my feet on the bed, reading, 'On the Road' again when there was a knock on my door.

"Yes?"

The door opened and Toby popped his head in. "Can I use your shower? Drew's been in the bathroom for forty-five minutes and I'm positive I do not want to go in there after him."

"Yeah, just make sure it's clean when you're done. I know how disgusting you guys can get!"

Toby wiggled his eyebrows up and down before shutting the door. I went back to reading, and when I finally heard my brother heading downstairs did I leave my room and head down myself.

On Monday morning, we were all standing around waiting for the bell to ring when Thea walked up behind me, grabbed my arm, and yanked me down the hall away from everyone else.

"What the fuck are you doing?" I snapped at her as I tore her hand off my arm.

"We need to talk about something and the rest of them don't need to hear it," she stated. I followed her out to the parking lot where a few students were still streaming into the building. She walked out far enough away from the building so we wouldn't be heard by anyone.

"Now what is so important?"

"How many attacks did this town used to get on a monthly basis?" she asked.

"Umm, maybe one, but sometimes we wouldn't get an attack for quite a few months. Why exactly are you asking me this?"

"Okay, how many have we had in the past month?"

"I don't know, three or four."

"And that doesn't seem odd to you at all?"

"Yeah, it kind of does, but what point are you trying to make?"

"The attacks started when Killian arrived here. It was less than a week after he got here when you, Sam, Micah, and Mason were fighting the Brothers on top of the Domus that just so happens to be the building that Killian lives in. I don't think him coming here was a coincidence. I think he came here with a purpose."

"What are you saying? That he works for our enemies?"

"I don't know. All I'm saying is be careful, Emily."

"I can't believe you right now!" I sneered. "You're the one who talked Lian into getting together with me and now you're saying he might have come here to give our position away?"

"Emily, he knows a lot about us. You know it's frowned on for us to be with a human anyway. It was a bad idea on my part. I should have kept my mouth shut and then you two might still not be talking or dating or whatever it is you have going on right now."

"You have a lot of nerve, Thea."

"I know you won't hurt me," she breathed as we stared each other down. A fight between us would not be evenly matched, and she knew that. Even without using our powers, I would still dominate her.

"No. I won't, but God knows I can't stand you right now," I spat before walking away before a fight did break out.

The bell rang on my way back into the building. I walked into homeroom after the bell rang.

"Do have a late slip, Ms. Porter?" Watkins asked.

"Fuck you!" I snapped.

"Emily," Lian breathed.

"I'm a minute late. It's not the end of the world."

"Would you like to go to the office?"

"YES! And give me detention or maybe suspend me. No, how about an expulsion? I'm sure you would love to not see me anymore. Am I right, old man?"

Watkins opened his mouth to say something I'm sure would really push me over the edge. Lian stood up and hauled me up and out of my chair.

"Give us just a second," he said to Watkins as he dragged me out of the room and into the hallway. "What the hell is wrong with you?" he whispered.

My hands tightened into fists and I saw Lian take a step away from me. I knew my eyes were glowing. They seemed to do that a lot lately. Part of me wanted to break Thea's neck. I didn't know what she was playing at. Saying that Lian could possibly be working for our enemies was ludicrous. But in the back of my mind, I knew that she would do anything to protect me and she would only tell me something if it was important, but that bit was being overridden by the illogical part of my brain, the part that was driven by my senses for fighting instead of talking and thinking things through.

"Emily? Your eyes," he said.

I blinked my eyes a few times. "Thea and I got into an argument this morning."

"About what?" he asked. I glared up at him. "Nope. Never mind. I know that look and I'm about to get a 'you're-not-Corlissian-so-it's-none-of–your-business.' I really don't want to start off the week with you pissed at me."

I ran my fingers through my hair and groaned. "Why do you put up with me?"

Lian started laughing. "Seriously? I think by now you should know that I'm in love with you."

"Why?"

His green eyes were wide. "Why am I in love with you? Are we really doing this now?"

I nodded my head and he let out an exhausted sigh.

"Okay." He let out a long breath. "You're beautiful and smart and sometimes you are hilarious. You are strong and independent and a complete badass. I love that you are moody as hell and that keeping up with you is a challenge for me. I love the color of your eyes, both colors. I love the steely gray looking back at me right now and I love when they glow violet. I love how your body fits perfectly against mine. I have favorite versions of you too: the pissed off Emily, the vulnerable Emily, the fighter Emily, and the sleepy Emily. I love knowing that you are very capable of taking care of yourself. I love what you have been dealing in life and how strong it has made you…"

"You can stop," I whispered.

"Really? I was just getting started, babe," he replied with a wink.

The door to homeroom opened and Watkins stepped out. "Are you two coming back in?" he said in a deep voice.

Lian nodded his head and walked back in the room. I didn't move immediately. Watkins raised an eyebrow.

"I'm sorry for what I said. I was mad at someone else and I took it out on you," I explained.

Watkins nodded his head. "Thank you for that, Emily. And you are forgiven." I was about to walk past him and into the room when he put up a hand to stop me. "Tell me how you shocked me?" he whispered.

I let out a snort. "That? It's just a trick of mixing fear with static. You can build up enough static to shock someone and when you mix fear in with that, it intensifies the shock, making it seem worse than it actually is. That's it."

Watkins just looked at me.

"Do you think I can actually inflict pain on someone? Look at me? I have no superpowers, nor am I big enough to hurt someone. It was a trick was all."

Watkins let out a breath. "It was a very good trick then. You had me quite scared there for a while."

"I tend to scare a lot of people," I muttered as I walked past him and into the classroom. The bell for first period rang and I grabbed my things off my desk and headed to my first class.

I hadn't spoken to Thea since Monday morning. She had tried to make small talk with me, but I didn't have anything to say to her… at least it wouldn't have been anything nice.

On Friday after lunch, we were at our lockers and she again attempted to speak with me.

"Emily, I am sorry about what I said."

I slammed my locker shut and glared at her. "Are you really?"

She focused on the contents of her locker. She moved her pointer finger around and I could see a piece of paper floating around.

"I'm sorry that what I said has you angry with me. You have been my best friend since kindergarten and I don't want to lose you. You have to understand that I am protecting you."

I let out a sigh. "I know you are, but you should know by now that you can't approach me like you did. I'm sort of a loose cannon."

Thea chuckled. "That's a good term to use. Oh! Hotch said training is canceled today. He has something he needs to take care of, so we are free," she smiled.

"Hotch never cancels practice… ever," I replied.

"I know, but I'm not questioning it. That means I get to spend more time with Toby."

"Ugh, I told you I don't care if you date my brother, but I just don't want to hear about anything."

"Oh, come on. You know you would love it if we were sisters," she said, shutting her locker.

"Yeah, but when we talked about being sisters when we were younger, it never meant that you had to marry one of my brothers," I stated as we made our way to class.

Thea laughed as we split up and went our separate ways.

I sat down next to Lian in science. "What are you doing after school?" I asked.

"Probably going home and waiting until you get done with practice," he said.

"I don't have practice today," I leaned in and whispered.

"You're not skipping, are you?" he asked.

"No! It's canceled for some reason. So, I am all yours after school."

He growled under his breath. "You can't say things like that to me when there is so much time left until the final bell rings."

"I just did and I demand that you take me to get coffee. Then we can do whatever you want."

"Please, I am begging you to stop talking," he insisted.

"And if I don't?"

"Now I am wondering why I put up with you!" he breathed.

I giggled as the bell rang for science to begin.

We walked to Grounders the way we had on the first day of school. That seemed so long ago that we walked to the coffee shop talking about our tattoos. We grabbed our coffees to go and began walking back to school.

"Let's cut through the woods. I kind of hope we get accosted by Midnight Brothers again."

"I kind of hope we don't. I don't have my daggers on me. Not that I can't do other fun things with my hands," I said, wiggling my fingers.

"Why don't you have your daggers? You always have them," he asked.

I shrugged my shoulders. "I took them off, since we weren't having practice. I suppose I should have left them on with all the attacks we have been getting in this town lately."

"Well, even without your daggers, I feel very safe with you," he said as we took the path to the woods. I needed to stop taking this shortcut. Only bad things seemed to happen.

"…and that's why Thea was mad at Toby earlier in the week according to my brother," I explained. My arm was draped through his as we walked out of the woods and onto the football field.

"That's kind of a bogus reason. We didn't have much time to think when the explo—" Lian started but was interrupted.

"Hello, Killian."

We both stopped dead. Standing just a few feet in front of us was a girl who looked to be about the same age as we were. She was a little shorter than I was, with long white blond hair that stopped about the middle of her back. She had an oval face and pale skin. Her eyes were big and bright green. Her nose was straight with a slight slope at the end and her lips curled up at each side, giving her a permanent smirk.

She closed the distance between us with a few steps.

"Are you not going to introduce us, Killian?" she asked.

"What are you doing here?" Lian asked in a deep voice.

She ignored him and turned to face me. "Well, I'm Phoenix, Killian's girlfriend. And you are?"

I yanked my arm out of Lian's and glared at him. "She is not my girlfriend. She was," he explained.

"And we never broke up," Phoenix threw in.

"Yeah, three years ago and then I left. That pretty much ends things. Now what are you doing here?"

"I've been tracking you for those three years, my dear," she said, glancing around. "And here I find you mixing with Corlissians."

That had me taking a few steps away from the two of them.

"Everyone assumed you were a traitor and they put a bounty on your head, but I knew better. So, I tracked you and I covered both our tracks very well as I did. I just knew I would find you. Now you can come home. Once they know the truth that you've been infiltrating Corlissian bases, you will be welcomed with open arms," Phoenix stated.

"What are you?" I whispered.

Phoenix started laughing and I tried to ignore her. Lian would not look at me though.

"Of course he wouldn't tell you, but I don't care. We're Talyrians."

The world around me started to spin and I felt like I was going to throw up. I brought my hand up to my mouth and forced myself to see straight. Lian was still looking straight ahead and not at me.

"And he's not just any Talyrian. His dad is the right-hand man of our leader," Phoenix added.

"Tell me she is lying," I breathed.

He took a deep breath and turned his body toward mine. There was a nasty curl to his lips and his eyes were glowing green.

"Sorry, babe, I can't," he replied.

"FUCK YOU!" I hissed.

"Fuck you? Oh, baby, I already did… twice," he replied with that smirk still on his face that made my skin crawl.

"Aww, she thought you two were in love. Poor little princess, still waiting for happily-ever-after," Phoenix crooned.

The realization hit me like a punch to the gut. Lian knew way too much about the Corlissians in this town and he knew entirely too much about what I was. He would undoubtedly go back to the Talyrian stronghold and tell their leader that the Corlissians had a powerful half-breed.

Lian walked toward me and I knew my eyes had changed color. I heard Phoenix let out a gasp.

"Don't worry, I won't tell them too much about what you are," he whispered in my ear. He placed a hand on my shoulder and kissed my cheek.

"DON'T. TOUCH. ME," I growled through gritted teeth. I felt his hand come off my shoulder and he took a few steps away from me.

"What is up with her eyes?" Phoenix asked. There was a touch of worry in her voice, and that brought a smile to my lips.

Lian knew me well enough to know that I was about to unleash hell on them. "We need to get out of here now. NOW!" he yelled.

He grabbed Phoenix by the shoulders and forced her away. "I can take her," she argued.

"Trust me, you can't," he said, leading her away from me.

It was quiet for a few minutes. Then I felt a drip on my arm and then one on my shoulder. Before long, it was pouring around me. My knees gave out and I hit the ground. My tears mixed with the rain running down my face. I was doubled over in the football field, crying my eyes out and soaking wet.

I don't know how long I lay there. When I finally sat up, they were long gone and I was utterly alone. I wiped my fingers under my eyes only to have black smudges on my fingertips.

Then I heard a female voice scream, "EMILY, HELP ME!"